# Stephen Challis

# The Dark Island

## A CAROLINE DE WINTER NOVEL

THE DARK ISLAND

**First edition. January 24, 2024.**

Copyright © 2024 Stephen C. Challis.

ISBN: 979-8989961900

Written by Stephen C. Challis.

# THE DARK ISLAND
## A Caroline De Winter Novel

Stephen C. Challis
This book is written in British English spelling.

# Prologue

The Dark Island is a sequel to Queen Ann's Curse and takes place in the year 2002. Caroline De Winter and Geoffrey Dawson's mutual attraction to each other has grown into engagement and then marriage. The story begins at their wedding reception and departure on a honeymoon to the Greek island of Crete in the Mediterranean, which is now a popular tourist area, but one with a dark history. It is one that will take the couple on a terrifying journey that plunges them into a conflict that links the paranormal to the living world and almost costs both of them their lives. It could threaten new world conflict from a long thought mythical source.

The Dark Island will question your faith, your scepticism, and even your very sanity. It's a story that links a group of people in 3 time periods. Carlos Santos, the conspiracy writer who is now a successful journalist, Leander Kosta, former communist partisan fighter during the war, aged police widow Christa Nomikos, whose past will finally catch up with her, and her son Dimitris, the local police captain and his English wife Angela, a fan of Caroline's books.

These diverse and unlikely characters are pivotal in bringing the secrets of The Dark Island into the light, and then consigning them back into history for eternity.

# Dedication

## Chapters

1. Crete Spring 1944
2. The Wedding Reception
3. Why is Sally Invisible?
4. Restless Spirits
5. Crete's Dark History
6. Hanna Vassal
7. A 50 Year Old Murder Mystery
8. Premonition
9. Christa's Old Flame
10. Menace From The Nazi Plant
11. Site Investigation
12. Rodin Point
13. Who's Bodies?
14. The Survivor
15. The Deputy Director
16. Christa's Big Secret
17. Die Glocke
18. Back From The Dead
19. Ghosts From Hanna's Past
20. Cora Kronos
21. Leander's Dark Secret
22. Reinforcements
23. Hanna Comes Clean
24. Violent Spirit
25. Dimitris Reaches Out
26. Sally Has Gone
27. The Stunning Spy
28. An SS Traitor or Hero?
29. Geoffrey's In Hospital
30. An Unexpected Visitor

31. Loose Ends
32. Destiny Angel
33. Gavdos Island
34. Stopping The Russians
35. Barbarossa's Cauldron
36. Caroline's Dying
37. The FBI Close In
38. Sea Chase
39. Where Is The Bell?

# Preface

As Captain Andreas Nomikos sped along the streets of the crowded capital of Heraklion driving his police Austin 8, which made him even more conspicuous, he had initially wanted to take a German Kübelwagen, but all of them had already been commandeered by fleeing German officers and other collaborators. In the capitol, he was relatively safe as not only a police officer, but the Chief Officer, because the Germans still had control.

Nonetheless, he knew he needed to ditch both the car and uniform if he were to have any chance of survival outside the protection of the Germans in the city. Slowly, a plan had formed in his mind. Here in the capitol he was well known, and therefore could not have pulled it off, but elsewhere, he was just another police captain. He turned off the main road out of town and took an alternative route; one that he knew would take him far ahead of the advancing partisans. There were other vehicles on the same road, but most were heading down toward the main route out of the city.

At these higher elevations, Nomikos could see the city and the flashes of gunfire marking the advancing army.

He slowed as he reached a bend in the road. Ahead was an old farm truck with three young German soldiers, most likely the truck was stolen. He pulled alongside and, in German, ordered them to pull over. The three looked worried, but complied. Unsure of what the police wanted, they played along. Nomikos stopped the Austin and walked towards them, keeping his P.38 hidden behind a clipboard. He spoke nonchalantly to them as he approached.

*"Are you boys heading for Heraklion?"*

The driver spoke up.

*"Yes, we got separated from our unit and are trying to catch them up."*

Nomikos nodded, before replying.

*"I see, well, in that case I may be able to assist."*

He moved the clipboard to one side, and too late, the soldiers saw the gun that Nomikos fired 4 shots in rapid succession from, striking them in the chest. They collapsed, blood spurting from their mouths. From here he had a good view of the road ahead, it was clear of vehicles for about two miles. He knew from the view he had in his rear-view mirror that before making the bend that the same applied behind him. Now, he had to work fast. Quickly, he dragged the bodies from the truck and selected one then quickly stripped off his uniform. Luckily, he had discarded his tunic in the rear of the truck, as had one of the others. He was about Nomikos' size and very quickly he dressed the German in his police uniform and had changed clothes. The remaining Germans he dragged over to the police car and laid them in front of the open driver's door. The one now dressed in his police Uniform, he put in the driver's seat. Finally, he took the Germans ID papers and placed his own police identity in the top breast pocket of the driver's battledress tunic. Satisfied, he took two Mauser K 98 rifles from the rear of the truck and worked the bolts firing three rounds. Two into the air, and the last at point blank range into the face of the corpse now seated in the front seat wearing his uniform. The ejected shell cases from the rifles he place strategically, two close to the police car and one on the floor well. He then took the p38 and placed it in the right hand of the corpse. Satisfied, he returned to the farm truck and drove off. He was sure that in the chaos of the retreat, it would be unlikely to have a thorough investigation, because the German bodies had wounds consistent with a small calibre handgun like Nomikos'.

The fleeing police chief was now confident that police captain Nomikos was dead, killed in a gunfight with two German deserters. Now He was just a scared German private looking to surrender to the allies.

# Chapter 1

### Crete Spring 1944

Commander Andreas Nomikos was as a very worried man, even though the last few years had been good for him. The young police Commander of the Heraklion district had at first opposed the massive German onslaught on his homeland in 1941, but soon realized that he was fighting a losing battle. Hitler's forces had not only conquered his homeland, Crete, but most of Europe as well. As a trained police officer the occupying Germans had need of him and others like him to maintain order and stop insurrections. Like many of his colleagues, he now worked for the Reich, but in mid-1944, things had gone horribly wrong. Now the scattered groups of Greek partisan guerrillas had grown into a powerful army and he and his men were the number one target for revenge. On June 6<sup>th</sup> 1944, allied troops had landed en masse on the Normandy coast and were advancing on all fronts. Russian forces were now advancing from the east and the beleaguered Wehrmacht army was being pushed back into Germany. For Muller, the writing was on the wall and he knew well that if he fell into partisan hands, he would be unlikely to ever see the inside of a courtroom.

When Christa and Nomikos first married, things were good, and she had made many friends, then the Germans arrived and it all began to change. The happy times were now just ancient history. Invitations to local events had dried up, invitations from her were politely declined and various excuses made. She knew her husband was collaborating with the occupying forces, but not to what extent. Of course they had discussed it, but he always told her that he had to work under them or risk being replaced and arrested as an agent of the resistance.

Under the German commander, Fredrick Wilhelm Muller, Nomikos had avidly pursued the resistance movement. He had played a pivotal role in the massacres of several villagers identified as sympathizers in what had become known as the Viannos Holocaust by early October 1944.

That had made him a special target for assassination or capture. His former protector, Fredrick Muller, had long since departed the island, having seen the inevitability of it falling into Allied hands. In fact, a few days before allied troops, 33 had overrun German resistance and had occupied the Greek mainland. It seemed like just a matter of time before they would launch a final assault on Crete. Hopelessly outnumbered, the German garrison faced annihilation in the coming battle, but the expected assault never came. Politics had now intervened. In Lisbon, a meeting between British and German officials had taken place and a formal agreement reached. Though not specifically a treaty, it allowed for Germany to withdraw its forces and allow the peaceful occupation of Greece. For that country, the war was effectively over.

However, Crete remained occupied by 17,000 German troops, and therein laid a problem. Crete was in effect, to be left alone and the agreement allowed those troops to remain in control and evacuate after the main German force had left Greece. But that did not mean peace was, in any way, the way of life in Crete. The partisan Army was not interested in the end of WW2. They were involved in a civil war the two sides, of which, were fighting to fill the vacuum that would be left after Germany departed. In such troubled times, German control was essential as a disciplined and well organized force. The allies would leave Crete alone. But for those who had collaborated with the Nazis and openly betrayed the resistance movement, there would be no respite.

That realization had now dawned on Nomikos. For him the stakes were far higher. As a collaborator, he may not escape justice at the hands of the partisans, but that was the least of his problems. He had to get off the island, not because of what he was, but who he was. Nomikos had a secret; a terrible secret that he knew would curse him and his family forever. The talk in the capital was, of course, of the war and a possible allied invasion of the island, but it had not happened. Suddenly, the explosions had occurred. That in turn prompted questions and rumours with many of those questions being directed at him. He had told them he knew nothing, but it was likely the Germans were blowing up surplus ammunition stocks and it did not concern the townspeople. That would have remained the case, had he not received an order from the acting commandant of the German Garrison, Colonel Kurt Franz Steinburg, to meet him at his headquarters.

No reason was given, but Nikos was now particularly worried. He wondered how much the Germans knew about his role in the event.

The Major greeted the police captain formerly and bade him take a seat.

He studied him for a moment before speaking.

*"Well, captain, I'm sure you've heard rumours of impending invasion and the German occupation forces being about to flee the island."*

Nomikos nodded.

*"The town is full of such rumours Major, but after many years in this job, I tend to treat them with, shall we say, a pinch of salt."* He smiled but noted the gesture was not returned.

Steinburg just nodded before continuing.

*"Well, I can tell you that there are no such plans in that direction, but there is a matter that will require your urgent attention. You are aware of a large explosion that took place to the east of Heraklion this week, plus reports of gunfire in the hills in the same area. Well, I'm aware that the word on the streets is we were disposing of surplus munitions. That is incorrect. At least in the main it is.*

*Our facility was engaged in the manufacture of a high grade chemical weapon system. We had recruited a team of top scientists and engineers in the biochemical industry, and brought them here."*

Nomikos assumed that recruited meant forced slave labour, but he was wrong.

*"You see, Commander, this work was vital to our winning the war, and it still is. These people held high regard in the Reich Council and received a generous salary. The only way we could ensure security. We have already removed the records and research material. So the only thing that remained was to just destroy the stockpiles."*

The police Commander remained silent for a few moments before asking the question that he already suspected that he knew the answer to.

*"And the gunfire?"*

Steinberg stared for a moment, as if his mind had wandered somewhere else, before replying.

*"Of no importance, a small group of terrorists attempting to steal fuel and weapons, they also made the mistake of assuming we were leaving."*

His answer seemed logical, but Nomikos knew it was a total lie. It also confirmed that time had run out, and he had to flee now. However, as he left the Major's office, he showed no sign of the inward panic that was now consuming him.

........................

Commander Nomikos was missing. His Deputy First Lieutenant, Tobias Papadopoulos, was now acting commander.

Papadopoulos had never been inside the restricted area. It was guarded by an elite unit of the SS who ran the site and never left it. In fact, though the Wehrmacht troops often frequented the town's bar and cafes, no SS men ever did. That was unusual, but not unprecedented. The day Nomikos disappeared, the morning tranquillity was shattered by a series of violent explosions followed by prolonged bursts of automatic fire, which most recognized as MP40 sub-machine gun fire. Following the noise, there had been nothing but silence, but soon black smoke was seen rising from the area. The cause was unknown. The mountain road up to the site was still guarded by Wehrmacht troops who forbade any persons to enter. At the time, few gave it any thought. As police officer now in charge, he felt the

Germans were probably destroying stockpiles of ammunition, which would be the norm if preparing to evacuate the island. He had expressed this opinion to various townspeople who had enquired that morning, until the report came in of a body found at the entrance to the plant.

When Papadopoulos arrived at the scene, he saw Steinberg's staff car and driver, plus the double crewed police vehicle whose occupants were talking to the German Commander. As he approached, he could not at first see any corpse at the scene, but then beyond the barrier he saw a small group of figures dressed in white chemical bio suits. The body of a young female lying on the trackway. The group were about 3 meters from the barrier.

The figures in white were holding some kind of grey tool and passing it over the lifeless girl. The tools were attached to a military grade grey box bearing a German eagle stencil. A high-pitched clicking sound was being emitted from the box when the tool was passed close to the body.

Steinberg blocked the police officers path with a raised hand.

*"Sorry Lieutenant, you cannot go any closer without protective clothing. I must ask you to be patient until Dr Wiess has finished his examination. He will explain further."*

Minutes passed in which Steinberg stated the girl was believed to be a local from the village. None of the small garrison knew her, but she was first spotted in a containment area where some equipment had recently been disposed of. After running off when the alarm was raised, she appeared to have collapsed here after covering less than half a kilometer. She had no apparent injury, but appeared dead when the guards reached her.

Already, Papadopoulos could see where this was going and was expecting a military clamp down with no chance of an investigation. But he could not have been more wrong.

Two figures in white approached and removed their protective helmets. They were introduced by Steinberg.

*"Lieutenant, this is Doctor Albert Wiess. He is a toxicology expert from the University of Salzburg, a civilian. His companion is Meijer Otto Diener, our divisional medical officer."*

Dr Wiess spoke first.

*"Well, Lieutenant, we have a serious situation here. The victim is showing clear signs of severe radiation poisoning. As far as I can tell, she contracted this exposure at a military installation. And this happened after the installation concerned had been cleared of all known contaminants. I have asked for permission for a team to examine the site first hand. Major Steinberg has agreed to this and has also acceded to the request that experts from them relative agencies accompany them."*

This news left him at a loss for words and it took a while for it to sink in. Finally, he spoke.

*"Just how serious is this matter, Doctor? What I mean is, how much of a risk is there to the local people here?*

The doctor became very quiet before replying.

*"At present, I don't know, but potentially the danger could not just be confined to this area. Conceivably it could be the entire island, or even further afield."*

......................

Papadopoulos was unexpectedly asked to attend an inspection of the site by a number of experts. He had pointed out that Captain Nomikos should really be the one to attend, as he was in charge. Steinberg, however, brushed aside the protests and refusal did not seem an option.

The following morning at 9 am sharp, Steinberg's Mercedes staff car arrived to pick him up. The City mayor was already in the car. Little was said during the journey. The two men had not spoken for over a year and it seemed that neither desired to change that situation.

As the car reached the site, it pulled into a parking area where chemical suits were being distributed. There was no sign of any buildings or structures, just a wide area of freshly levelled earth. There was, however, a large military tent. Once the suits had been distributed, the two men were asked to enter, but leave their protective hoods off. Inside the tent was a small number of chairs, most of which were occupied. In front was a table where Major Steinberg and Dr Wiess sat. A third man dressed in civilian clothes was with them. After they had taken their seats, Steinberg rose to address the group.

*"Gentlemen, I thank you for attending this meeting. As most of you know, there was an incident at this site over 2 weeks ago. A powerful explosion destroyed a military facility here and released a very toxic chemical as well as some residual radiation. We have been busy up here with engineers and experts and can now say the situation is contained. We will go up to the site shortly and I will explain what precautions we have taken. We have provided you with suits as a precaution and also this yellow badge. If there is any radiation present, the badge will change colour, but so far, we have not detected anything. However, the Radiation is not our primary concern. As mentioned, there was a large release of a chemical toxin agent that cannot be so easily contained. Our only choice was to bury it in concrete with a 3 meter layer of earth on top. If this agent was ever exposed to the air, then the consequences would be incalculable. May I introduce Professor Ludwig Erikson, of Zurich University; he has been invited to join us to explain the high risk to this area. I'm afraid he speaks German and French, but not Greek, so I have invited Captain Nomikos here to not only view the facility, but to also interpret as he speaks German.*

*"Professor, you have the floor."*

The professor nodded and stood up. He was a clean shaven man in his mid-50s, as far as Nomikos could judge.

He addressed the Group in German.

*"Guten Morgen Meine Herren"* he began.

Then asked how many of his audience could understand German. To his surprise, most, including the mayor raised their hands. That made his task easier. Nomikos knew most of the non-military people there, and was fairly certain that the mayor knew few words of German, but guessed correctly that he did not wish to have to ask him to translate. As the meeting progressed, the Germans, backed by the Professor, made a credible case for ensuring the site remains sealed and off limits for at least 100 years. This was the assessment given by both Dr Wiess and Professor Erikson. Nomikos however, could sense there was something that was being kept from the group. He put his hand up as the meeting drew to a close, asking one poignant question.

*"Major Steinberg, can you expand on the chemical agent you have referred to; its properties and purpose."*

*"No Captain, I cannot. This is classified as military information. I have told you all we can in the interests of public safety. The rest is up to you."*

# Chapter 2

## The Wedding Reception

It was of course unlucky for the bride to see her groom before the ceremony on the day of her wedding, but neither retired Chief Inspector Geoffrey Hawthorn or his bride, Caroline De Winter, cared to much about such things. The two had met the year before in traumatic circumstances that had involved Spencer's son and the well-known psychic, who was to become his wife today.

Geoffrey's daughter- and son-in-law were both police officers, formerly stationed in Portsmouth. But due to the events of the previous year, they had been posted at their own request to Aldershot sub-division in the Rushmoor division in the North of the county. The stories of the supernatural events surrounding the Mary Rose museum and a mysterious ring had been all but eclipsed by the terrorist incident the previous year that had claimed the life of a female police officer and had critically wounded his daughter.

Now, in the summer of 2002, that all seemed like a distant and unpleasant memory. The current topic on TV was over the abduction and murder of two young girls, Holly Wells and Jessica Chapman, from the town of Soham in Cambridgeshire, and the arrest of a young couple Maxine Carr, a teaching assistant at the local school and her boyfriend Ian Huntley. Every police officer had their own theories, of course; many comparing Carr to the infamous child killer, Myra Hindley.

Debbie and David Spencer were no exception. Both had since been promoted, but due to police regulations were not stationed together. Debbie was now a duty Sergeant at Farnborough, and David a DS at Aldershot, both within the Rushmore division about 5 miles apart. The Chief Inspectors of both sub divisions had ensured that they worked matching shifts, so there was no unnecessary upset on their social lives. Today, however, the family were all together for the ceremony and a celebration afterwards at the Netley Police Club where Caroline and

Geoffrey had first met. The service was to be held at the Portswood registry office and was full of many guests. It included some high-ranking police officers, one of which was the Chief Constable, Paul Kernaghan, who had met with Geoffrey briefly in 1985, when they were both attending an anti-terrorist convention in London when Kernaghan was a senior officer in the RUC. Of course, the chief constable was fully aware of the incident in Portsmouth, and his background with republican terrorism made him a great asset to the force.

He had accepted the invitation to attend the wedding on the advice of other senior officers who knew that Geoffrey was a popular commander before his retirement, and attendance would be appreciated by rank-and-file officers.

Even so, he wisely made no reference to the actual events in Portsmouth the previous year, other than comment that he was pleased that Geoffrey's daughter had made a good recovery.

He continued

*"So, have you and your wife decided on a honeymoon destination, Geoffrey; somewhere away from the madness of police work?"*

The retired Chief Inspector took another sip of champagne, before replying.

*"That may be difficult, sir, having spent most of my life as a copper, but we have chosen somewhere that seems quiet and less touristy, Crete. Full of history and it appeals to Caroline, ancient ruins and the like. I will probably fit in well."*

Kernaghan smiled diplomatically at the quip before replying.

*"Good choice, Geoffrey, sun, sea, and I believe no crime wave, as far as I know."*

Geoffrey saw Caroline approaching and turned to introduce her.

*"Sir, May I introduce the lady who unfathomably has just become my wife; and Caroline, may I introduce Sir Paul Kernaghan, the Chief Constable of the Hampshire Constabulary."*

Caroline smiled sweetly, well aware that the chief knew very well who Caroline was, and likely did not approve, but the formalities played out.

*"Delighted to meet you, Mrs. Hawthorn, Geoffrey is a very lucky man."*

Of course, the Chief Constable may not have known that Caroline had continued to use her public name, Caroline De Winter, for business reasons, the name for which she was known as an author and clairvoyant, (she preferred the title Psychic). Or if he did know, he diplomatically avoided it.

There was, of course, good reason for the chief constables' concerns. The previous year, Caroline De Winter had been involved in an incident that had had psychic undertones for the force which involved Geoffrey, his daughter, and son-in-law.

It could have proved pretty embarrassing to the force, however; before things had spiralled out of control, a terrorist attack in Southsea that had killed one officer and critically wounded Debbie. The incident completely overshadowed the ghost stories and paranormal rumours. There was no person happier about that than Paul Kernaghan. He had, of course, researched Caroline De Winter, before attending the wedding, but had found nothing to raise suspicion. He had even noted that other police forces had, in fact, sought her help in some cases; though of course it had been kept very low key.

———————————

Both Debbie and David drove the honeymooners to Gatwick Airport for their flight.

In fact, both had approved of the choice of destination and would love to have joined them, except of course that honeymoons are strictly two person affairs. As the Boeing 737 climbed up into the clear blue skies over southern England they could not have dreamt of the turmoil to come.

During the flight, Caroline had been reading the history of Crete, and in particular, the connections with ancient Greece. Her husband had settled down to watch an in-flight movie with headphones.

The guide book included a small section on WW2 and the battle for Crete. She paused momentarily as a sudden flashback entered her mind, a dream; or rather, a segment of a dream from a couple of nights before; a scared woman and a rising feeling of panic that had awoken her. There had been more, but now it was faded. No matter, she continued reading, but the vision had troubled her. In normal people, such an occurrence was quite common and would have been quickly dismissed. But Caroline was no normal woman. A better description would have been one she often applied to herself in interviews. Someone with a brain highly tuned to outside communications like a highly sensitive radio antenna. But these messages were not generated by radios. Over the years, she had learned not to dismiss them lightly. The previous year she had been aware of the catastrophe of 911 as it happed and felt the anguish experienced by those killed in the attack on the twin towers.

# Chapter 3

### Why is Sally Invisible?

Captain Dimitris Nomikos was spending today with his mother, Christa. Of course a policeman is never off duty, so he had his pager with him, but had left strict instructions that it should not be used unless for the matter of upmost urgency.

Today was his mother's 70$^{th}$ birthday, and he had arranged for her and his wife to visit the Palace of Knossos historic ruin. It was a popular tourist attraction, built by the Minoans at around 1950 BC. The early 20th century restoration team restored $^{the}$ site, making it one of Crete's top destinations today, mainly due to its close proximity to the Capitol Heraklion. It also boasts of the temple's notoriety as being the home of the Minotaur, a half bull half man creature that inhabited a legendary maze, and where Greek hero Theseus slew it. Whilst experts still argued about the truth of that legend, it nevertheless provided good tourists dollars.

Dimitris was not in uniform, but had arrived in an official police vehicle and was openly wearing a holstered pistol. Of course, most residents knew him anyway. Most people largely ignored the three individuals sitting in the restaurant area. Except that was not the case for the middle-aged English couple seated a few feet away.

Caroline and Geoffrey had picked up things that were out of the ordinary. Geoffrey had recognized immediately that Dimitris was off duty by law enforcement, probably of high rank. Of the two women accompanying him, the younger one stood out obviously, not Greek, but of European descent, likely British or German, but American was also a possibility.

As a woman whose career was interacting with many people, it was obvious to Caroline that they were a family group; mother, son and wife. This was a little game they played often; the former police superintendent and an internationally renowned psychic and Medium. It happened at almost every social event. Of course, no one was aware that they were the subject of a form of psychoanalysis. Caroline had once quipped to Geoffrey that if any of the guests could read minds, then they would probably be ostracized from society. However, neither had noticed that they were being closely observed by a young female student who finally got up and approached them.

*"Excuse me, but aren't you Caroline De Winter, the medium?"*

Caroline looked up, but strangely, her husband did not; neither did Dimitris or his family. Almost as if they had failed to notice her. The young student looked nervous, wondering if she had made a mistake. Caroline smiled - replying.

*"Yes that's me. For my sins, can I help you miss, err..."*

*"Sally. Sally Knight."* she replied, now looking somewhat relived.

*"What can I do for you, Sally?"*

*"Well, I am a great admirer of your work and I wondered if you are here on a case? You see, I am studying physic research and would love to interview you sometime."*

Again, there was no response from Geoffrey. Caroline smiled faintly as she realized the reason why, before replying in a low breath that was almost inaudible.

*"No, I am not on a case, as you put it. I'm here on my honeymoon with my husband. He knows all about cases, he used to be a policeman."*

She smiled again. Geoffrey, as she expected, did not respond.

Sally looked up nervously as he glanced in her direction and sighed.

*"I'll contact you later."*

With that, the young student vanished into the crowd.

A few feet away, ever the on duty police officer, Dimitris noted Caroline's and Geoffrey's description down in the small notebook he always carried. He did not know why, but their presence on Crete seemed be an indication of noteworthiness. His wife had noticed this and leaned over to him disapprovingly.

*"So, what's so suspicious, darling? I don't think they are international terrorists or drug lords, just tourists."*

Dimitris put away the notebook and smiled.

*"Probably, but I would like to check them out."*

The smile on his wife's face faded, and she turned to face him with a flash of impatience written on her face.

*"Well, that's simple; forget the police checks and the subterfuge and contacting Interpol. I have a better idea."*

With that, she rose from the table and walked over to Caroline's table. Both she and Geoffrey looked up as she spoke in perfect English.

*"Excuse me, I couldn't help overhearing. You are English are you not? So am I. Did I hear you mention that you are on your honeymoon, if so, may I offer my congratulations?"*

Caroline smiled and extended her hand.

*"Thank you. Caroline and Geoffrey Hawthorn; are you on holiday too?*

Before the visitor could reply, a young man sporting an expensive SLR Camera approached them and interrupted.

*"Excuse me Mrs De Winter; can I get a shot for our local paper? You have many friends in Heraklion and it is an honour to have you here in person."*

He took the photo before Caroline could answer. Geoffrey looked a little annoyed, but was by now used to the reduction in privacy that comes with being married to a celebrity. His wife just smiled and said;

*"Thank you young man but, no interviews please. My husband and I are on a private holiday and will not be doing any public engagements."*

The young photographer nodded and left.

Only now, up close, and because of the photographers' interruption, did Dimitris' wife recognize Caroline. Her picture was on the cover of the book she had just bought with the catchy title, 'The Soul Never Dies', but had not yet started reading. She had also read about her recent wedding on Google, while deciding whether or not to buy the book.

She continued the introduction.

*"Sorry, I should have recognized you earlier. My name is Angela Dimikros and I see we have another thing in common. I too am married to a copper. Unfortunately, mine is not retired."*

Caroline smiled and extended her hand, replying;

*"Sometimes I don't think mine is. This is my husband, Geoffrey. We are here on our honeymoon. Why don't you and your husband join us? I assume he is off duty?"*

Geoffrey extended his hand, before adding;

*"Yes, please do. Do I detect a slight Welsh accent there?"*

Angela smiled.

*"Very good, Chief Inspector; Swansea, but I am trying hard to lose it."*

She left the table briefly and returned with her husband and his mother. More introductions and handshakes followed.

As Caroline took the older Ladies hand, a shock went through it. Flashes of chaos and screaming enveloped in a kind of fog. This had happened before, and by now she had learned to control it so no one outwardly noticed, but Dimitris did. Nevertheless, he said nothing. The group sat down and Geoffrey ordered another bottle of wine. Introductions over, the conversation turned to history after Angela warned her husband.

*"No police talk Dimitris, we are on holiday today, and don't you agree Caroline?*

Caroline shot a wry smile at Geoffrey and nodded. She was beginning to like this young police wife.

Then she turned to Dimitris' mother.

*"So, Christa, have you lived here all your life? I bet you have seen many changes."*

Christa smiled somewhat shallowly, as if she was remembering many events that were perhaps best forgotten, before replying in heavily accented English.

*"Yes, enough to last a lifetime. Some good, others not so good. The war was hard for us; I lost Andreus, my husband, and Dimitris' father. All of us suffered, but I suppose other countries had it worse."*

Though Caroline suspected that the war was likely the source of Christa's unease and likely the reason for her visions, she wisely decided to move on.

Geoffrey had also sensed there was something in the past that was troubling not only Christa but also Caroline. He tried a different track.

*"So where did you and Angela meet?"*

Angela looked across at her husband and smiled warmly, then answered for him, (a common trait among English women, and most likely elsewhere.)

*"At Cambridge University, we were both undergrads, and he looked, well, you know, kind-a cute and lost."*

If Dimitris was embarrassed, he did not show it, simply commenting;

*"We were both reading politics and economics. It was my father's wish I got a proper education and made something of myself. Well, I got the education and something more precious."*

He raised his glass and smiled at his wife, who returned the smile, and raised her glass in agreement.

Caroline nodded, and this time noticed a slight flush of embarrassment on Dimitris's face. Then she made a comment that seemed innocuous,otherwise. but Geoffrey knew otherwise,

*"Do you remember your father? you must have been very young when he died."*

She noticed a sudden flash of panic in his mother's eyes, which dissipated at her son's reply.

*"A little. I was 4 years old. I remember he was quite stern and slapped me on the leg if I was cheeky, but that's all."*

There was an awkward pause, broken by Caroline, who sat back in her chair

*"Well, Crete has a fascinating history, including this temple. It's great to see the historic location of the labyrinth and the temple. I am in awe of the meticulous attention to detail you have put into recreating it."*

The conversation then drifted into history and even briefly into the science of the paranormal. But both Caroline and her husband knew that something was wrong. Years of interviewing witnesses and suspects had given him an insight into evaluating words against body language. In the police world this is known quite simply as coppering. But Caroline, whose mental perception vastly exceeded the ex-Chief Inspector, saw something else beyond deception. Fear, real, cold and overwhelming fear, of what or whom she did not yet know.

For a while, Caroline's unease had abated, but destiny would dictate it would not stay that way.

# Chapter 4

### Restless Spirits

Geoffrey had noticed that Caroline was a little distracted since the meeting with Dimitris and his wife. He put it down to her general lack of interest in police and law enforcement matters. However, as often was the case, he was wide of the mark. Caroline was neither bored nor disinterested, her mind was elsewhere nor at a place her husband could not follow. Try as she might to push this aside and enjoy her honeymoon, the malevolence of the psychic force was too powerful.

This was why; when Dimitris offered to show Geoffrey around his office and introduce him to his colleagues, she pressed him to accept. While grateful, Angela had come to her aid by pointing out that she and Caroline could go and have a quiet coffee and talk about the life of an ex pat in Crete, and Greek cuisine.

Caroline did not know what was disturbing the spirit world, but did know it had something to do with Dimitris and his mother. Spending some time with Angela may help.

........................

Christa Dimikros was a worried woman. The arrival of this English couple and their mention of her husband had stirred a vivid memory of the last time they had met. It was 1944, so many years ago, but still so very clear in her mind.

Nomikos had returned from a meeting with the German regional commander, Major Steinberg. He had told her the meeting was about a loud explosion in the hills outside that had worried the residents. Of course, she was aware of the incident and saw nothing amiss in the German Commander speaking to the local Police Chief about it. However, when he got back from the meeting, he was a totally changed man. Gone was the efficient unflappable police Commander who was always calm and collected. In his place was a frightened, jumpy man whose eyes projected both horror and fear. Of course, she had asked him what was wrong, but he ignored the question and put his hands firmly on her shoulders, staring straight into her eyes, which now began to seriously alarm her.

He told her that she must be prepared to trust him totally and do whatever he said. Then, himself, as he sensed her concern, he sat down. After taking a moment to compose himself he began.

*"There is no way I can explain this to you, but you must believe that nothing means more to me than you and Dimitris. For that reason, I must leave you both immediately. I do not know if I can return or when. In the days to come, you will probably hear many stories about me and evil deeds I have done. Some may be true, but the worst will not be. For Crete, the war will soon be over; and God willing, peace will once more come to our family.*

*For me, I am not sure if there will ever be a peace. I know I am asking a lot, and you deserve an explanation that I cannot give. This may well be our last meeting. If Fate determines that to be so, then I can only say having you and Dimitris share my life was the happiest period in it."*

Tears filled his eyes as he rose, kissed her tenderly, and put on his cap. He paused momentarily as he reached the door when he heard Christa call his name, but only momentarily. Then he was gone. He never returned. At least not in person, but often in her dreams, he came to her. She had never stopped loving him, and never believed he was dead. Not even after she was visited by one of his fellow officers who broke the news. He confirmed his body had been found with those of two German deserters on a mountain road. He had personally seen the body, along with a German officer, there because the incident involved German personnel. It was not recognizable due to the facial injuries, but he was dressed in his uniform. He produced the wallet ID card and a photograph of her and Dimitris that she knew he always carried in his tunic pocket. The facts seemed clear enough.

But Christa had never really accepted it. It made no sense. In the days that followed, militia groups began rounding up those accused of collaborating with the Germans, but no one called at her home. However, with the breakdown of basic law and infighting among groups, Heraklion had not become safe, so she had moved out of the city into the country. Gradually, Nomikos became just a memory, but there were still those nights that he came to her in her dreams. Now 70 years later, those fading memories suddenly grew in magnitude, and she didn't know why. But she did know it had something to do with the woman, Caroline; who she had met today. She got up slowly and walked to the dresser. She opened a drawer and took out a picture of Nomikos, taken on the day he was appointed as chief of police. How smart and proud he looked. She remembered that day. Now she knew she must find out the truth, her daughter-in-law could help. And that is why she had asked her to find out a bit more about the enigmatic Caroline De Winter.

................

The coffee tasted different in Europe. There were many different brands. French and Brazilian had very distinct flavours. In England, instant coffee ruled the market, Nescafe and Maxwell House. But here it was a little tricky. Angela had anticipated this and had chosen one of the few cafes that served Maxwell House. A girl brought the tray, and the two women sat back and relaxed.

*"So, how's the honeymoon going?"*

Caroline smiled

*"Well, so far so good. We haven't quarrelled since we landed, so that's a good sign."*

Angela smiled

*"Oh, give it time; he will soon start bitching about how stuff is much cheaper in England."*

Both women chuckled. As intended, the quip broke the ice, enabling Angela to open up on her background. At first, she talked about university and how it had been a life-changing moment. Then she paused before continuing.

*"So, tell me what brought you and Geoffrey together? I would have thought that a senior police chief would have been the last choice for a psychic, or did you see something deeper?"* Her half smile showed she was following Angela's drift. *"Actually, he was very much a sceptic, but his son was having real issues. My daughter-in-law is also a police detective, and she met up with me after I offered to help. Those kids were pretty mixed up and were unable to fathom that the cause of their problems was a malevolent spirit from England's history. When I had done that, it was plain sailing."*

Angela sat back in her chair and thought about the statement for a brief moment before commenting.

*"So you exorcised the evil spirit?"*

Caroline threw her head back and laughed.

*"No Angela, that's not what psychics do. You're confusing me with a priest. Exorcism is a religious rite carried out within the Christian faith. Priests can talk to a spirit and call them out, but it is a one-way conversation. The Spirit is unlikely to hear, let alone reply. If the so called possessed subject believes the Priest will solve the problem, then lord be praised, it's a miracle."*

*"And if it doesn't work?"*

Caroline took another sip of coffee.

*"Ah well, that's when they usually call me."*

Angela did not reply for a moment, taking time to digest Caroline's answer. Then she looked up with a serious expression on her face.

*"Caroline, this is not a spurious question, but can you really, like you write in your book, actually talk to the dead?"*

Her reply was equally serious.

*"Oh yes, Angela; I can - and do, and usually not by choice. In the spirit world, some have a desperate need to pass messages on. They use psychics to do that, but I do not usually get involved in those cases. Now, can I ask you something? What's troubling your mother in law?"*

The question took Angela by surprise; she hesitated and searched frantically in her brain for an answer before deciding to reply.

*"Well, I think she is a bit scared of you. I told her you were a famous clairvoyant, and that seemed to upset her. I really don't know why. I'm not sure if she even knows what that is."*

*"Well, that may well have confused her. A clairvoyant is someone who sees into the future, and who often charges exorbitant rates to inform someone they will meet the right man, or woman, will have children and live a happy life. A psychic is just a conduit; a sort of postman or messenger between the living world and the spirit one. When I shook her hand, I felt a strong bond from a spirit trying to channel me."*

Angela looked puzzled, but seemed very attentive.

*"Channelled?"*

*"Sorry, channelled is a word used in the physic realm; it means to use someone to make a connection."*

*"So, are you saying a spirit or something is trying to contact Christa? Why would they do that?"*

Caroline sat back in her chair.

*"Frankly, I've no idea, but it must be important."*

Angela sat back for a moment digesting what Caroline had said, then offered a suggestion."

*"Could it be her husband's spirit? He died in the war."*

Caroline shook her head.

*"No, it was a female. I don't know who yet, but I think she will make contact again. Look, Angela, I wouldn't mention any of this to Christa or your husband, at least not yet. If you've read my books, you will understand why."*

She nodded and was about to admit that she hadn't actually read 'The soul Never Dies'. She had bought it out of curiosity and just hadn't got around to starting it yet. That would change - starting tonight.

Caroline dropped Angela off at the station house using the Avis rental car before returning to the hotel. Dimitris had already agreed to drive Geoffrey back later. That suited Caroline and it gave her the chance to get a shower and change. She smiled to herself, thinking of her likely scanning through the book and trying to get up on the world of psychic phenomenon. The warm shower felt so good after the sweltering heat of the island.

Stepping out of the shower, Caroline slipped on her towelling robe and wrapped a small towel around her still wet hair. Suddenly, her smile faded. She looked up in the reflection of the mirror as a shape began to form behind her.

*"Hello Sally, I wondered when you would show up."*

# Chapter 5

## Crete's Dark History

It was around 8 pm when Geoffrey returned, later than he had promised, but then what else was new. It was a fine evening, and he had picked up a couple of Kababs. And thoughtfully, Caroline had obtained a bottle the local Ouzo wine, which was on ice in the Fridge. The holiday apartment was on the first floor, but had its own balcony, affording a good view out over the sea; a perfect setting worthy of any travel brochure. Although they had not been married for more than a couple of days, Geoffrey, although appreciative of the romantic gesture, had no problem seeing through it.

*"Okay, sweetheart, what is it?"*

In a scene reminiscent of a femme fatale from a Bond movie, Caroline raised her eyes, looking at him over the top of her wine glass, and then she broke into a giggle.

*"Damn you, Geoff, you could always see through me. Ok, there is something, not sure if you can help though."*

Geoffrey put his glass down.

*"Let me guess, something to do with the paranormal that requires input from the living world; something that may involve our friends, Dimitris and Angela."*

Caroline sat back in her chair, slowly shaking her head, but not in denial.

*"Partially right, honey, but not them. More so, it's Christa; I need to know if there is any record of an old murder case dating back to 1944. A young resident named Sally Knight."*

*"Okay, I'll see what I can do; Dimitris may have access to some old records. So, may I ask if she's the reason you've been distracted lately?"*

Caroline nodded

*"She is possibly the key to all of it. She has reached out to me with an intensity I haven't felt since the Mary Rose case involving your daughter.*

*What she is saying, if true, has the potential to threaten lives, thousands of lives. I have to be sure about her and everything she told me. If it checks out, then we need to do something. And fast."*

*"Do what exactly?"*

Geoffrey's question was a fair one, and Caroline knew it. She said nothing for a moment, as if searching for the right words. Finally she replied.

*"I don't know; I just cannot assimilate this at the moment."*

She got up and walked to the balcony rail before turning back to face him.

*"Look Geoff, supposing someone reported to you they had just killed someone at their home and the body was there in the house. This had happened 10 years ago, and that they now wanted to confess. You wouldn't just arrest them and call it 'case closed,' would you?"*

Geoffrey shook his head

*"No, you know I couldn't do that. So what you are saying is that you need to find out if this Sally Knight really existed and how she died, why she died, and who killed her*

Caroline sighed.

*"Well, sort of. I know in my heart why she died and who killed her. Its verification and motive I need. Most of all, Christa is a big part of this, but I cannot approach her directly. The poor woman is scared to death of me, and her son- and daughter in law are very protective."*

Geoffrey nodded understandingly

*Well, there are sure to be people here who remember the war. Why don't you check out the local museum while I speak to Dimitris and see if there are any records of the late Sally Knight? Now, can we get back to the seductive and mysterious woman I married who has designs on me this night?"*

.....................

Clio Nikolaou did not look up from her desk as Caroline entered the Museum of the Battle of Crete and National Resistance, situated close to the Heraklion Archaeological Museum in the city centre. Many tourists casually visited to browse during the day. And only if approached directly with a question, would she start a conversation? Clio had worked in the museum for almost 40 of her 60 years and seemed to be a good starting point. Hopefully she spoke English.

She looked up as Caroline approached her desk.

*"Good morning madam, I am researching the history of this area in 1944 for a book. I was told this is the place to visit."*

Clio nodded, replying in heavily accented English.

*"Well, we have a pretty unique collection here, covering both the occupation and period leading up to the German, Italian occupation."*

Caroline glanced around.

*"So I see, I am more interested in life here during the occupation years, everyday stories and experiences, including, if possible, any eye witnesses that are still living here."*

If Caroline's reply surprised her, it did not show.

*"Well, madam, those were dark times for our community. We have some albums and some ID cards and passes issued during that period. A lot of artefacts were looted by the communists after the Germans left. We do, however, have a good selection of uniform items and Partisan equipment. Let me get some albums for you to look at. As for surviving witnesses, I suppose I would count as one, though I was only 8 at the time."*

Clio produced a large photo album and put it on the table, followed by a second one.

*"These cover 1944. We can let you have photocopies of anything you wish to use. Just call me over if you need anything else."*

Caroline opened the first album. For 5 minutes, she went through the pages, meticulously examining each page. There were two photos she bookmarked before she called Clio over.

She pointed to one showing a police officer standing by a marked police car, the other of a German Officer talking to the same policeman.

*"Can you identify these two people Madam? The Policeman seems a bit familiar to me."*

Clio looked at the black, and white images before replying.

*"The Policeman is Andreas Nomikos, the commander of police here at the time, a much hated man. The German is the Garrison Commander Colonel Kurt Franz Steinberg. His son Dimitris now occupies that same position, which is why Andreas may seem familiar. You may have seen him around town."*

Caroline nodded

*"Yes, of course. I met him yesterday and his wife as well. I did not know his father was chief here during the war, strange he never mentioned it."*

*"Strange, well if I was an outsider I would agree, but not if you were here then, or since."*

Caroline's interest was now peaked, and she pressed the point.

*"That's fascinating. So what caused the rift?"*

*"It's not really my place to say you being friends with Dimitris and all. I don't want to say anything that may cause a row, don't want to be the cause of any upsets."*

Clio hesitated

She moved to walk away, but Caroline had no intention of leaving it there.

*"Please Madam; I assure you that everything you can tell me will be confidential. Dimitris and his wife are not friends; they're really only two people we had a drink with. So in case we see them again, it would be wise to avoid any subjects that may be awkward."*

Clio nodded understandingly and returned and sat down at the Table.

*"Well, Andreas was nothing like his son. He was a German collaborator and fled the city after the Germans left. If he had stayed, it was likely the partisans would have shot him."*

Clio stayed at the table and identified the other photographs. Captions for each were carefully put in the notebook and added to the photocopies. The task took almost an hour, but Clio seemed happy to help. Caroline thanked her for her cooperation and offered to pay her for her time; the offer was declined, so the two women agreed that Caroline could make a donation to the Museum. Then Clio added;

*"Funny that you are asking about 1944. Most enquiries are more general. Sometimes tourists, both German and British, are looking for relatives, but yesterday another lady came in, a German who specifically asked about Andreas and the German presence here. I think she was looking for a relative also, but she never said so. She seemed more interested in the contamination zone in the hills."*

Caroline's interest now sparked something that Sally had said to her about the no go area being the key.

*"So, what is the contamination zone? There is nothing in the guidebook about it."*

Clio shook her head.

*"You won't find it in any guidebook or map, for that matter. The island depends on the tourist trade, so it is not mentioned. It was a camp, or plant, during the war, very hush-hush and guarded by the SS. It was blown up when the Germans left, and sealed off. The military detected dangerously high levels of radiation there in the soil, so they covered the ground with tons of soil and sand, then sealed it off and posted warning signs. It's a pretty hefty fine for anyone caught up there."*

...............

Caroline left the museum with a bundle of papers; photocopies of the photographs in the albums, it was a start. Now she had another line of enquiry to pursue. Further progress would depend on Geoffrey, and more importantly, with co-operation from Dimitris. On her return, Caroline half expected another visit from Sally's spirit, but that never happened. She turned on her computer and started a google search using Crete forbidden zone and no-go areas, but got no useful returns. After 10 fruitless minutes, she paused her search and decided a good margarita was called for. It took a couple of minutes to mix; she took a sip as she returned to the laptop. She touched the spacebar to reactivate the screen, then saw new search criteria in the search box; it read 'SS in Crete ww2'. Strange, she did not recall typing that or even thinking of it, but she hit the search button, anyway.

The screen brought up an article written in 1965 regarding the presence of a military outpost staffed by a small SS detachment. The article was from a fringe ww2 conspiracy magazine called, 'Forbidden Facts' that promoted a number of since debunked theories, such as Americas plan to make the UK a state of the USA, and that the Duke of Kent was negotiating with Hitler to allow Britain to remain neutral while the Third Reich over ran Europe. Which was why Hitler's deputy, Rudolf Hess, had flown to Scotland in a well-publicized event before the US got involved in the war.

Such theories still had their proponents today, but this article, written by a man called Costa Santos, seemed different. As Caroline read through the text, it had a ring of sincerity about it. The author made no wild claims about motives or master plans, but did pose the questions that many people both on and off the Island had asked. Such as what was the purpose of the SS detachment? Why did they never visit the town, and what was the plant or research station actually involved in? The museum curator had indicated radiation contamination, but that in itself posed more questions.

...............

Dimitris was puzzled by Geoffrey's request to check on police records for a case so long ago, often people made similar requests regarding current or recent crimes. Usually these were reporters, and department police dictated that all such requests be denied or referred to the Department of Justice, but in this case it seemed innocent enough. He had told her that Caroline was researching law and order under the occupation, and the name Sally Knight came up as a murder victim in 1944. There were no news reports available dating from that time, but he wondered if the police files may contain something.

*"Well, I can check Geoff, we do have some stuff from the period but at the time we were overseen by the German governor and they could, and did, censor or remove items. Still, ill see what's there."*

Geoffrey thanked him and the conversation moved on.

Back at their apartment, Caroline's research was broken by a phone call. She glanced at her watch: 7:30; Probably Geoff, she mused as she picked up the receiver.

*"Hello, Is this Frau De Winter?"*

A female voice with a marked German accent. She did not recognize it, but replied.

*"I am Caroline De Winter. Who is this?"*

*"I apologize for calling you like this, but I got your number from the curator of the war museum. My name is Hanna Vassal. I am carrying out enquiries about the disappearance of a relative who I have discovered was here in 1944, working for the Reich administration at a military plant. I understand you are also making enquiries about the area. Is it possible we can meet up at some time?"*

Caroline knew that Geoff may not be so keen on her carrying out investigations on a 50 year old mystery during their honeymoon, but she nevertheless agreed. Taking her number and telling her she would call her tomorrow to fix a time. As she hung up Caroline had already decided to push Geoffrey to Tag along.

# Chapter 6

## Hanna Vassal

Geoffrey had not put up any real objection to Caroline meeting with the German woman, and in truth was a little intrigued by the co-incidence. They had arranged to meet at a small bistro that was close to the apartment. Geoffrey would have preferred to have waited until he got something back from Dimitris, but there was no guarantee he would have any useful information, anyway. So now they sat in a quiet corner at the appointed time and place.

Caroline spotted Hanna the moment she arrived; a slim, well-dressed woman in her mid-40s carrying a small briefcase. She stopped and scanned the customers in the Bistro before approaching them. Caroline looked up as she approached.

*"Good morning, Frau Vassal I assume?"*

*"Yes, you must be Caroline. It was good of you to see me. I know it must seem odd to get a request like this out of the blue."*

Geoffrey Smiled broadly before replying.

*"Not as odd as you may think, Ma'am. In fact, since I've known Caroline, you might say it's quite a common occurrence."*

Caroline feigned slight annoyance before replying.

*"As usual, he has to but in; Hanna, this is my husband Geoffrey. Ignore him Hanna; he's in a funny mood this morning. Now I understand you are enquiring about the no go area here, something about a missing relative?"*

Hanna hesitated for a few seconds before replying.

*"Well, that's what I told the curator, because I couldn't say much else. Really, I am trying to track down events that occurred here in late 1944. My grandfather came here with my grandmother to work on a project. They were virologists working for the German Government. They were not alone; apparently there was a group of around 20. My mother told me the story and said they arrived here, but were never heard from again.*

*All attempts to find out more have been unsuccessful. There are no official records of them since they left Germany. Of course I would like to find out what happened to them, but it's more than that. All records of them, work history, and identity documents are missing. It's as though someone is deliberately trying to erase them from history. Why would they do that after all this time?"*

Neither Caroline nor Geoffrey could think of a logical answer, but decided to talk a little about their interest in the incident. Caroline began.

*"Well, Hanna, we are interested in this quarantined area, but for different reasons. However, we may spread some light on this. The area was a military research station of some kind and was run by a detachment of the Waffen-SS. The station was destroyed by a large explosion towards the end of the war. And it has been off limits to all personnel since. The ground is apparently still contaminated with some chemical agent or radiation. There are signs posted at the gate on a fence that surrounds the site warning of hefty fines and imprisonment for anyone trespassing."*

Hanna nodded

*"Yes, I've seen them. But I still don't understand why you are interested in this place."*

There was another awkward moment of silence broken by Geoffrey.

*"Well, that's complicated. Do you know who my wife is?"*

Hanna lowered her head and replied softly.

*"In truth, not until yesterday; when I got her name and checked it on Google. I'm afraid I am not really into this psychic paranormal stuff. Are you saying that this is the reason for your interest?"*

Caroline nodded

*"I'm afraid so. I had no knowledge that this place existed last week. We are here on our honeymoon, believe it or not. But someone interrupted that; a powerful presence that compelled me to help."*

By now, Caroline was beginning to sense a growing scientism in Hanna's facial expressions.

"Help, I do not understand Help who?

Caroline sighed

"That's the problem, I'm not sure. All I know is that there is a great surge in the spirit world that is targeting me. I do know that it concerns this place and the people who died here in 1944. I also know that I need to deal with it to clear my mind and get back to a normal life."

Hanna remained silent for a moment, and then stood up.

"Well thank you for seeing me, Caroline, but I do not really think you can be of assistance in this matter."

She smiled briefly before turning around and leaving the Bistro.

# Chapter 7

## A 50-Year-Old Murder Mystery

Geoffrey was surprised at getting a call from Nomikos, asking him to drop by the office later regarding his missing person enquiry, but happily agreed. He had felt sure that there was no way he could have found too much after such a long time. Caroline, however, was very enthusiastic to hear what he had discovered.

Nomikos saw him enter the front office and come forward, with hand extended.

*"Geoffrey, thank you for coming in, I have found something that I think you, and especially Caroline, will find most interesting."*

He led the way into the office and closed the door behind them. After motioning Geoffrey into a seat, he picked up a file from his desk.

*"In 1944, your Sally Knight was a young student here in the city, much like now the student population was hostile to authority. She was on a watch list compiled by my father and supplied to the German authorities. In most cases, she would have been called in for questioning, but at the time the allies had requested the garrison remain in the city, assisting the police to ensure a smooth transfer of power after the war ended. In fact, we did have a number of former garrison members settle here after the war. Most are still here.*

*Sally died in somewhat mysterious circumstances at around the same time as the explosion at the plant. There was suspicion that the Germans killed her, but according to the autopsy report, she died from radiation poisoning, a very high dose. The body was cremated, and the ashes disposed of in secret to ensure there was no radiation risk."*

Geoffrey had listened carefully to what had been said, and took a few moments to assimilate it before speaking.

*"I see. So was there any reason uncovered how she was irradiated?"*

*"Not officially. There was a note in the daily diary that my father had been invited with other town officials to the plant where a German-led*

*enquiry was taking place. There is nothing here regarding what was said at the meeting. In fact, that is significant to me personally."*

Geoffrey noted the change in Nomikos manner as he asked; *"Why?"*

His reply was unexpected.

*"Because my friend that was the same day my father was found dead outside the city, with the bodies of two German soldiers. I recently came into the possession of a notebook belonging to one of his colleagues here. He recorded in it that my father was apparently involved in a gunfight. Over what, we can only speculate. A lot of reports and witness statement appear to have been lost in what is known in England as 'The Fog of War'.*

*Your investigation has exposed some information that has given me a renewed inspiration to look further into my father's demise. I confess, initially I had been told the locals considered him a traitor and a German collaborator. I suppose the truth is that I just did not want to dig too deeply into that aspect. After all, no one likes to think that their father betrayed their country.*

*So I let it be. But there were problems with doing that. Some things do not fit, such as why my father's pocketbook was missing from his body. My mother told me he always carried it on duty. Also, she never attended the funeral. I do not even know if there was one. He never came back, and I kept asking her why, finally she said he had died in the fighting to free Crete."*

Now Geoffrey was really paying attention.

*"So is there no record even of the funeral or where he was buried. I find that more than a little odd."*

Dimitris nodded.

*"Not just odd, it's almost unheard of, even taking into account the chaotic conditions at the time. I therefore am looking at the whole situation differently. I think that your wife may be able to make sense of it all."*

Geoffrey nodded understandingly.

*"One of the problems with Caroline is that she works on a different plain to people like us, police officers who assess guilt or innocence on evidence. Caroline also converses with witnesses and assesses their veracity and truthfulness. The problem is that these witnesses are not of the living world. They cannot be interviewed or cross-examined.*

*Last year we were both engaged in a case in England where I witnessed her extraordinary power to solve an 800 year old mystery by both researching history and interacting with these spirits. So I am unable to debunk this power, but neither can I rationally explain it. However, I do think she may be able to move us forward."*

It was now that Dimitris demonstrated the benefit of a British University education.

*"Well, as your William Shakespeare put it; 'there are more things in heaven and earth than were dreamt of in your philosophy.'"*

Geoffrey smiled, *"Hamlet to Horatio; well done and well-remembered."*

.....................

While Dimitris and Geoffrey were meeting, across town a troubled Hanna Vassal was not having too much luck in tracing anyone who knew anything about the prohibited area or the people who may have worked there. The nearest she got was a reply that they were Nazi, very bad people. But no one would or could elaborate. It was frustrating, to put it mildly. She walked over to the kitchenette and poured herself a drink from the half-finished bottle of ouzo on the countertop.

*'What are you doing, Hanna?'* she said quietly under her breath. *'Chasing a 50 year old mystery that no one even remembers. For what?'*

She took another drink; at first she did not notice the temperature drop. Then, at the extreme limit of her peripheral vision she saw the figure standing close to the kitchen door. She had not heard the door open and no one had knocked.

Quickly, she turned to face the figure

*"Who the hell are you? I'm certain I locked the door."*

She blurted as the figure came into focus. A young, pretty dark skinned teenager stood in the room. She had dark brown hair and wearing a light yellow dress. She studied Hanna for a few seconds before replying.

*"You did lock the door. Miss, I'm sorry if I upset you, but you are making a mistake."*

Hanna saw no threat from the confused looking teenager and sat down. That's all I need, she thought to herself. Some lost kid looking for cash or a handout.

*"A mistake about what exactly, young lady? maybe you should explain yourself."*

The girl shook her head and looked down before responding.

*"No one knows your real purpose for being here. You are moving into an area that you cannot succeed in. Why do you insist on speaking to the wrong people?"*

Hanna looked up at her.

*"Wrong people. Who exactly are you? I've spoken to everyone who matters. Nothing you say makes any sense."*

Hanna saw the determined look in the teenagers' eyes and assumed she was the daughter of one of the opposition. She softened her tone and smiled.

*"So young lady, I am making a mistake, am I. OK! Who do you suggest I should be speaking to?"*

The teenager looked up and spoke.

*"Caroline De Winter"*

Then her image blurred and just faded away. The girl's image vanished in front of her eyes as a wide eyed Hanna screamed and dropped her glass, which shattered on the tiled floor.

# Chapter 8

### Premonition

Caroline was finally beginning to take hold of herself. Three days after starting their holiday, she decided to firmly put her paranormal feelings to the background. She decided that the most likely cause anyway was restless spirits trying to reach out to relatives in the living world. This was her honeymoon, and she was determined to put that and her relationship with Geoffrey front and centre. Dimitris had supplied some background information on Sally Knight, but though interesting, it did not really move the narrative. Angela had taken it on herself to act as a volunteer guide on places of interest. Rarely did she discuss the paranormal, though by now she was well into Caroline's book. Geoffrey had been chatting to his daughter and indicated he had a couple of other calls to make. So she called Angela and asked if she would like to join her at the Bistro.

It was while enjoying that coffee this morning that she saw a familiar face. Hanna Vassal was seated alone at a table near the patio entrance. Caroline was sure she had noticed her, but she made no attempt to show that she recognize her or even pay her any attention, seemingly focusing on the laptop computer in front of her. Not in itself an unusual activity but Caroline wondered why she had come here to this Bistro. She surmised that it was not because of the coffee. Her suspicions were right.

Hanna had been hoping to catch Caroline alone, but was disappointed when she saw Angela with her. In any case, she was still unsure what she was really going to say, since her experience with the apparition her careful plans had been knocked off course. Hanna was not seeking a lost relative; she was in fact an imposter, a woman with an ulterior motive, one that certainly did not concern a psychic. She had already approached the police post and delivered the letter endorsed by several Greek politicians, but had received a lukewarm response.

That in itself had raised her suspicions even more. Of course, no one except the police knew the real reason she was here, least of all Caroline. Her cover story had been accepted by all, including the curator of the museum. But try as she might, the apparition had rattled her. A casual remark to a waitress had supplied the name of Caroline's companion. It had dictated her next move. She asked for the bill and left without even a glance towards the two women.

......................

The morning had started well for Dimitris. His mother had departed for her weekly visit to Catholic Sisters of Mercy Hospital, situated 5 miles outside the city in a small hamlet. The hospital was in fact, little more than a clinic and rarely had more than 6 patients. Most were there because they had little income and support. Average age was 80 to 85, and the clinic provided basic care and a light daily meal. Christa knew most of them, and in particular, an elderly fisherman with an unkempt beard and greying hair who kept to himself most days. The sisters tolerated him and sometimes rebuked him for blasphemy when he cursed, but old Kriss was harmless enough. He did, however seem to interact with Christa and would speak to her often about the good old days and how the youth of today lacked respect.

Today she greeted him with a wave and he waved back with less enthusiasm; muttering that the sisters were spying on him again. It was a frequent charge and by now the sisters were well used to it. Christa suggested they go for a walk away from them, and he could tell her all about it. Of course, old Kriss was not the only patient that Christa saw. Nor was she, by any count the only volunteer the sisters could count on. But in truth, the sisters were grateful that she was one of the few that could put up with Kriss' moods and not lose patience. Maybe the reason was that she was closer to his age. In fact, all the patients were old enough to remember the war, which was a subject that usually dominated the conversations. Few had any time for the younger sisters whose conversations were limited to us all being god's children and deserving of respect.

Christa stayed for a couple of hours, making sure verbally, to reassure Kriss that she would reveal nothing he had said; not that they would have been the slightest bit interested anyway. As she boarded the bus for the return trip to Heraklion, she thought again of the English couple who had unnerved her. Her son had told her that the man's wife was well known in the psychic world as a person who knew a lot about the afterlife, and that her husband was a retired senior police officer who had worked in England. She knew Dimitris had long been an admirer of the British Bobby, a name that British police officers were known by. And also that he was a fan of some of the British TV police shows that he had on tape. That was most likely the reason he had befriended the couple. Still, there was something about his wife that unnerved her, something almost chilling. She had noticed it the first time they met. And as far as she was concerned, the sooner their honeymoon was over, the happier she would be.

........................

Back in Heraklion, Dimitris was reading a reply from the Justice Department. It was not the news he had hoped for. Hanna had been given permission to visit the prohibited site to check for radiation and take samples of the soil. Apparently, the department thought that it was not worth creating a fuss over that may attract bigger press attention right in the middle of the tourist season. As far as he could recall, the site had not been tested or examined for at least 10 years. Certainly, if there was no more danger, then the area could be opened for recreation use, such as camping or hikers. He had been granted one concession, in that he is allowed to accompany her and bring a bio chemist to also take samples. He picked up the phone and dialled Hanna's number.

........................

Back at the apartment, Caroline had enjoyed her day. Dimitris and Geoffrey's absence had given her the space she needed to finally put the whole psychic thing to the back of her mind. Now back at the apartment, she and Geoffrey had a little time to themselves. For Hanna, however, that was not to be. Elated, following the call from Dimitris, she decided to spend the evening making plans for the coming visit. She was a little worried that there could still be problems, but the thought of the rewards and the boost to her career put that aside. She decided to make it an early night. Closing the laptop, she took off her top and skirt, and was preparing to take a shower, but the effects of the ouzo had made her sleepy.

"*Sod it*" she said softly, "*Shower can wait till the morning.*" She turned out the bedside lamp and pulled the bedcover over her as the room began to grow colder.

......................

Across town, Caroline was talking softly to Geoffrey. They had been in bed only 20 minutes when suddenly she stopped mid-sentence. She stood up and grabbed her purse, hurriedly searching through it before grabbing a card and picking up the phone.

Geoffrey also stood up.

"*What's up love?*"

Caroline ignored him. He could hear the phone connect and the ring tone on the line.

"*Pick up Hanna, for God's sake, pick up.*"

Now Geoffrey was really alarmed. He grabbed her shoulders and pulled her around to face him, repeating,

"*What's the matter Love, you look like you've seen a ghost.*"

He paused as he realized what he had just said.

Caroline, however, was in no mood to discuss it. She shook herself free and glared at him.

"*Hanna's in danger, real danger. It may already be too late. We have to get there now.*"

Quickly, she slipped on her slacks and T-shirt, grabbed the car keys and headed for the door with Geoffrey in tow. Geoffrey used his mobile phone to call Dimitris, who, fortunately, had given him his private number. To his surprise, Dimitris already knew the address. Hurriedly Geoffrey finished dressing himself as he was being towed out the door.

Dimitris was already there when Caroline pulled up. An ambulance was also parked outside. Despite the hour, a small crowd of tourists and locals had gathered, being controlled by two Greek police officers. As she got out of the car, two paramedics emerged carrying a stretcher. Geoffrey noticed the face of the patient was uncovered, which was a good sign. Dimitris emerged about a minute later, speaking to a police officer. He looked up as he saw them both and walked over.

*"Well, she's unconscious now. She was not breathing when we got here, but she has a chance."*

Caroline looked relieved and only now turned to her husband.

*"Sorry for the shut out Geoff, but I didn't have time to explain."*

Dimitris then spoke up.

*"So, what's going on Geoff? I take it you know this Hanna Vassal somehow."*

Geoff shrugged

*"Not really, we only met her once. She's looking for a missing relative and thought we may be able to help. I think Caroline scared her off. We haven't seen her since."*

Caroline interrupted

*"Oh, I have. I was having coffee at the Bistro near our apartment with Angela when I noticed her sitting alone working on her laptop. Didn't speak to her though, and she left. I think she may have been avoiding me."*

Dimitris shook his head

*"I doubt that. You see, Hanna Vassal is no tourist. She's a high-priced lawyer working for a developer. They are interested in the quarantine area, or at least that's my guess. She has gained permission from the ministry to visit the area and take samples for analysis. She has the support of a*

*number of parliamentarians. We were supposed to go up there tomorrow, but that seems to be off the cards now."*

Geoffrey seemed deep in thought, and then spoke up.

*"Seems a bit of a coincidence; any idea what happed here tonight?"*

Dimitris smiled.

*"Do we suspect foul play you mean? Sorry to disappoint you, this seems like a stupid accident. We will of course carry out an enquiry and hopefully be able to question Hanna if she recovers. But for now, it seems she left the gas cooker on and had a bit too much wine. She probably owes her life to you Caroline, but I have no idea how I can put that in my report."*

Geoffrey grinned as he replied

*"Thankfully, I no longer have that problem friend, it's your investigation. Of course, if you need me -you know where to find me, but it's late and I think we'll call it a night."*

Once in the car, Caroline, though no longer tense, was aware that all was not as it seemed. Finally she said;

*"I don't buy it Geoff, none of it. Ok, Hanna was not the person we thought she was, but she was shrewd and level-headed. I cannot see her leaving the gas on, or for that matter, cooking anything."*

*"You're saying you think someone broke in and turned it on?"*

Geoffrey's question was a good one, tinged with a hint of sarcasm. But Caroline didn't bite.

*"No, not someone, some thing, and that is the most worrying aspect. I've come across this phenomenon before we met. That time I was the victim, but I've learned a bit since."*

*"Are we talking Spirits here? I thought that only poltergeist's could move things around."*

Again, the observation seemed fair, but as usual incorrect, due to his lack of understanding of the paranormal, at least in comparison with Caroline. She considered trying to explain, but really just wanted to get home, so she just answered;

*"No sweetheart, the two entities are different. Let's talk about it tomorrow."*

.....................

The events of the previous night troubled Dimitris. He knew nothing about the paranormal, but had done his own research on Caroline. In particular, he noticed she had been used, though unofficially by several police agencies, to assist with some murder enquiries. He did note that his wife was now nearing the end of Caroline's book; he decided to ask her what impressions she had of her and her claims. Her reply was unexpected. She told him that the book had changed her in a very fundamental way. She now had no fear anymore of dying. The book had shown her that there was another life after death, and that fear of death is misplaced. To Dimitris that sounded like something the priest would say at a funeral, though Angela had not shown any real interest in religion before.

Still it could do no harm and if it made her feel safer, then that was fine by him. It was 24 hours before Hanna regained consciousness. By which time Dimitris had the preliminary report by the investigator in charge.

As expected, the report included that the gas dials on the gas stove were turned down, but not completely off. There was a half empty bottle of ouzo wine on the kitchen counter top, but the investigator was not one to have jumped to conclusions. She had also noted that there was no sign of any meal being prepared. A check of the waste bin showed no used plates or food. This was an anomaly, but though noted, was not enough to alter her preliminary report that this appeared to have been an accident. He put the report down, and wondered. He himself had to force the locked door open to gain entry after getting no response; therefore the victim had locked herself in.

Still, there was little more to be done until the hospital said they would be able to interview Hanna. Until then he had a big city precinct to run.

Hanna Vassal was a lucky woman. She heard those words faintly through the pain of the mother of all headaches that greeted her as she slowly regained a semblance of consciousness. The speaker was male; there were other voices, but jumbled and indistinct. Slowly she opened her eyes; the glare of light forced her to instantly close them again. Then slowly she opened one eye, squinting to adjust the glare. The green curtain surrounding her, the realization she was lying in a stark single bed with an iron frame, she could hear people talking and moving about beyond the curtain, she took a deep breath which produced a fit of coughing. That, in turn, brought a woman into the bed space from beyond the curtain.

Hanna recognized a nurse's uniform.

*"Good morning, Hanna. How are we doing this morning? You had us a bit worried."*

It took a few seconds for the words to register before she was able to reply.

*"I feel like shit, to be honest, with a blinding headache for a start. Am I in hospital?"*

*"Yes, you are lucky to be alive. Maybe you should be more careful with the wine. Here. Now lay still and I'll get you something for the headache."*

Hanna did not need a repeat of the instruction. She closed her eyes and tried to remember what happened last night. The nurse had indicated wine, but she had only had one glass. It didn't make sense. Then she remembered something else, the meeting. God! The meeting, she would be late for the meeting. She tried to sit up, big mistake. Her head hit the pillow fast. She fought to get control of her senses and looked round as the nurse returned, this time accompanied by a man in a white light coat she assumed to be a doctor.

*"Well, good morning, my dear. I would just lie still for the moment. The nurse will give you something for the headache and it will ease after a while. We have no idea of your medical history, so we have a few questions we need to ask."*

*"You and me both, doctor."* she muttered, then more clearly.

*"Sorry, I understand, but I too have questions; like what happened to me and why am I here."*

The Doctor smiled understandingly.

*"Well, you are here because you fell asleep in your apartment with the gas stove still on. The result was you have inhaled a dangerous amount of Carbon Monoxide gas. Quite frankly, you are a very lucky young woman. Had the police not found you Tuesday night, we would not be talking now."*

Hanna looked confused.

*"Tuesday night, you mean last night; today is Wednesday - right?"*

The Doctor shook his head

*"No Hanna, today is Thursday, 9:30 am to be precise. You've been out for almost 25 hours. That is unusually long for gas exposure. I suspect that you were also a little overtired - yes."*

The news hit her like a bolt from the blue. Then as it slowly sank in she repeated what she had just heard,

*"I've been here for 25 hours?"*

The doctor nodded. Hanna lay back on the pillow and closed her eyes.

*"I had a meeting this morning; I mean yesterday morning, with Captain Nomikos at an old site outside town, I must call him."*

*"Well, that will not be necessary, Hanna, he wants to see you and has asked to be informed when you are able to answer a few questions. In the meantime, we need your medical history. Just take it easy. The nurse has a form to fill out regarding allergies, medications, and such. With your permission, I'll call the captain and tell him you're awake. If you don't feel up to it, I can ask him to call later this afternoon. In any case, it is my advice that too much activity may not be conducive to a good recovery. Any meetings and such can wait. Let's get you back on your feet first."*

..................

As Hanna was coming to terms with her situation at Heraklion Police Headquarters, Dimitris was speaking to Officer Cora Kronos, the investigating officer who had filed her preliminary report. He asked if there had been anything unusual at the scene, regardless if she thought it relevant or not. The officer thought for a moment before replying.

*"Well, sir, one thing did seem odd. It may be nothing and I am sure there could be a hundred and one reasons, but the gas stove was lit, albeit on a low setting. Indicating she had forgotten to turn it off. But there was no sign of anything being cooked or prepared. It was a very warm night, so why did she turn the gas on?"*

*Dimitris nodded*

*"Yes, I noticed that, it's as you say; odd."*

He was interrupted by an officer from the office who told him the hospital had just called to say Hanna was now conscious, and would he like to speak to her? He nodded and asked her to transfer the call. The receptionist smiled and disappeared. The deck phone then rang, and he picked up the receiver. He spoke to the caller for a couple of minutes before turning back to the incident investigator.

*"Well, Cora, it seems as we will soon know. Hanna Vassal has woken up and should be OK. She has agreed to see me at 3. Would you like to come along, Cora?"*

*Kronos smiled*

*"Yes sir, thank you."*

...................

Having heard nothing from Dimitris, Caroline and Geoffrey had settled down a little. As promised, Caroline had attempted to explain the difference between a spirit and a poltergeist. It had not made much sense to him, but he knew better than to risk an argument, so he decided to accept that in the world of the paranormal, there was a difference. As far as he could tell, Poltergeists were troublemakers whose purpose was to scare people with stupid pranks; whereas spirits were departed souls that could, and sometimes did, make contact. He decided that was enough for a level-headed ex-cop. So he paid it no more heed. He was, however, a little intrigued as to what the deal was with the quarantine zone. So much so that he decided to ask Dimitris a few more questions about it. But for the moment, he would keep Caroline in the dark. No sense in upsetting the honeymoon any more than they already had. Five days had already passed of the 14 days break, and enough of it had been wasted already.

# Chapter 9

### Christa's Old Flame

Carlos Santos read the email twice. It brought back some good memories of the 60s. Of protest marches and music you could really dance to.

'Dear Mr Santos,

You don't know me, but I recently came across an article you wrote in 1965 for a magazine called 'Forbidden Facts'.

It was about a military installation on Crete in 1944.

I am currently on holiday in Crete and am investigating the same location. I wonder if it would be possible for you to call me on my cell phone, 0224.03.4548.

I would really appreciate your input.

Sincerely,

Caroline De Winter'

The email did intrigue Carlos and also brought back memories. That article written when he was 19 had been the first he had been paid for. It had arguably started his career in journalism. 1965, it seemed so long ago. He picked up the receiver of his desk phone and pressed 0.

*"Jenny, can you place a call for me to a cell phone number, 0224.03.4548, a Miss Caroline De Winter. She's in Crete in the Mediterranean. If my calculations are correct, it should be around 5 pm there."*

*A* female voice acknowledged and hung up.

..............

In her apartment in Heraklion, Caroline was stepping out of the shower, her second today. The dry heat of the island made this a necessity for most westerners. Geoffrey was out on the balcony, admiring the view. It certainly looked idyllic. He had not heard from Dimitris for almost two days. That actually really suited him. He had hoped that this honeymoon would be memorable for both of them, provided this wartime mystery would just go away. Then Caroline's cell phone rang. He picked it up noticing it was a UK number. He glanced towards the bathroom, noting the shower was off. He answered the call, partially out of curiosity. An English female voice came on the line. Geoffrey knocked on the bathroom door.

*"Honey, you have a call from the Spectator Magazine; from one of the editors, a Carlos Santos."*

Quickly, Caroline emerged from the bathroom, securing the towel around her head. Back in London the Phone rang on Santos's desk. He picked up the receiver.

*"Mr Santos, I have Miss De Winter on the line, transferring you now."*

..........................

As she slowly regained her strength, Hanna had been transferred to an observation ward. It allowed her to continue to review the past 3 days in her head. Of course, the investigation was important for her career, but she could not put the sight of the vanishing teenager out of her mind. That was no dream. Nothing made sense. There was no rationality to it, but nevertheless she knew she needed to discover more. This Caroline De Winter woman seemed to be a good place to start. She had asked someone to bring her laptop from the flat, which the Police had still taped off. Cora Kronos had delivered it, giving her the chance to ask Hanna a few more questions. Now, with access to the internet she was able to research Caroline. Very quickly, the screen filled with images of her books and biographies. Of course, there were the debunkers and conspiracy nuts too. Finally, she found the latest one reporting on her upcoming marriage. It showed a picture of her and Geoffrey. After 20 minutes, she realized that she still knew little about the woman herself. But she did know she hadn't imagined the ghostly vision, which was real, despite the whole notion flying in the face of reason. Quite simply, she had to speak to this woman.

# Chapter 10

## Menace from the Nazi Plant

*"Well, that's a turn up for the book. The deceptive high flying lawyer wants to consult with the psychic who she thinks is a fake, but who just happened to have saved her life."*

Geoffrey's sarcasm showed in his comments as he added.

*"I would have told her to drop dead."*

Caroline laughed at his suggestion.

*"Really, what happened to the Masons code of being non-judgmental? Did you leave it behind at Portswood lodge?"*

There was an awkward pause before she continued.

*"Actually, Geoff, I welcome the chance to speak to her. The fire may have tempered some of that scepticism, and I am interested in her welfare. I still believe she is in great danger. The only problem is, she doesn't know it."*

An hour later, Caroline parked the rental car in the hospital car parking lot and walked into reception. The Nurse on duty had been informed that Caroline would be coming in and she directed an orderly to escort her.t her.The Nurse on duty had been informed that Caroline would be coming in and she directed an orderly to escort her. She knocked at the door he showed her to and was somewhat surprised to see Hanna answer it. After being released from the ICU ward, she was transferred to an observation public ward, where she was granted access to a small office to meet with her visitor.at.

Hanna stretched out her hand, and was relieved that Caroline took it warmly.

*"Thank you for agreeing to see me, Mrs. Hawthorne, and first let me apologize for both deceiving you and my attitude to you when we first met."*

Caroline smiled and put her hand up, palm outwards.

*"Well, we often jump to conclusions in such cases, think no more of it, and please call me Caroline. Mrs. Hawthorne makes me sound like an old schoolmarm."*

*"Well, no problem there, but I want to ask you about Tuesday night. The Police told me it was you who called them. Of course I'm grateful, but I have to ask how you knew?"*

Caroline nodded

*"Of course you do. The truth is, I knew; call it a sixth sense if you will. Let me tell you what I saw, dreamt if you prefer. You locked yourself in, poured a drink, and had an early night. While you slept, your gas burner on the stove was turned on low, so it would take a while for the gas to build up. That's why I got up and alerted the police. To anticipate your next question; I do not know the identity of the being that turned the gas on. I do know the reason they did it. It was to stop your investigation. I think you suspected this all along, which is why you are here. I also think a young girl, Sally Knight, gave you a warning, probably during the last few days. How am I doing?"*

Hanna looked pale and sat down on the office chair, trying to take in what she had just heard.

*"So, are you saying this spirt, Sally Knight, tried to kill me, because I was investigating the quarantine area?*

Caroline shook her head.

*"No, Sally is not responsible for the attempt on your life. She just tried to warn you. She died there in 1944 and knows the truth. I know this, because she gave me the same warning. What I still don't know is what is so dangerous about this site. I'm afraid I don't buy the radiation scene. It just seems too convenient. Now I know you have your own reasons for opening the site. They do not concern me. Frankly, I could not care less if its built on, preserved, or used as a retreat for the Hare Krishna's. My concern is to avoid more deaths and suffering. In my experience, powerful unrest in the paranormal world usually is a portent for something that will have grave consequences."*

Hanna was now more confused, but pressed on.

*"Look, I do not even pretend to understand the paranormal, but I have read up on some stuff and from what I've read, spirits are the souls of those who have died. They will not harm us and are incapable of interacting with the living world. I mean, the idea of my great grandmother or grandfather wishing me ill is just, well, it wouldn't happen."*

*"Yet you are here talking to me because you may not believe all I've told you, but you believe the evidence of your own eyes."*

Caroline's comments hit home, and she realized they were also undeniable. After composing herself for a few seconds, Hanna replied.

*"So, are you saying this spirit you call Sally will keep appearing to me?"*

Caroline reached out and took her hand. Her voice became notably softer.

*"Well, that will be up to her, but I doubt it. She delivered the warning, and that was done independently. Younger spirits rarely act independently, to answer your question fully, I need to find out who is guiding or controlling her. That will not be easy, especially if that spirit does not wish to reveal itself. However, I will try. If you wish, I can update you on my progress. And of course, you know you can call me at any time if you think I may be able to help."*

......................

The conversation with Christa had really unnerved Angela. Now she felt threatened and vulnerable. She did not understand this, any of it. Angela knew that Dimitris' father, who had been chief here during the war, was killed during the evacuation. Christa herself had told her that. Now Christa was telling her something else - or at least, appeared to be. By the Time her husband got home, she was trying to calm her nerves and was on her third glass of sherry. It did not take a policeman's mind to realize something had happened while he was at work. In fact, Dimitris had never seen her like this.

She looked up as he came through the door. Put the glass down and rushed at him, throwing her arms around him in a tight embrace.

*"Dimitris, don't leave me. I could not stand it if you are taken from me. I'm not as strong as Christa. Please don't go."*

Dimitris took a moment to recover and gently kissed her tear stained face before speaking.

*"Go? I'm not going anywhere. What brought all this on? What has happened today? Tell me."*

Angela took another sip of sherry and sat back on the couch. Dimitris sat down with her and put his arm around her as she related her conversations with Christa; asking a few questions and trying to play the part of a supporting and understanding husband. However, as he listened, he realized more and more that his wife did not need a shoulder to cry on. She needed answers. The same answers to the questions that he was asking himself, answers to questions that up until now he had been ignoring.

What happened that day his father visited the plant? Was his death connected to that visit? Why was the whole incident now coming to the surface? It was past time to turn a blind eye. It was 40 years ago, but there were still people living in the city today that remembered those times. One thing was certain; he now had to start asking those questions. Even if the answers were unpleasant and even if it affected his position in the Police Dept. His marriage was more important than that. He had even considered asking if Caroline could channel his father somehow to seek answers. All he knew now was that he could not ignore it. He turned to Angela.

*"I have enlisted Geoffrey and Caroline's help in trying to make some sense of what is happening. We both believe that it has something to do with the quarantined area and what happened there in 1944.*

*Hanna has got permission to visit the site from the ministry in Athens, with a number of scientists to take samples of the soil and test it. I have asked to attend, because someone needs to ensure nothing else is done by*

*Hanna or the team with her. They have strict criteria to follow. We will be accompanied by a squad of my police officers, and the military will have the site under observation from the air during the time we are there. Once her work is done, we leave. This is not 1944, the Nazis are gone; the war is over, and the plant no longer exists. Now I am waiting for Hanna to contact her team and I will let you know the date. So, how about you stop worrying and we get an early night."*

# Chapter 11

### Site Investigation

Caroline received a surprising call from Angela, who asked if they could meet for coffee at the Bistro. She gave no specific reason, but her tone projected anxiety. This was confirmed when she followed up by asking if she could see her alone, because she needed what she described as, girl talk Geoffrey had just settled down to watch an episode of Midsomer Murders Dimitris had loaned him, so was happy to let her go. When she arrived at the Bistro, Angela was already there and waved her over.

*"I took the liberty of ordering two Maxwell Houses for us, is that Ok?"*
Caroline just replied
*"Fine"*

Even now, Caroline sensed something was wrong. Angela's voice was noticeably nervous, and she gripped the coffee cup tighter than normal. She took a sip and then began.

*"Look, Caroline, I'll come to the point. Today I'm in need of a friend. All my friends are Greek, and today I need a fellow Brit. Dimitris has gone up to the quarantine zone with that German woman and some others, taking samples of something. But to tell you the truth, I'm scared to death."*

Her hands were now visibly shaking; she put the cup down, fearing she would drop it or spill the contents. Caroline put her hand out covering hers as she guided it safely to the table.

*"Well, this visit has been in the making for a few days. I know you must have known about it, so why are you so upset?"*

It was a fair question and Angela knew it, but now she struggled for an answer.

*"Christa; I told her about the visit, just in passing, but she became almost hysterical. She said I had to stop him and he would die up there like his father did, unless I stopped him. I think she would have gone up there herself in order to stop him, if she had been able."*

Caroline was now beginning to understand. Of course, she knew more about the reasons for the trip than Angela did, which she had obtained from Hanna. And in turn, Angela did not know of Hanna's vision, nor would she, at least not from Caroline; whose very reputation rested on confidentiality. She liked this woman, naïve and over confident at times, but she was determined to make a life abroad for her and her man. She chose her words carefully.

*"I see. So, have you spoken to Dimitris about all of this?"*

Her reply was instant and delivered with a tone of resignation.

*"Yes, of course. He just said that it was routine and that he would not be alone. There were scientists and other police officers that would be there and even a flipping army chopper, and that it was his job. I even asked if I could go, but he said it was a police and government operation and not even the press had bee,mnnjklkoooiiujun invited. I know that is probably right, but I cannot shake the feeling that he will be in danger."*

Caroline understood what she was saying; the difficulty was that she also had misgivings and felt that Dimitris may be in danger. Of course, she could hardly admit that. For some days now, she had been aware of a disturbance in the spiritual world, having heard many voices and had short visions. Of course, this may have nothing to do with Crete or Dimitris. The Island's history is steeped in many battles and sudden deaths that spanned the centuries. Still, none had directly tried to channel her, so it was safe to assume the matter did not concern her directly.

........................

Hanna's first view of the area that had been out of bounds since 1944 was hardly inspiring. A mound overgrown with vegetation and grass, little to indicate it was once a top secret industrial plant. Rabbit droppings and gorse and bramble bushes were slowly reclaiming the ground. Dimitris and two officers had arrived in a landrover, and after unlocking the barrier, had posted two officers at the site entrance.

Hanna and her party had followed him up the partially overgrown track in an ex-army personnel carrier.

After parking the vehicles, Hanna and two companions donned silver NCB suits with hazmat helmets before producing two instruments that resembled some kind of metal detectors. In fact, they were military grade Geiger counters attached to metal handles. They started sweeping the mound, first in front and then over it. The machines made a spaced out clicking sound. Dimitris knew enough of the system's workings to know a sudden increase in clicking accompanied by an increase in volume would indicate high radiation levels. After 10 minutes, there was no such signal.

Finally, one of her companions waved for the geology party to approach that were carrying their sample cases. The sound of an approaching aircraft broke Dimitris's concentration, and he looked up as a small OH 58 Kiowa helicopter with army markings flew overhead. So far, the operation was going as expected. Dimitris just hoped they would finish on time and he could get back to Angela. Her welfare was uppermost in his mind. Then one of the geologists shouted out, not to Hanna, but to Dimitris. As he approached, the geologist was calling for everyone to move back. They needed no second telling.

.................

While the investigation was underway on Crete, Carlos Santos was boarding a 737 at London's Gatwick airport; it had been many years since he had been on the island. A visit that had led to the article that Caroline had called him about. His mind went back to those years in the early 60s, a time so vastly different from today's world. He was a young student, protesting against almost anything the government supported. Ban the bomb, social justice, and the general establishment. He was a wholehearted supporter of, Peter Hain, a friend who shared his views, and had moved on to a senior position in the government he was protesting against. Of course, he too had changed, now that he was a senior journalist with a top rated magazine. He had persuaded his wife to stay home, pressing that it was a working weekend and would involve a lot of political interviews, and knowing that would alley any fears. In truth, he was eager to avoid any awkward moments.

There was a person probably still living there who once had meant a great deal to him. He knew he would find it difficult to resist looking her up, or at least enquiring about her. He also knew that by now she would likely be married with grown-up kids, and she may have long departed.

As he reached his assigned seat, he opened his carry-on bag and took out a book before he settled into his seat and secured his seat belt.

As the flight attendant moved through the cabin, checking seats were upright and cell phones were put away, he grabbed the book, 'The Soul Never Dies', by Caroline De Winter. He turned it over and studied the photo on the rear cover and then read the brief biography. The plane reached the runway threshold and turned into wind. The engine noise grew to a crescendo as the Jet accelerated down the runway, shaking as it gathered speed. Then the shaking stopped, and the jet rose smoothly into the sky above the west Sussex countryside.

Carlos opened the book and began to read.

# Chapter 12

## Rodin Point

Geoffrey and Caroline were aware, of course, that today was the day Carlos Santos was flying in from England. They had agreed to meet him at the airport, and reserved a weekend room at a small hotel in the city about a quarter of a mile away. They were also aware that Dimitris was supervising the testing of soil in the quarantine area. As for themselves, there seemed little more to do.

Carlos's plane was due in at 3 pm local time. Plenty of time to have a light lunch down on the seafront and do some souvenir shopping. On the way, Geoffrey noticed that there seem to be some activity at the Police headquarters building. Four vehicles, including a paramedic fire truck, were exiting the yard with sirens and flashing lights. All of them were heading out of town.

*"Just another car accident with British tourists who forgot which side of the road they drive on here. No longer your concern. Dimitris and his boys can handle it."*

Caroline commented after seeing Geoffrey's head turn, following the vehicles.

*"Sorry,"* he replied. *"Force of habit."*

There was a pause and a faraway look pass over his face that his wife picked up on.

*"Do you really miss the force?"*

She added

Geoffrey smiled and shook his head.

*"No, not at all. I'm happy to be retired and here with my talented young wife."*

Caroline threw her head back and laughed.

*"Not so young these days, but thanks for the compliment. There's something on your mind, so give."*

Geoffrey glanced at her momentarily before returning his eyes to the road.

*"What, the famous psychic cannot read my mind. Wow! I must make a note of that."*

Caroline was not amused, and it showed in her face.

"Alright, there is something niggling me. It's Dimitris's father. Recently, he told me he is beginning to doubt the accounts, such as they are, of his death. I know it is troubling him, and there is also the fact that he cannot really question Christa about it, for fear of upsetting her. But there is something odd."

*"Odd in what way?"*

*"Well, there is no apparent record of the funeral. The authorities discovered his ID on the body, but his notebook was missing. Every cop I know would always carry his notebook while on duty, even here in Greece. I would like to help him clear the matter up, but it's complicated. In England, I would have the contacts and records to help, but here, records are sketchy and no one wants to remember the bad times. Also, there is a danger that if we both discovered the death was a cover up, then what really happened and why the deception?"*

Caroline nodded in agreement.

*"Has he asked for your help?"*

*"No, at least not directly, but he did confide in me about it and asked my opinion. He has an enquiring mind, doesn't like loose ends, he reminds me of me of when I was a young DS. Still, I would like to help if I could."*

........................

Back at the Rodin Point quarantine zone, Dimitris had established a perimeter zone and awaited the re-enforcements he had called for. As they arrived on site, the senior detective approached him.

The two men walked towards the area now marked by red flags. A small trench dug by the geologist revealed what appeared to be a human skeleton. It was in remarkably good condition and had the remnants of a white garment around its shoulders. After testing the soil for radiation and using a gas detector to show there was no danger, he summoned some officers who began to carefully excavate the body, only to discover it was not alone. Three other sets of human remains were also present, and a pair of wire-framed spectacles. From the initial inspection, it was not possible to tell how long the bodies had been in the ground. That would take forensics, but Dimitris's guess was around 40 years, maybe longer. The ground was very dry and sandy, which may impede decomposition.

The team slowly expanded the gravesite. After several hours, the team had discovered other artefacts. Notably, a fair number of spent 9 mm shell cases together with several aluminium flasks.

By the late afternoon, an incident post had been set up, which included a small 20 ft. accommodation trailer and a large canvas tent equipped with tables, chairs and some scientific instruments, including a microscope and a soil analyser. It was clear that this was not going to be a quick job, much to the annoyance of Hanna, who had hoped by now to have gotten conformation the ground was safe.

..........................

At Heraklion police headquarters, someone passed Dimitris' report to the Brigadier General, who up until then had shown little interest in the case, except for giving the green light to Hanna's mission. The follow up report indicating a possible mass grave, peaked his interest. He read the report carefully, then picked up the phone and dialled a number.

*"Deputy Director Adamos, I have a job for you, probably right up you alley; echoes of Crete's World War 2 history. I have a report from Heraklion station on the city's outskirts, a Captain Nomikos, the senior officer there. He and his men have uncovered a mass grave left over from the occupation years in the hills outside the city limits. Probably nothing to it, but I would like you to take a trip over there, just in case. We have a German Lawyer who's representing some land developer. She has been given permission to carry out some soil testing there. It's an area that's been*

*out of bounds since 1944. I think it was her digging about that led to the discovery."*

At the other end of the phone, the Deputy Director had suddenly experienced a cold shudder, causing him to sit down. He was quiet for a few moments, prompting another statement.

*"Adamos, are you still there?"*

*"Yes, sir, sorry, I knocked on the phone. Heraklion station, you say? Would this be the old SS plant at Rodin Point we are talking about?"*

*"Yes, that's the one; do you know anything about the site?"*

Know anything? That's a damn understatement, he thought to himself before replying.

*"Not really, sir. Only that the SS were manufacturing something that was highly secret and had to be destroyed. At least that was the rumour at the time. I'll take a ride over and see the Captain, could do with a change of air."*

After he hung up, a thousand fears and questions filled his mind. Why, after all these years? What could they possibly find? And that name, Nomikos, it sounded familiar, but he could not remember why.

# Chapter 13

### Who's Bodies?

Caroline and Geoffrey watched from the terminal building as the British Airways 737 jet touched down at Heraklion airport. Aboard, Carlos Santos, had still not finished the book, but was almost three quarters of the way through. He now had a pretty good idea of who Caroline was and wondered what she was investigating.

On emerging from customs, Carlos saw Caroline's sign, 'SANTOS' and approached her, smiling.

*"Mrs. De Winter, I presume; delighted to meet you."*

The two shook hands and Carlos answered the expected, how was your flight question.

As they drove out of the airport, Caroline started the conversation.

*"So, is this your first visit to Crete, Carlos, or have you ever been here before?"*

*"No, I was here in the 60s, which is when I heard about the plant. I must say, it has grown quite a bit from the island, I remember. The fashions have changed a lot too. Back then, the women were all wearing full length black dresses and rarely spoke, especially to men. Although in my case, there was one I got to know very well. Luckily, she was a widow, and it was sort of allowed."*

Geoffrey smiled in apparent agreement.

*"Yes, indeed, times have certainly changed. Everything is allowed now. The swinging 60s have a lot to answer for."*

Caroline said nothing; she sensed it would be inappropriate to comment on men's talk, deciding to bring it up later when she and Geoffrey were alone. Instead, she spent the rest of the trip to Carlos's hotel, bringing him up to speed on the current situation at the plant.

Carlos seemed generally interested in the renewed activity and suggested they meet up later that evening to discuss the matter further, maybe over a drink in the bar. However, Caroline was not keen on the idea of meeting in public. Expressing her concern over local earwigging (*An English expression meaning eavesdropping*) Geoffrey agreed.

"*The locals and the police are already a bit edgy about the whole thing. It has stirred up a lot of unpleasant old memories.*"

In view of this, Caroline suggested they invite Carlos to dinner at their apartment. Of course, she had no intention of cooking or preparing a meal herself, and contacted a local restaurant to prepare one in advance. A custom take away. At around 7 pm Geoffrey picked up Carlos from his hotel and they settled down for a quiet evening. Caroline was eager to hear more of the mystery that surrounded the Nazi plant in the 60s as opposed to the current situation. Carlos, in turn, was keen to learn what had sparked the current resurgence in interest.

............

As Carlos and his hosts were enjoying dinner on the balcony in the Heraklion district of the city, approximately 16 miles away, the campsite had grown quiet. Most of the team had packed away for the night and returned to their hotels in Heraklion. There was however a small security detail left on sight comprising 3 police officers from Dimitris's station, 6 Military police personnel that operated a 2 man shift system at the road entrance, and an official from the Ministry of the Interior who had brought his own camper. A single military portable gas generator provided security lighting at the site. Dimitris had received information that a Deputy Director from police headquarters would join the group in the morning and would travel to the site with the Captain from the station. Joining them would be Cora Kronos at Dimitris' invitation.

On his return from the site, Dimitris found Angela somewhat relieved. She was, however, none too happy to hear he had to return the following day with a senior officer from police headquarters. In her mind, this meant she needed to spruce up the place a bit, despite his assurance that the officer concerned would be unlikely to even come to the apartment. In fact, Dimitris was really annoyed at the discovery of the mass grave. He decided not to mention it to either Angela or Christa, reasoning that it may trigger questions about the war best left forgotten. However, he did call Caroline, he was not sure why, but it seemed important.

They spoke only briefly, as she explained she had a visitor from London coming to dinner this evening, but nevertheless was very interested in the discovery, especially when he confirmed the remains were likely those of people who were at the plant in 1944. Of course, he added that there had to be tests to confirm that. As she put down the phone, Caroline seemed deep in thought. Finally, she turned to her husband.

*"That was Dimitris; he said they have discovered bodies up at the plant, five so far."*

*"Germans?"*

Caroline shook her head.

*"No, at least not soldiers, more like workers, no uniforms, at least that's what he said. He also told me the Headquarters are sending a Deputy Director up to check it out in the morning."*

Geoffrey didn't seem surprised.

*"No different here than back home. The brass have to poke their noses in, in case it's a big story involving the press. Can't let a mere Captain, take the credit."*

......................

The restaurant had done them proud. The meal of fresh lobster and appropriate sides went down very well. As the sun set over the blue Mediterranean sea. It almost seemed inappropriate to talk of war and death, but Carlos was a mine of information. Caroline specifically asked about his visit in the 60s and what he had learned then.

*"Well, it was a different time then. The war was still very fresh in the minds of the people. Not just World War 2, but the civil war that followed. Most of the men had been around then; some were combatants, some*

*were just observers. We had Communists and collaborators and everyone had exaggerated stories to tell. The plant incident was the same. The most prominent was that the Germans had destroyed the plant and all civilian staff with it, to cover up what they had been up to. There was no love lost for the police, either. Their head was a corrupt pro-Nazi who fled the city. He got bumped off later by the Germans."*

Caroline saw a chance and took it.

*"Do you remember the police chief's name?"*

Carlos shook his head.

*"Not really. Some Greek Commanderder. Christa did not believe it though; she saw the good in everyone."*

The statement by Carlos stopped the conversation dead. There was an awkward silence before Geoffrey commented.

*"Christa. Who's Christa?"*

Carlos looked a bit puzzled.

*"Sorry, Christa was the widow I told you about. We hung out together. Anyway, she thought they were prejudging the issue without knowing the facts. Apparently, it was all a big conspiracy to cover up the actual truth. Peter was a great one for conspiracies. It was her who told me about the plant. Probably all bunkum, but in those days it was dynamite. As a young student in London, we all believed in conspiracies. It made a good story. And as I said, it got me into journalism. Peter Hain, one of my cohorts in those days, had connections and put me on to the magazine that published the article."*

Geoffrey chuckled,

*"Ah yes, Peter Hain, the hell raiser of the LSE, I remember him alright."*

Carlos did not show any offense if he was offended and merely stated;

*"Yes, he was, so was I. Now he's a respectable Labour MP in the Commons. I am a journalist with the New Statesman and you are a*

*retired Police Chief inspector. The world turns Geoffrey and whether or not we like it, we turn with it."*

Caroline smiled, muttering Touché under her breath, before moving on.

*"Well, it seems as if the past has an annoying habit of catching up with us. Now the police and geologists are crawling all over the old plant site because of some property company being keen on building up there. Today they found some bodies. It may be a good time to consider writing an update to your original piece."*

.........................

The sun had now set over the activities at Rodin point. The temperature had cooled. An eerie silence had descended over the site, broken only by the monotonous thump, thump, of the generator. A single light burned in the small accommodation trailer where Salvi Dante, the interior ministry representative, was working on a report of today's finds. He had come prepared with reports of Nazi activities on the island and another classified document that detailed the demise of a student who died at the plant just before it was destroyed. This document was compiled by both German and Crete investigators, and had been sealed under a secret classification by the Greek military who had released it to his department. Dante did not know if the death had anything to do with the operations at the plant. But he noted that the cause of death was severe radiation poisoning. It was evident from the readings that the girl had experienced radiation exposure at levels 10 times greater than those observed at Hiroshima after the nuclear blast. The researchers concluded that her exposure must have happened within 30 minutes of finding her body. That there were no residual radiation readings now present on the site was primarily the reason Dante was here. The exposure must have occurred elsewhere.

The first days excavations had also uncovered several black Bakelite name tags from the fabric remnants on the bodies. The team placed these in plastic bags, which are now in the evidence tent. Plastic sheeting now covered the excavated area.

Outside, two of Dimitris' officers surveyed the scene. One lit a cigarette and offered his companion a second one; the glow of the lighter lit up their faces momentarily and masked the greenish glow now forming over the site.

# Chapter 14

## The Survivor

Five AM the bedside phone rang in Dimitris' apartment, rousing him from a troubled sleep. Angela had answered it, but had to lean over him to get it. Why does he insist on keeping the phone on his side when I am always the one who has to answer it, she muttered.

*"Yes!"*

*"Good morning, Angela; is he there?"*

She snapped irritably.

*"At 5 in the morning, he had damn well better be"*

She passed the phone to Dimitris.

Angela flopped back on the pillow, but became concerned when she heard the duty officer on the end.

*"Sergeant, sir, there's been an incident at Rodin Point. One of the military guards called up after the 4 am relief failed to show up. He got no reply from the site, so he drove up. He has requested your immediate attendance and also medical back up. I tried to find out what the problem was; he sounded frightened and just said, get the captain here now, and then hung up.*

Dimitris replied

*"Right. On my way."*

Before turning to Angela

*"There's been an incident at Rodin point. It may be that you will have to meet the Deputy Director when he arrives. Give him my apologies and ask if he could drive himself up here. You can give him directions, can't you, sweetie?"*

Then he was gone.

...........................

As Dimitris approached the entrance to the plant site, he saw that something was defiantly wrong. Four armed soldiers guarded the gate. After checking his pass thoroughly, they allowed him to continue up to the site. On arrival, he saw three army helicopters parked on the ground, a Kiowa and 2 Bell Hueys, one with medical markings. As he parked the police car, he drew the attention of an officer in combat overalls and displaying the insignia of a brigadier. He greeted the captain with an informal salute.

"*Good morning, captain. We have a bit of a mess here, so I have imposed a military lockdown. My men have orders to let no one on site without my direct permission.*"

Dimitris returned the salute.

"*Understood, sir, so what exactly are we dealing with?*"

"*Well, sometime overnight, there was some kind of intrusion. We have 3 dead and one delirious. Two of the dead are your men, the other, one of mine. The crazy one we found in the camper. The camper was locked, and there was no sign of damage or forced entry. Of course, we are waiting for our medical team to finish a preliminary examination of the bodies.*"

"*Are there any signs of injury or clues on the bodies, gunshot wounds or the like?*"

The Brigadier shook his head.

*My men found nothing visible, but they discovered two individuals facing the excavation area, both holding rifles with bayonets affixed, as though they were challenging someone, and suddenly collapsed where they stood. My men found your man inside the equipment area.*

Dimitris looked across the camp before asking.

"*And the other officer? Where is he?*"

The Brigadier looked puzzled.

"*What other officer?*"

"*I left two men here last night. Where is the second one? I do not see him?*"

The brigadier paused for a moment before replying.

"*Then it appears we have one missing. I'll order a search of the immediate area.*"

. . . . . . . . . . . . . . . .

Caroline had experienced anything but a restful night. Visions and voices were a constant interruption. At one point, she got up as quietly as she could to avoid waking Geoffrey, and stepped out on the balcony. It was a cool night and relatively quiet. She walked over to the rail and looked out over the sea. Apparently, this part of the Med was named the sea of Crete, possibly after an ancient Greek named Krisa, but Caroline, being the romantic she was, preferred the less popular theory that it was named after a local woman who married Ammon Zeus, the god of the air, but she didn't care. It was tranquil and lit by a waning moon. Out to the west she saw, or thought she saw, a faint blue glow, but it seemed to disappear when she looked at it, a peripheral phenomenon that often occurs. She took a deep breath and momentarily closed her eyes. A flash of image occurred. A figure of a charging soldier attacking what appeared to be a Greek police officer. Then it was gone. A millisecond that seemed to last a lot longer. She sat down on a sun lounger as the figure of her husband appeared in the doorway.

*"What's wrong, sweetheart can't sleep?"*

Caroline snapped back to reality and tried a weak smile.

*"Something like that. I think there a battle coming; not sure when or even where, but it's coming, like a runaway train and I'm standing in front of it."*

..........................

Dimitris's cell phone went off at 0845, and Angela's name appeared. She spoke briefly. The Deputy Director had called, and she gave him the message. He thanked her and replied that he didn't need directions, as he knew the location well. After closing the phone, he briefly spoke to the Brigadier, informing him that a senior police officer from Heraklion was on the way and requesting the guards to be informed. Now it was just a matter of waiting.

Meanwhile, Deputy Director Adamos was leaving the city and was around 30 minutes out. He was a little worried after being contacted by the force and being informed of the incident at Rodia point. He had also discovered the Captain on site was the son of the officer that had dominated his waking hours for the last 50 years. How much did he know? Who did he tell? What records may still be at the site? All pointed questions. His mind went back down through the years. Back then, he had been a rookie constable, attached to the premier station in Heraklion. Then it was not even the Capital city. That honour went to Neighbouring Chania. Everything was controlled by the Germans, a fact that annoyed him, but that his boss accepted. That made him the perfect choice to enable the Germans to hide their most outrageous project. Yes, a brilliant plan, but Nomikos had not performed as expected. True, he had died, but not in the way intended. He recalled the conversation he overheard between Colonel Steinberg and an SS officer in a bar that fateful night. The Officer was wearing a topcoat and a small trilby hat, but his collar tags were visible beneath the buttoned-up coat.

He only heard one part of the conversation, which was in German, and was that of Steinberg.

*With luck, the outraged populace will blame and charge our clueless police chief for the entire episode, swiftly executing him. While you, my friend, can return to Germany to continue the war. You must act tomorrow at first light."*

Those words had haunted him.

So many questions, and now, as he reached the entrance, he may finally get some answers.

...........................

Caroline was surprised to get a phone call this early from Angela in a panic sounding state. She asked if she was watching the local TV news. Caroline tried to calm her down, pointing out that the local news stations were in Greek, a language neither of them spoke well. Regardless, she pressed on.

*"It's all over the news what happened last night at Rodin Point. The army has cordoned it off and there have been deaths. I tried calling Dimitris, but he has switched his phone off. I knew something bad was going to happen, I told him."*

Caroline quickly made a decision.

*"Angela, listen, I need you to come over here and we'll watch the TV coverage together."*

Angela interrupted.

*"I can't leave Christa, she's been watching too, and is scared."*

*"Alright, bring her with you. We can watch and wait here together. Make sure you bring your phone."*

Caroline put down the receiver; Geoffrey had already switched on the local TV channel. An image appeared of a Greek female news anchor broadcasting from outside the site entrance. Four Greek armed soldiers appeared in the background around 30 yards from the camera crew. Geoffrey surmised that this was a distance set by the Army and would be about right for such an incident. Now there was little they could do until Angela got there. Only then did Caroline remember Carlos was due at 9 am for a day of exploration, together with the opportunity to compare notes, in the event this could prove precious in unravelling what was happening. After 10 minutes, Angela and Christa arrived, and they quickly began to translate. At just after 9 Carlos's Cab arrived.

The knock at the door came as a surprise, and both Christa and Angela looked up. Caroline quickly explained.

*"Ah! That will be Carlos, a guest here for the weekend; he is also here about the plant situation. In fact, he wrote an article about it years ago."*

She went to the door and opened it; she began to introduce the others. Angela smiled diplomatically and said;

*"Welcome, Carlos, another English voice."*

She extended her hands. Christa looked up, and her face changed as she studied the journalist slowly, a shocked look came over her as she stood up.

*"Carlos Santos, you've aged a bit and put on weight, but I'd know those eyes anywhere."*

She quickly crossed the room and embraced him. In turn, he smiled and looked back at her, suddenly kissing her passionately on the lips, before gently pulling free.

*"Christa, it's been a long time. Did you miss me?"*

While a confused, Angela waited in vain for an explanation.

.......................

Back at Rodin Point, Deputy Director Adamos and Dimitris had reported to the Brigadier on site.

He returned their salute.

*"Well Deputy Director, we seem to have a conundrum here; several bodies, no injuries, and no obvious causes of death. Take a look and see what you make of it."*

With the Brigadier watching, the two junior officers began examining the corpses in the makeshift morgue tent, their temporary home while awaiting transportation to Heraklion for a full autopsy. There indeed seemed to be no signs of injury, but both soldiers had an expression of terror frozen on their faces. Dimitris remarked the soldiers were both gripping their AK74 rifles with magazines attached. Safety catches were off, but the dead fingers were clamped firmly around the fore stocks. As though they were threatening an adversary, but not yet ready to shoot. The other body Dimitris recognized was Zenos Gabris, a young corporal who had been with the station 3 years and had been promoted only 2 months previously.

In contrast to the others, Zenos was frozen in the act of drawing his pistol from its holster. The weapon just clearing the holster and his mouth was open as if shouting or crying out.

Dimitris turned to the Deputy Director.

*"Have you ever seen bodies like this before sir, it's as if time stopped in a split second? Like pausing a video"*

Adamos nodded slowly in agreement, but in truth had hardly heard the comment. His thoughts were elsewhere.

*"Well, I'm sure the medical boys will have an answer, Captain. Till then, tell me a little about yourself. I understand your father was also a commander here, so you seemed to have followed the family calling."*

Dimitris shrugged his soldiers

*"Most people say that, but in truth, I barely knew him. Back then, it was a different world with the war then the civil unrest. I am grateful for one thing, though. His insistence I get a formal education at a top university in England. It was there that I met my wife. From then, life's been good."*

Dimitri's comments gave the Deputy Director some reassurance. On the face of it, not only did Captain Nomikos not remember his father, it would appear he had heard nothing about his activity in the war, either. To avoid questions, he wisely decided to leave it there.

The Brigadier had seen enough and decided to return to his headquarters. Before leaving, he addressed Adamos.

*"Right, Deputy Director, I think I can leave this one in your capable hands. Send me a full report when you get the autopsy results."*

With that, he strode off towards his car calling out to his driver, who seemed to have taken a liking to Cora, Dimitris's young crime investigator. He quickly broke away when the Brigadier called his name. Adamos and Dimitris watched them leave, and then Adamos turned back to Dimitris,

*"A bit of a conundrum seems a bit of an understatement to me. It all seems a bit too mysterious for my liking captain, what say you?"*

Dimitris smiled faintly before responding.

*"I have to agree, sir. I am used to facing unanswerable questions, but there is usually a logical explanation. Here I cannot see one. With your*

*permission, I would like to speak to my crime investigator; she may have noticed something we haven't."*

*"Three heads are better than two, eh? Well, by all means."*

Dimitris nodded and called Cora over to join them.

*"Cora, this is Deputy Director Adamos, who is the incident commander here. We would be interested in your take on this incident."*

Cora shook her head.

*"Nothing seems to add up, sir. Maybe we should be consulting Caroline De Winter."*

Although the comment was not meant to be serious, Dimitris chose not to smile and replied.

*"Yes, the thought had occurred to me, too."*

Adamos looked confused.

*"Sorry, who is this, Caroline De Winter, one of your staff?"*

Dimitris turned to the Deputy Director.

*"Hardly, sir. She's a celebrity clairvoyant on honeymoon here with her husband, who is an ex chief inspector from England. It was her that alerted us to that German girl Vassal, who almost gassed herself. No idea how she knew, but there is no doubt she saved the woman's life. However, I don't think she could help matters here; more likely just muddy the already muddy waters. No sense in rocking the boat."*

One of the search party members abruptly interrupted their conversation as they found the missing police officer, who was injured, unconscious, but alive. It appeared that he had fallen off a ledge in the darkness and fallen about 30 feet. By the time Dimitris and the Deputy Director reached the scene, army medics were already in attendance with a stretcher.

*"Well, hopefully he will be able to shed some light on the mystery, eh, captain? We really could do with a live witness at this point."*

Adamos' remark seemed a little trite, showing little concern for the police officers' condition. As an apparent afterthought, he added.

*"Check his condition with the doctors and stay with him until he comes round. He will probably be reassured to see a friendly face."*

With that, the Deputy Director returned to his vehicle to make a call, having promised the Brigadier he would update him on the current situation. Dimitris turned and walked back towards the medical tent.

# Chapter 15

## The Deputy Director

Carlos had gotten over his surprise at seeing Christa, and she quickly stifled any queries from Angela with a short, but informative comment.

*"Angela, I'd like you to meet a very special friend of mine, Carlos Santos. We haven't seen each other for many years, we met when Dimitris was in University, where you and Dimitris met, but lost touch. He is visiting me because of his interest in the Rodin Point affair. In the 60s he wrote an article about it. Carlos, may I introduce Angela, Dimitris' wife."*

Carlos extended his hand.

*"I see that a fine education was not the only thing young Dimitris found in England. Nice to meet you, Angela."*

Introductions over, all eyes now returned to the screen. The TV anchor was stating that the operation was being overseen by two senior police officers, Deputy Director Adamos and Captain Nomikos. Both officers' pictures appeared on the screen with their names on a banner underneath. Christa Stood up and paused the TV, staring at the Deputy Director's picture.

*"That Deputy Director, I know him, he was at the headquarters building with Dimitris's father in the war. He seems to have come up in the world. In fact, it was him who told me of his death and brought me back his personal effects. I wonder if he's mentioned that to Dimitris."*

Angela looked up at the screen.

*"Oh, I doubt it. Dimitris told me last night that he was assigned there by headquarters to ensure that the credit for any discoveries up there doesn't go to a mere captain. I doubt that they are even speaking much."*

......................

Constable Nico Makris slowly began to stir. He could hear voices. He opened his eyes, blinked and closed them again. Doing this repeatedly as he tried to orientate himself. It was daylight, and he was lying on a camp bed in a military green tent. He tried to remember how he got here. An army medic came to the side of the bed and checked his eyes, one at a time,

*"Good morning Nico, how do you feel?"*

Realizing that the medic was male, he answered curtly.

*"Like fucking shit. How did I get here?"*

"You apparently ran over a cliff, Nico, last night. - what were you running from?"

Nico recognized the Captain's voice and turned his head to look at him, his voice now moderating as he recognized the speaker.

*"A crazy soldier, sir, he tried to kill me, he looked weird, ran at me with his bayonet. Why would he do that? Wait, the light, that blue light, what in hell..."*

He stopped in mid-sentence, and threw his head back on the pillow with a loud scream, which attracted the attention of several people outside, including the Deputy Director; who wasted no time in getting to the tent.

As he entered, Dimitris was talking softly to the distraught officer. His words seemed to have a calming effect.

*"Okay Nico, just relax. There is no light anymore, no threats, no bad things, just me and the medics. Now I want you to describe what you saw last night. What did you see in the light, try to remember? Was it a person?"*

Nico's breathing became more measured, slowing, as he tried to put into words what he saw.

*"It was persons. I think they were 4 or 5, not real live persons, sort of misty, like a horror film. They were wearing white overalls, or coats. They were angry, mad, and threatening, pointing at us, screaming like demons from hell. I pointed my rifle at them and yelled for them to stop."*

Deputy Director Adamos now moved forward, trying to maintain Dimitris's softer tone.

*"Why did you not fire at them? Were they not close enough?"*

Nico turned to him, barely recognizing his rank, before replying.

*"We tried. The gun wouldn't fire, sir. Gabris was yelling, 'shoot them', but we couldn't. Gabris dropped his rifle and went for his sidearm. At least I think so. Nothing made any sense. These phantoms were yelling at us."*

*"Yelling what?"*

Adamos demanded.

*"What were they saying?"*

*"I didn't understand it, I think it was German. I don't speak German."*

Dimitris understood the injured officer's dilemma. He told him it was all right and just to rest. Then he turned to the Deputy Director.

*"I don't think we'll get much more out of him today Sir, how do you wish to proceed?"*

Adamos nodded.

*"I think you're right, Captain. We'll have to wait for the autopsy to gain anything else. For the moment, we need to keep your man in confinement. With the press poking their noses in all over the place, the last thing we need is ghost stories. I've sent in my report and Headquarters will be putting out a press release at 6 pm. Until then, suspend all work on the site. We'll use the excuse of finding unexploded ordnance being found, and clearance operations will take a while."*

As the Deputy Director walked away, Dimitris removed a personal tape recorder from his tunic pocket. He glanced down and pushed the off switch, stopping the tape. The recorder had been running for almost 50 minutes. It had not only recorded the conversations with Gabris, but also everything while he was unconscious. The words were in German, yet Gabris had told him he did not understand German. Was he lying, and if so, why. Until he found out, he decided to keep the recording to himself. His German was not that good, but he knew someone who was better at it.

....................

It was almost 7 pm when Dimitris arrived at Caroline's and Geoffrey's apartment; having been told that Christa and Angela were there watching the TV coverage along with a friend of Christa's. He was about to suggest he go home and let them join him, but having both Caroline and his mother there seemed a good chance to get some details. He knew that, unlike him, his mother spoke excellent German, a legacy from the occupation.

On his arrival, Angela was bubbling with questions, but Dimitris just kissed her lightly and told her she knew very well he wasn't allowed to discuss an investigation while it was underway, but added everything would be back to normal in a few days. She seemed annoyed, but knew the rules. Crete was not England and different standards applied. He accepted a coffee from Caroline and then asked Christa if she could spare a minute, then he walked out onto the balcony and shut the patio door after she joined him. Once alone, he produced the recorder, rewound it and set it to the required section, then handed it to her with an earpiece. She sat down and listened intently before switching it off.

**Sie haben keine Ahnung, was Sie getan haben. Indem Sie uns getötet haben, haben Sie sich selbst und Ihre Familien sowie noch ungeborene Familien getötet. Ihr werdet euch nicht aufhalten, also müssen wir euch aufhalten.**

Christa handed him back the recorder and looked up at him.

*"Where did this recording come from, Dimitris, and who is the man speaking?"*

Dimitris shook his head.

*"I can't tell you that, Mother, at least not yet, but it is important. My German isn't as good as yours, but I think it seems to be a warning about stopping killing, and a threat about consequences. I will tell you that it seems to have something to do with last night. It may be very important."*

Christa smiled.

*"Isn't it always?"*

Dimitris handed her a piece of notepaper.

"*Can you write down the exact translation? I don't want to involve you in this, and I haven't informed Deputy Director Adamos of its existence yet. It would be easier if I just hand him the translation.*"

Christa asked him to reset the tape and give her the earpiece. She began writing, then when she finished, she handed him the notepaper. Dimitris looked at it without comment before tucking it in his tunic pocket. The two then returned to the lounge where the TV Station was starting its scheduled evening program.

Christa was now moving towards making a momentous decision, one that would affect all of their lives. But before that, she needed to talk to Carlos.

# Chapter 16

### Christa's Big Secret

Carlos was a little surprised to get the call from Christa. Initially, he suspected an attempt on her behalf to rekindle their relationship. However, her tone of voice quickly dispelled that. At 3 pm, she rang his doorbell.

After making herself comfortable and accepting the Whisky Mac she had requested, she opened the conversation.

*"I'm in a very uncomfortable place, Carlos. To come to the point, I have been hiding a secret that no one knows, especially Angela and Dimitris. At first, I was unable to breathe a word of it. To do so would have put many lives at risk. But they say your past will always return to haunt you."*

Carlos put a comforting hand on her shoulder.

*"Perhaps you should start at the beginning, then."*

Christa took another drink.

*"The beginning, alright Carlos, you are the only person I can trust with this. To be frank, I do not know which way to turn. But I do need your help.*

*Do you remember when we were a real item in the 60s while Dimitris was at university in England? You asked me about Dimitris's father."*

*"Yes, to be honest, I had ulterior motives for that."*

Christa smiled weakly.

*"I know you wanted to be sure there was no avenging husband that would cramp your style. At the time, I told you he had been killed in the war, because that was what I had been told. Since then, I have discovered the truth. Dimitri survived the war. I only found out in 1986. I received a message from the sisters of the Sisters of Mercy Catholic Care Hospital that I work part time at. It said they had a recent patient that was a bit of a recluse, but he had seen me on my last visit and had asked my name, he told them he thought he knew her. They did no more than pass on the*

*information, and did not request a visit to him, but I was intrigued. All they knew about him was that his name was Kris and he was a retired charter boat captain. Like all their patients, he was referred to them by a care agency, in his case, social services.*

*Well, when I first met him, he was unkempt and had a thick shaggy beard. At first, I didn't recognize him until he spoke. He said, 'Hi sexy, how have you been?' That's it, no apology or explanation. For over 30 years I had convinced myself I would never see him again. Then he pops up, like he had just stepped out for a beer. I very nearly slapped him, but as the sisters were looking on, I didn't. I knew I needed answers to questions, so we spent the following visits going for walks out of earshot. He told me that I could tell no one that he was still alive. And if I did, it would put both of our lives in danger.*

"Whatever he did during the war was surely immaterial after all this time."

Carlos's words were quickly dismissed by Christa.

"Maybe, but recent events have somewhat overshadowed that."

Carlos was now intrigued.

"In what way?"

"The recent events at Rodin Point and these weird spooky events with Angela's new friend, the equally weird Caroline. What's her name?"

"De Winter."

"Yes, that's her. Well, it seems to me that somehow this is tied to Dimitris's father and his faked death. Whatever it is, it goes well beyond world war two. An incident occurred the day before yesterday at the site, it was not publicized, but a police guard from Dimitri's unit suffered a blackout, and when he awoke, related he has experienced an impossible nightmare."

She then produced a folded piece of paper and handed it to Carlos.

"This is a transcript of a recording Dimitris made of the tape, it's a copy. He has the original."

Carlos took the paper and opened it.

*Sie haben keine Ahnung, was Sie getan haben. Indem Sie uns getötet haben, haben Sie sich selbst und Ihre Familien sowie noch ungeborene Familien getötet. Ihr werdet euch nicht aufhalten, also müssen wir euch aufhalten.* **Translation** 'You have no idea of what you have done. In killing us, you have killed yourselves and your families, and families yet unborn. You will not stop yourselves, so we have to stop you.'

'The guard cannot speak German and it makes little sense. Today, Dimitris is handing over the transcript and tape to his superior officer at the site. I think when he does so; all traces of it will suddenly disappear. To be frank, Carlos, I am concerned. I need advice, and you are the only one I can trust.'

Carlos folded the note and asked if he could hang on to it for a while. Then he asked;

*"Have you spoken about this to Caroline De Winter?"*

Christa shook her head.

*"No, I've told no one."*

Carlos sat back in the chair and for a moment said nothing. He was thinking, and then he said quietly;

*"Your husband and Caroline have never met, have they?"*

Christa shook her head. Carlos continued.

*"I have an idea, for now; let's keep Angela and Dimitris out of the picture. Now here's my proposal...*

....................

Dimitris was already on site when Deputy Director Adamos arrived. He immediately went over to his car and saluted him.

*"Deputy Director, I have some information that may be of importance concerning yesterday's incident. It had slipped my mind until after you had left, but during the session with Officer Makris, I had left my voice recorder on in my tunic pocket. When I remembered, the tape had run out, but it did record everything Makris had said. My mother can speak German, so last night I asked her to translate it. Of course, I didn't tell her*

*the source, just that it was an apparent threat made by a boy against a girl in some domestic case."*

He handed the note to the Deputy Director, adding;

*"Don't know if it's important, but this is such an unusual case. I thought it best to tell you as soon as possible."*

The Deputy Director read the note and thought for a moment, before surprisingly handing it back.

*"Your mother's translation is accurate, but at this stage, I cannot see it is relevant to the matter in hand. But keep it safe for now. You never know."*

As the Deputy Director walked away, he seemed calm, but appearances can be deceptive, especially when practiced by a seasoned police officer. In actuality, his mind was racing. He knew he needed to speak to someone, someone not connected with the force. He knew the very person.

.................

Caroline was surprised to receive a call from a Deputy Director in the Hellenic police, and also a little intrigued. He had requested a strictly off-the-record meeting that concerned an incident in his past concerning 1944 and events that had affected him personally; saying he had heard that she was aware of some of these incidents. He stressed that this was in no way an official enquiry and, if asked about it later, he would deny ever meeting her. Though she was suspicious, she was also intrigued. She agreed to meet him at the museum in one of the reading rooms, where he could be sure there were no eavesdroppers. Caroline Arrived on time, as did Adamos - wearing civilian clothes. He collected a number of books and greeted Caroline, thanking her for taking the time to help with his research, of course, it was a charade put on purely for the benefit of the curator and her staff. Once in the reading room, he put the books on the table and sat down. Caroline studied the man before her; he seemed nervous and unsure of himself.

The complete opposite of what one would expect of a senior police officer. She opened the conversation.

*"So! How can I help you Deputy Director?"*

Adamos sat back and began.

Inevitably, his mind went back, back to that fateful night....

.............

*Well, I understand that you are, shall we say, looking into the events that are under investigation at Rodin Point."*

Caroline watched the man before her and knew that she had to proceed carefully.

*"May I ask where you came by that information Deputy Director?"*

Adamos nodded

*"Well! As this conversation is not officially happening, my driver told me he got the information from one of Dimitris's officers. But that isn't important. What is, however, is that I find myself having to ask for help, from, shall we say, unusual sources?"*

Now Caroline understood. It was certain that the Deputy Director had checked her out online, and the computer has no secrets.

*"Alright Deputy Director, suppose you tell me a bit about the history of this place, and in turn, I will try to fill in some gaps."*

Adamos nodded and began.

*"As you may know, in 1944, I was a young corporal attached to Andreas's police post here. Unlike my superior, Andreas Nomikos, I was none too happy with the German occupation of my homeland. Frankly, I had seen much abuse of the principles of law and order that I had cherished before the war. However, after the occupation we found ourselves subject not only to police supervision but also German oversight. Well, there was a Christmas party held at the town hall that I had been invited to attend as part of a delegation from the station. A better word would have been, ordered. We were instructed to mix with the guests and keep our ears open for any signs of dissent or unrest.*

*We were instructed to attend out of uniform to allay any suspicions. As I entered the hall there were several German soldiers and officers in uniform drinking casually and obviously relaxing. There was also a small group of young women. He ordered a drink and spoke to another officer he recognized from the station. I said to him, "Haven't seen those girls around, who are they?"*

My companion smiled and replied.

*"Students from the language collage here, mostly French and Scandinavian, also a couple of Europeans. We have been warned about them. They are on our monitoring list. The Captain doesn't trust them. Most do not speak Greek well, just French. I think some speak English, but as I speak neither English nor German, I'm giving them a pass."*

Adamos smiled as his memory of the event came back.

*"Of course, I was young and thought myself god's gift to women, as did we all. I remember saying, "Well, I speak a little English, mostly picked up from American Hollywood films, and a British friend of my mother's from before the war." As I got up, my companion warned me, "Best of luck Nico." Adding, you'll l need it; under his breath.*

I chose my moment carefully. The band had stopped playing and its leader announced it was time for a more reflective number.

As the opening bars of silent night filled the hall, I made my move approaching a slim blond girl and asked if she cared to dance. She smiled at him, replying in hesitant Greek.

*"Dance, yes, is good."*

Pointing at herself and him as she got up, one of her companions spoke to her in English.

*"Watch yourself with these Greek boys Sally; they're not all as chivalrous as Achilles."*

That was the first time I met Sally Knight.

At the mention of Sally's name, Caroline's attention sharpened, but she gave no outward indication. Adamos continued.

"Well! As the dance began, several Germans broke into the German version Stille Nacht. It seemed so perfect. We danced close together, but not too close. I remember asking her;

*"So, you speak English? Where are you from?"*

Sally seemed surprised, but appeared happy that we both shared a common language. She said;

*"From Ireland, my parents are still there. I was able to come here last year to study, because Eire is a neutral country. How about you?"*

I hesitated briefly before replying. Young people even then had a deep mistrust of authority. So I told her;

*"I'm from Crete, but I was born here. My name is Nikolaos Adamos, but Nico to my friends."*

She smiled a sort of, impish grin really, and then she dropped the question.

*"What do you do, Nico, from Crete?"*

Well, I thought, here goes, and said something like;

*"Not sure I should tell you. My friends say it would kill any conversation dead."*

Sally gently pushed me back. And I remember her next words

*"Not telling me could have the same effect, Nico."*

Her smile was infectious. So I took the plunge.

*"Well! You asked for it. I'm a policeman attached to the local station, but tonight a strictly off duty one."*

She showed no adverse reaction, but just grinned and said;

*"I shall have to watch my step."*

She gave me a quick kiss on the cheek as the song ended.

Adamos smiled to himself as he recalled their first meeting.

*"Yes, a great memory. That was the Christmas of 1943. How could things have gone so wrong?"*

Caroline was now beginning to sense the reason for this Deputy Director's unease. She nodded understandingly before saying;

"*It sounds very romantic, Deputy Director. What was it that changed?*"

Adamos shook his head before continuing.

"*I suppose the war interrupted. As the New Year began, Sally had begun to change; she often made excuses as to why they couldn't meet, or had to leave early. It was Andreas who first alerted him that something was amiss. He informed him that Sally was now under observation on the orders of the German commander, Major Steinburg. She had been seen in the company of known partisan sympathizers. I had expected to be ordered to drop the relationship, but to my surprise the Captain told me to maintain it and see if he could get information from her. This was in effect asking me to spy on her for the Nazis, something I just could never bring myself to do. It seemed I was going to betray the girl I had fallen in love with or to refuse a direct order. That left me with only one real choice, a very dangerous one. I arranged to see her in a remote park area after dark and had decided to tell her she was under observation, and that his captain, and therefore his German handlers, knew of her associations.*"

She had listened quietly, not saying anything. When he finished, she looked a little shaken, then she replied.

"*Why are you telling me this, Nico? Your Commander could see it as collaboration. The Germans could have you shot me too, likely.*"

I had expected the question and had already prepared the answer, the most truthful one I could, so I told her.

"*I am Greek, not German. The war is coming to an end and there is talk that there is an agreement between the allies and Germany that will allow the German garrison to retain order until Crete is returned to civilian power. In that event, I do not want to see anything happen to you. I do not want to know what the partisans are planning; I just want to see an end to the war and a future for all of us.*"

It was the truth, but though I didn't know it then - that answer saved my life.

Twenty yards away, a Greek partisan, who unbeknown to me, had overheard and lowered the .32 Welrod pistol and trained it on my back. Moments later, he emerged and spoke.

*"Fine words, officer Adamos. Those are the thoughts of all Greeks, but I fear it is too late."*

I turned and saw the gunman, and my first thought was that Sally had set me up. Before realizing that if it had been an ambush, I would be dead by now. It was Sally who broke the ice.

*"It's not the town or your commander, or even this stupid arrangement between the Allies and Germany. It involves the plant run by the SS. They have developed a super weapon and one capable of giving Germany total victory in just days. There is no one to stop them; if we tell the allies, then they will seize the weapon for themselves. Same with the soviets. The world cannot be trusted with such a weapon. If we say nothing, then Germany gets the weapon, same result. Now, I have persuaded my friends not to kill you for one reason, the murder of a Greek police officer at this time would stir up an investigation, which is the last thing we need. I'm afraid we can't risk setting you free. I'm sorry, but you are going to be absent without leave for a couple of days. Hopefully, we will get to see each other after that."*

Adamos sighed, as he remembered, with tears now beginning to form.

*"That was the last time I saw her, young and defiant. As she left, I was led away. After the Commander's death, they let me go; in fact, they even concocted an alibi to explain my absence."*

The years had not dimmed that memory, not even after the passage of so many years.

*"Now I am aware that you are working on some aspects of this matter and my research on you has shown me you have been helpful in various police enquiries. Of course, I know Sally died later that night. I need to know how, and if I was in any way responsible?*

Caroline had always been an excellent judge of character and was satisfied that this meeting was genuine. She replied.

*"I don't know the full answer to that yet, but I can tell you that Sally has been in contact with me, and I believe others involved in the matter all concerning the old plant. There is a big secret there that no one is talking about. I am aware that you and Dimitri are investigating the deaths that have occurred up there. I also know that there is a real danger at the site, that none of us appreciate. Sally was a brave girl. I know the SS killed her and I think I know why. I do, however; discount the theory of radiation poisoning. Thank you for being frank with me today."*

# Chapter 17

## Die Glocke

Leander Kosta was quietly enjoying a beer with two friends in the small village about 6 miles from Heraklion when he received a call that would upturn his life.

*"Hello Leo, its Christa. I know we haven't spoken in a while, but there is something I need to ask you. During the war, did you ever run across a young girl called Sally Knight?"*

Unsure of what the purpose was of the question, Leander was guarded in his reply.

*"The name sounds familiar. Why do you ask?"*

*"Well, it may be nothing, but her name has come up. My son has a police file on her; I came across it cleaning his desk up. Seems Odd it's an old file from 1944, detailing her death. Not only that, but some other people have been here this week carrying out some research into the old SS Plant. I also heard her name mentioned by them. I just thought you might know something more. I don't suppose it matters too much anyway, if she died in 1944. It's all ancient history."*

*"Alright, Christa, I'll do some checking with my former colleagues and see if I can find anything. Can I reach you on this number that you are calling from now?"*

Christa confirmed he could - and hung up.

So many years had passed. Of Course the war was an unpleasant memory for most Greeks, and Leander was no exception. But the mention of Sally, the brave young resistance fighter, stirred greater memories. It was she who had persuaded him not to kill the police officer that night. Looking back, she was wise beyond her years. Against all odds, the actual activity at the plant had remained a secret. The world had moved on. Now humankind had travelled into space and walked on the moon. Those involved on the German side were, as far as he knew, all dead. The allies had captured much technology and scientists involved in the V1 and V2 rocket programs. This technology had been shared between the Russian and American nations.

...................

Christa was more than a little apprehensive about Involving Carlos in her decision to 'resurrect' her dead husband, but deep down she knew it was likely only a matter of time before Kris's true identity was discovered anyway, and she knew her options were narrowing fast. However, there was something else bothering her. Angela had taught her to use the computer and the search engine facility. Like many women of her time, she could not resist looking up her old flame, primarily to see if what he had told her was, in fact, borne out by the data. But an entry on Wikipedia had caught her eye, it was an article written in the late 90s concerning secret weaponry of the Third Reich. She could not find the actual article, but a synopsis of it mentioned an anti-gravity experimental aircraft called 'The Bell' that was so dangerous that in 1944 it had killed a number of scientists that were working on it. It was, of course, most likely a co-incidence, but she knew she would have to approach him with it before he met 'Kris'.

She picked up the phone and dialled the number.

...................

Opening the door, Carlos was surprised to see that Christa was not alone. He did not recognise her companion, a Greek of medium stature with a greying bushy moustache. He judged him to be old, around 70 plus years. Christa quickly introduced him.

*"Carlos, I want you to meet an old friend of mine, Leander Kosta. He has information on the wartime activities at the old SS plant at Rodin Point. At the time, Leander was a member of the communist resistance here. I felt you two should meet."*

Carlos looked puzzled as he took Leander's outstretched hand, but Christa was unphased.

*"I know you wrote an article some time back on a German Wunderwaffe, code named Die Glocke. I believe that this entire episode at Rodin Point is connected to that weapon. So does Leander."*

A look of understanding came over Carlos's face; he motioned them to sit down and began.

*"Well, first of all, the facts over this weapon are, at best, muddled. I cannot verify any of them really, but I did interview a polish journalist, Igor Witkowski, back at the time. He provided much of what remains as evidence today."*

*"But let's start at the beginning. The Third Reich was a political idea that gained power in the 30s. This, of course, you all know. Hitler was elected on a wave of patriotism mainly fuelled by the sense of injustice felt by the terms of surrender imposed after the armistice that ended World War One. Hitler had fought in that war and shared that resentment. Once elected Chancellor, he of course became de facto head of the Armed forces, the Wehrmacht, the Luftwaffe and the navy, including the Kriegsmarine. But Hitler did not trust the military high command. He formed a paramilitary organisation known as the Schutzstaffel, or as we know it today, as the SS, which was charged with ensuring the security of the Fuhrer and its leadership. They could be loosely described as the equivalent of the Praetorian Guard of ancient Rome.*

*The SS, although unpopular among the rank-and-file members of the Armed forces, had complete authority. Hitler appointed an uninspiring figure called Heinrich Himmler to head up the organisation. Himmler, now an infamous Nazi, but then relatively unknown, had attended one of his rallies and got to speak to him at the time. Himmler was apparently so inspired, he immediately signed up to the party, and Hitler immediately felt this was a man he could trust.*

*He, along with the rest of the SS, had the ear of Hitler and was given wide powers over the regular forces. Inevitably, the SS became itself split into various factions. Among these was the Einsatzgruppen that travelled with the military and were tasked with the rooting out of all civilians deemed to be a threat to the Reich; in effect, their extermination wing.*

*Prominent among these men was a senior officer and scientist named Hans Kammler. I'll have more to say about him later. But among the most secretive were those attached to the Project Riese. Established in Poland, it was this science research station complex run by a specialist SS unit where the Bell was developed.*

*So, let me go back to the journalist now, Igor Witkowski. He supposedly had interviewed a senior Nazi engineer, an SS officer named Jakob Sporrenberg, aged 77, shortly before his execution by the allies as the principle architect of the Final Solution. Unfortunately, there was no way of verifying the story. It may be that he escaped execution. There is some evidence that he was switched with another prisoner; it was all hearsay. Officially, both Sporrenberg and his boss were dead. So the case closed.*

*So now back to Hans Kammler, another shady character who disappeared in 1944. He was presumed dead, but also rumoured to have been taken to Russia or the US to work on their respective rocket programs. I published the article, but it was ridiculed at the time, my credibility as a writer took a knock, so I left it at that. It taught me a valuable lesson. If you can't verify, don't publish."*

Leander had listened carefully and now spoke up.

*"But it is true that some of these scientists did indeed help the allies after the war, isn't it?"*

Carlos nodded.

*"Yes, this was code named Operation Paperclip. Its purpose was to round up the elite of Germany's rocket engineers and bring them to the US. One of Hitler's chief scientists was a young engineer, Dr Werner Von Braun, who had designed and built the massive Saturn 5 rocket that had spearheaded the Apollo program. It was not too well publicised that the Saturn 5 was an adapted intercontinental ballistic missile design that had been designated to the V 12, Its original purpose was to deliver nuclear payloads onto British and American cities.*

*What the allies knew, but kept pretty quiet, was that Von Braun was not the only German scientist working on German Rocket Technology. Another one ostensibly of greater importance was the aforementioned SS-Obergruppenführer, Dr Hans Kammler, a 39 year old General Lieutenant in the Waffen-SS, and a Luftwaffe engineer. Not to mention the infamous Dr Kurt Debus, another brilliant scientist working in the spectrum of magnetic fields and propulsion systems. A fanatical high-ranking member of the SS, he ended up as director of the J F Kennedy space centre at Cape Canaveral in Florida, working closely with Von Braun."*

Carlos paused at this point to allow the information to sink in before continuing.

*"Prior to taking over the SS V weapons programme, Kammler's claim to fame had been expanding the size and efforts of a mysterious and highly classified 'anti-gravity' device known as Die Glocke, or The Bell. Some described it as a flying saucer. It was by all accounts a very dangerous device that used some sort of anti-gravity propulsion system.*

*Apparently, they never did perfect it and it killed several of the luckless bastards who were working on it. I cannot find any verifiable documentary evidence, so we perhaps we will never know, but to my knowledge the Bell technology had remained a secret. There was no mention of The Bell in any surviving documents, but this was in Europe. I don't see any connection with Crete or Greece."*

Leander had listened carefully while Carlos was speaking. Now he spoke up.

*"So, you're saying that the United States ignored the crimes of these Nazi fanatics just to use their expertise. It sounds almost unbelievable."*

Costa nodded.

*"You must remember, these were very different times. The Americans knew that many of the Nazi rocket engineers had been commandeered by Russia and were no doubt working to enhance their military defences;*

*what history calls the cold war. To the allies, making a deal with the devil made sense if it kept America safe."*

Leander sat back in his chair.

*"I am now beginning to understand. Earlier, Christa asked me about a young girl named Sally Knight. I'm afraid I was less than honest with her then, but in fact, Sally was the bravest girl I've known. The night she died, she was leading a small group of the resistance members in an incursion to the SS plant. They intended to hit the accommodation block and abduct some of the science team. About a week before the raid, one of our informants who they were unaware of that spoke German, had overheard a conversation where Die Glocke was mentioned. It seemed like some kind of supercharged aircraft that nobody could shoot down and had unlimited fuel. Sally was the only survivor of the raid and she died mysteriously. There may be something in your theory about Rodin Point; if only we had been able to talk to Sally..."*

# Chapter 18

## Back From the Dead

The venue was a modern hair salon in the small town of Malia,high-flying around 20 miles from Heraklion city. This was a traditional style hairdresser who did not cater to the high-flying tourist trade. Most of the customers were local and appreciated a no nonsense traditional barber. The owner was a former army sergeant, Castor Dukas, who had worked most of his service acting as a barber and used that time to enhance his skills. He had little opportunity to diversify when army regulations gave strict guidelines. He had left the army 5 years ago and one of his first acts was to go to a salon in the city for a real modern look. The reason he had chosen this salon was solely because he had recently met one of the stylists and mustered up the courage to ask her out on a date. They had now been married 4 years and Castor had used part of his army severance pay to buy the salon. It was very reasonably priced, most likely because at the time it was off the main tourist track.

But today they had a challenging customer brought in by a middle-aged man who identified himself as Costa Santos. Castor did not know him and reasoned he must be a tourist. This elderly man was going to be a real challenge to his skills; he looked around 70 years old, but was possibly older. He had a mop of unkempt white hair that was pretty matted looking. He sported a large bushy white beard and wore a black woollen fisherman's cap that seemed almost as old as he was.

Costa spoke first.

*"Good morning, sir. You have been recommended to me as someone who relishes a challenge. This is Kris. He has had a pretty hard working life, most of it running his own fishing boat. Lately, he switched to charter trips. However, his son has recently tracked him down and wishes to visit. Old Kriss has not seen him since he left for serve in the army and has*

*asked me to help in cleaning him up a bit. We chose you because, being an ex-soldier yourself, you would understand his dilemma."*

Castor nodded and extended his hand.

*"Happy to help, Kris. So, how long since you've seen your son?"*

Kris took the hand extended to him and replied hoarsely.

*"Around 15 years, maybe longer. The army kept him moving around a bit. He never wrote, at least if he did I never got any mail."*

Castor smiled as he motioned him into the chair and produced a white cloth.

*"Yes, they have a habit of doing that. Still, let's see what we can do."*

He started with standard scissors, cutting back the beard and evening it up, then he laid a hot towel over his face while he mixed up the soap into lather.

Outside the Salon and in a small car park, Christa and Angela waited in a rented Range Rover. They had decided not to invite Dimitris along, primarily because he was a well-known figure and his appearance would no doubt raise questions. At this time, questions were the last thing they needed. In any case, Christa needed time to set up a private meeting. She was still unsure of what she was going to tell him. She had asked Angela along and had waited until Carlos and Kris had left the car before she had dropped the bombshell of Kris's true identity. It had taken a minute or so for the news to sink in.

Finally,me. she spoke.

*"I don't understand any of this, you're telling me. Dimitri's father is alive, and he doesn't know. You never told him? Why would you do that?"*

Christa was expecting this kind of reaction and had been preparing in her mind for the answer.

*"As far as everyone knows, Andreas died during the war. He had to; otherwise, the resistance would have had him killed as a collaborator.*

*At first I believed in the official account; one of his men had attended the scene and confirmed he was shot dead during a traffic stop. He had retrieved personally his personal effects and given them to me. Only later did I find out that the body was not Andres, but another man who had been shot and dressed in Andres Uniform."*

Angela shook her head.

*"But surely you had to identify the body?"*

*"No, they said he had been shot in the face at close range and it would be better if I remembered him as he had been when he was alive."*

Christa could see"

Christa could see that Angela was having a hard time digesting all of this. And who could blame her. After a moment, she gave voice to her thoughts.

*"So, where has he been all this time?"*

*"Well, after the funeral, obviously, he had to lie low. He moved to the mainland and grew a beard and moustache. He was an experienced fisherman, so got a job on a tuna boat. With the turmoil following the war, no one bothered too much about papers and ID. He gave a false name and vanished into the fishing industry. But so long as there were people alive who sought retribution, he could never come home. I'm sure you are wondering why he has now come back?"*

Angela nodded.

*"But the resistance must all be dead by now, or at least very old. Surely, they still can't hold a grudge."*

Christa smiled and laughed briefly.

*"Oh my girl, if only that was all. There would be no problem. The truth is that it is not the resistance that is the danger, it's closer to home. It concerns that damn Nazi plant and what really went on there. Many high-ranking politicians and intelligence services in America, Russia, and here in Greece would be happier if he stayed dead. Unfortunately, thanks to that damn German woman and your fortune teller friend, Caroline, he cannot stay 'dead'. Only a few of us know the truth. Carlos suspected something, and I updated him, which is why he has agreed to help us now; also, an old friend from the resistance who you do not know, Leander Kosta."*

Angela shook her head and put up her hand in a stop gesture.

*"Whoa, hold on there. Are you saying you were in the resistance as well? This is all too much at the moment. I need to get a perspective on this."*

Christa smiled and stretched out her hand and patted her knee gently.

*"Yes, I'm sorry, I do realize this is a lot to take in, but Dimitris and you need to know this. Even Andres does not know it all, but he knows enough to realize that the time for secrets is gone. Keeping silent is no longer an option."*

Angela nodded slowly.

*"It's that damn plant, isn't it? I knew it was a threat. I told Dimitris not to go there. Call it a premonition, or whatever, I just knew it was dangerous."*

While Christa was delivering her bombshell news to his daughter-in-law, inside the salon, Castor was expertly removing many years of growth with his expertise using the cut throat razor removing the stubble without so much as a small nick or cut. He then applied another hot towel to remove the remnants of dry skin. Finally, Castor pushed the control pedal, returning the chair to its upright position. Only now could Andreas stare at the face he had not seen for decades, the youthful looks now weathered and creased with age. Sadness filled his eyes as he thought of the missing years and the time stolen by events beyond his control. As Castor turned his attention to Andreas's matted hair using a stiff brush and oversized comb. He wondered what Angela would make of the transformation. More importantly, what would his son make of it. Seated behind him, Carlos had the same thoughts. He surmised that after such a passage of time and the excesses of Nazi Germany being just an unpleasant episode in history that it was unlikely that anyone would recognize him today. Especially as everyone knew for a fact that Andreas was killed in 1944, and any suggestion to the contrary was just a madcap conspiracy theory, so popular among the student youth of today.

Almost an hour had passed before Andreas got up from the chair. He was now a transformed man. Smiling, Carlos handed him is old cap, which he briefly put on. Both Carlos and Castor laughed as it fell forward over his eyes.

*"I think I'll keep it as a reminder of what I had become."* He chuckled.

Carlos stepped forward, taking out his wallet.

*"An expert job Castor, how much do I owe you?"*

The veteran soldier shook his head.

*"You owe me nothing. Helping a Greek father whose son is serving his country is reward enough. In fact, I am grateful that you brought him to me."*

Carlos thanked him but had no intention of not paying the debt. He resolved to ensure Castor received payment, especially as the job had been done under false pretences. He produced a new baseball cap with the logo of the temple of Knossos logo.

*"Try this for size, Kris"*

He called to Andreas, who deftly caught it and placed it on his head before giving a passible salute.

Christa was the first to spot Carlos as he approached. Then she saw her husband. It was as though he was back from the dead, now older and walking slower. But those eyes were unchanged. Ignoring Angela, she exited the range rover and threw her arms around his neck. Carlos got into the driver's seat and motioned for Angela to join him. She did not raise any objection. In fact, she agreed that her in-laws deserved to be together. Christa opened the rear door,husband, then turned to Angela.

*"I know it's been a confusing day, but no matter, may I introduce my husband, Andreas, your father-in-law."*

Angela looked up and extended her hand.

*"I know it's unbelievable, but I would have known it even without the introduction. You have your son's eyes. It's a pleasure to meet you."*

Carlos gave a relaxing smile.

*"Well, the easy part is over. Now comes your husband, it may not go as smoothly."*

# Chapter 19

### Ghosts from Hanna's Past

Hanna Vassal was feeling pretty down. Banned from the site and pretty much ignored, she had become enveloped in a web of deceit of her own making. By her own reckoning, she had started with the truth, lied about it, and then lied again to keep out of trouble with the police. Now the police were making life difficult for her, and any day now, her firm may start asking questions. Yesterday had been a blur; she had slept on and off most of the day, and was now on her last bottle of wine. As she poured it, she caught sight of her reflection in the mirror, mangled, ratty hair and puffy red eyes. She was wearing only her silk underpants and realized that she looked anything but attractive. It had also been around 4 days since her last shower and the body odour was strong, even to her clouded brain. She stared at the reflection and raised the glass.

*"Hey, beautiful, fancy a shag?"* she muttered before draining the glass and throwing it at the mirror. It did no damage, as the glass was plastic, fake, just like her life. She fell back on the bed and quickly passed out. She wasn't aware of anything, and the temperature beginning to drop.

Hanna had no recollection of how long she had been asleep when a sporadic shiver brought her round. Her shoulders were cold, and she instinctively reached for the bedcover, only to realize she was lying on it. Resigned to that fact, she now had to move. She opened her eyes and rolled over. At first, her fogged brain did not notice the figure in the back of the room as she pulled the loose cover over her shoulder and flopped unceremoniously back on the bed. Then as her senses returned, she opened her eyes, realizing she was not alone.

A woman in her early 40s was standing in the room about 3 feet from her. The woman shook her head before speaking.

*"You, my dear, are one sorry example of a member of the master race. What in God's name are you doing here?"*

*"Hell, lady, you got real confused, this is my room and what I do here is my own damn business. I don't need counselling or advice, so fuck off."*

Hanna closed her eyes, but someone pushed her violently off the bed. That got her attention. She got to her feet angry and in fighting mood. She slapped the intruder hard across the face, or that was her intention. In reality, her hand passed through the woman's head without resistance. The action threw her of balance, as unimpeded, her hand continued it track before striking her left shoulder, sending her crashing back onto the bed. This had the effect of clearing her head instantly.

*"Another damn ghost."*

She exclaimed angrily.

*"So who are you, Sally's mother?"*

The figure's expression changed and her voice grew softer.

*"No, Hanna I am Heidi, your Grandmother. I am, unfortunately, the reason you are here."*

She sat down on the bed beside her and continued.

*"You thought you were so smart, changing your story from facts to business, trying to find answers to at Rodin Point. And sparking an investigation that has consequences you cannot even begin to contemplate. As it happens, the fact is, you are here. Since I know that you have the family trait of stubbornness, I also know that you will keep digging. It's in our nature. Stay away from Ronin Point and the police.*

*Caroline can assist you, as no one else will take you seriously. Clean yourself up, drink some coffee and get something to eat, and most definitely, take a bath, you smell like a Jewish whore."*

*Hanna closed her eyes. The warmth of the bedcover felt good. After a few minutes, she opened her eyes, but she was alone. She sat up slowly. The room looked the same. Had she dreamt it all? She got up and crossed the room to her purse lying of the carpet where she had dropped it the night before. She carefully extracted a faded photograph from a rear compartment. The print showed a couple in their 30s. Now she looked at it with a deeper vision, concentrating on the woman and seeing her for the first time as a living person, not just an old sepia family print.*

........................

Back in Heraklion, Christa Angela, Carlos, and Andreas had ordered coffee at the bistro and were joined by Geoffrey and Caroline. The choice of venue served two purposes; first - to see if anyone recognized Andreas, and secondly to decide how to break the news of his 'resurrection' to his son. Although he could speak a little English, Christa advised Andreas to stick to Greek. With her husband now committed at Rodin Point almost constantly, Angela was reluctant to drop this on him now, but equally knew that it would be unfair to keep him in the dark too long. Angela knew she was going to have to be the one to tell him. As his wife and the one closest to him, there was no other choice. Christa would be there to support her. After some debate, they had decided their course of action.

There were, of course, risks. Dropping news like this on Dimitris, who was the lead investigator in one of the most important events in the area, may well reflect on his ability to put full attention on the job at hand. Geoffrey, above all, pressed this point. However, Christa pointed out that Dimitris was no longer the lead investigator. That responsibility had passed to Deputy Director Adamos, who reported directly to the Brigadier General.

Caroline said nothing, well aware that the group did not know that she and Adamos had met. And that Andreas would no doubt have information that the Deputy Director needed. Also, most of the group needed to know what had happened to Andreas after his visit to the plant in 1944. Christa was now aware of the true facts, following conversations with her husband during the past two months. But as far as she could tell, she was the only one.

Back at Rodin point, the subject of their intense debate was spending some time discussing some of the less controversial aspects of the case. With the bodies now having been transported from the site and the mass grave having been covered with a tarpaulin, the main work was done. Dimitris remarked on this to Costa, adding;

*"I suppose that German woman will be asking for renewed access before long."*

Costa turned quickly to face him, her expression betraying almost an apology.

*"Hanna Vassal, I almost forgot. One of the sergeants gave me a message last night. She has not been totally honest with us. Her law firm told us that she is on vacation in Crete and was due back in about a week. They didn't give any indication that she was on a case. The Sergeant felt it best not to enquire further until he had spoken to you."*

Dimitris took a moment to digest this before replying.

*"Well, maybe they were just covering for her, not wishing to say too much to the police"*

Costa shook her head.

*"I don't think so, sir. The sergeant did not identify himself. He merely asked to speak to her."*

Dimitris smiled.

*"That was pretty smart. What's this sergeant's name?"*

*Sergeant Leo Helios, sir. Between you and me, I think he fancies himself as a detective."*

# Chapter 20

### Cora Kronos

Hanna Vassal was now a woman in turmoil. She had no doubt that the spirit she encountered the previous night was real. Still not ready to accept the fact that her dead grandmother was able to talk to her from beyond, she spent the morning searching online for more rational explanations. Most delved into the realm of psychotic delusions and mental disorder. Nearly all recommended the sufferer seek professional medical attention.

That would hardly enhance her already shaky professional career. She was already on her third cup of coffee when the phone rang. She stared at it for a few seconds. No one had called her in the last 48 hours, and she had no friends here. However, on the fifth ring, she picked up the receiver.

*"Miss Vassal, I don't know if you remember me, Cora Kronos, we met while you were in hospital. I'm a criminal investigator working with the police on your case."*

Hanna did remember, and also that Cora was sympathetic and a good listener.

*"Yes, of course, I do Cora. How is the case going?"*

She tried to sound as normal and businesslike as she was able.

*"It's progressing, but I cannot really discuss it, but that isn't the reason I called. No one has seen you around recently and, quite frankly, we are a little worried. At least more accurately, I was a little worried. I can understand that you must be a little unsure of where you go from here. I know, believe me. It sucks when your senior managers block you, when you know you are right."*

*"Well, I can't deny the last few days have not been the best in my career. But it's more than that, I don't know, it seems as though everything is running away from me in directions I have no control over. Have you*

*ever heard the expression, 'It's all Greek to me.'? Well, that's the closest description I can think of at the moment."*

Cora had vaguely heard the expression, which was British in origin, and was used by both Caroline and her husband, according to Dimitris. She thought for a moment, then replied.

*"Caroline and Geoffrey apparently use it a lot. Look, I'm not on duty this evening. Dimitris has given me the night off, and the Deputy Director has his own people, anyway. How about meeting up for a drink and chat?"*

......................

By the time Cora had changed and made her way out to her hotel, Hanna had showered, changed, and managed to clear away a number of empty wine bottles. She slipped on a loose-fitting pants suit and tied her hair back, as an alternative to trying to shampoo it and style it. She saw Cora's gold Fiat Spider pull up outside the hotel and watched her exit the car with a bottle of something wrapped in a brown paper bag. In less than a minute, she was at the door.

*"Hey moody, why the long face? Were you expecting someone else? Well sorry, Leonardo DiCaprio sent his apologies. He can't make it."*

Cora's smile broke the ice and brought a giggle from Hanna.

*"You're crazy, Cora, thanks for coming, but your boss may not be too happy."*

Cora laughed briefly.

*"Well, I didn't ask him. I told you, I'm off duty. Here's a gift to calm your nerves a bit."*

Hanna took the bottle and began to unwrap it, then paused, pointing the neck towards Cora and said; "Beware of Greeks bearing gifts; my boyfriend told me when I left Germany."

She smiled and then unwrapped the bottle. A bottle of champagne from Germany, labelled Deutscher Sekt. Hanna knew the brand which was popular in Germany and also with the tourists.

*"Wow, where did you get this?"*

Cora took the bottle and placed it on the table before replying.

*"Never mind. Call it a welcome present."*

Hanna produced two glasses and half-filled them before making herself comfortable on the settee, then motioning Cora to join her. For a while, the two chatted about Crete and why her boyfriend hadn't joined her. Hanna was beginning to relax, which showed in her reply.

*"It was a business trip. But anyway, who wants a boring boyfriend along while holidaying in Crete?"*

After a few minutes, Hanna grew serious.

*"Cora, do you know Caroline De Winter?"*

Cora nodded.

*"Yes, I met her at the hospital with Dimitris. She's a fascinating woman. Unofficially, I think she is helping Dimitris on this case. Why do you ask?"*

That remark really got Hanna's attention, but she was aware that Cora would be unlikely to say anything further, considering her job. However, she tried to test the waters a little further.

*"You know, I had a weird experience. Call it a vision if you like. Caroline said it was unlikely to happen again, but if it did, I could call her."*

Cora sat back and took another sip of champagne.

*"And so have you called her?"*

Hanna shook her head.

*"No! To be honest, I don't know if I should. It may make things worse. There is still stuff I would rather keep under wraps."*

Cora leaned forward, her voice now more measured.

*"You mean, like the fact that your firm does not know anything about the investigation, and thinks you're on vacation here. And the fact, or call it woman's intuition, that the initial story about checking on a relative was closer to the truth. Dear Hanna, police officers expect that sort of thing. Your involvement in this matter is of no consequence, anyway. You are not, as far as I know, suspected of anything. But if you really need answers, call Caroline. Tell her what has scared you. Another Vision?"*

Hanna looked totally shattered. She lay back on the settee with tears forming in her eyes.

*"I came here seeking information on my grandparents. Well, I got more than I'd bargained for. Now I wish I had never come here, never met Caroline, or got involved."*

She drained the glass and poured another, noticing that Cora's serious expression remained.

*"Okay! Okay! I'll call her."*

Cora knew it was more than likely she would not make the call. She topped up her own glass before taking out her cell phone and dialling a number.

*"Hello, Caroline, Its Cora Kronos, someone her would like to talk to you."*

She handed the phone to Hanna and said;

*"I'll be on the patio admiring the view."*

Hanna took the phone, swearing under her breath, and glaring at Cora as she left the room.

..................

Dimitris was puzzled to get a call from Caroline, who asked for a meeting with him alone. Stressing that the matter was extremely important, and that it was unconnected with the investigation he was working on, but concerned his father.

Dimitris was surprised and asked for further information. But Caroline was firm.

*"Sorry, Dimitris, I can't go into any details on the phone, but I would not be calling you if it were not of the utmost importance. Only a handful of people are aware of this. They include Angela and Christa, who will be here when you get off duty.*

*Trust me on this, Dimitris. Do not file any reports at this stage or contact the Deputy Director. You will understand when you've spoken to Angela. What time can you be here?"*

Dimitris paused. This sounded fishy, but he trusted Christa and his wife.

*"Alright, Caroline, I should be home around 4. There's nothing going on here at present and probably won't be until the autopsy results get here. Cora said they should be here first thing in the morning. One thing though, would I be right in thinking you may have made contact with my Father's spirit?"*

Caroline smiled, glad that this was a phone call."

*"Yes, you could say that. Speak to you later."*

She ended the call.

# Chapter 21

### Leander's Dark Secret

Geoffrey was getting concerned. It seemed that things were moving at way to fast a pace. This was defiantly not the honeymoon he had envisioned. Caroline was at Dimitris's house, apparently meeting with Angela, Crista and Carlos. He had no idea why, and more troubling was that Caroline had refused to tell him. Of course she had pressed him, but she was adamant, saying that he would just have to trust her, but it was important. Furthermore, she had said that the following day she had agreed to a meeting with Hanna Vassal at her hotel. At least this time she did offer a reason, saying that she had been badly frightened by the spirit of her dead grandmother, who was one of the scientists killed at the plant. Normally, he had kept out of commenting on his wife's paranormal activities, but this time, he felt he had to at least make a point.

The fact was that Caroline was well aware that she was asking a lot of a man who was, to say the least, unconvinced of the world of the paranormal. He remembered the last words she had said when she left for the meeting.

*"Sweetheart, I know this is a strain, but in 24 hours I will give you a full account of what's going on. By then I will know where it's heading, and regardless of the consequences, you will be in a position to judge my actions and hopefully be there to support me. I have a feeling I will need it."*

......................

Dimitris Nomikos was trying to stay focused as he left the site with Cora. He was trying to figure out what was so important that his wife and mother were so adamant that he meet with them and Caroline. Once in the car and clear of the site, he decided to see if Cora could be of any help. He started by asking if she had spoken to Hanna recently.

*"Yes, as a matter of fact, I did. I heard she had not been around for a couple of days, so I called her and sort of invited myself over. In fact, I'm glad I did."*

Dimitris looked at her briefly before returning his eyes to the road. *"How so?"*

*"She was in a pretty rough state. She asked for a couple of hours as she had things to do, but that wasn't true. I am sure she spent the time cleaning up the place, showering and making herself presentable. A good try, but when I arrived I saw through it. The empty wine bottles were barely hidden and the strong smell of air freshener was a bit of a giveaway. Plus her make up looked hurried and seemed to be, well, a little slapdash."*

Dimitris smiled.

*"Perhaps you're not her type."*

*"Maybe, but seriously, she was more than a little spaced out. It seems she had another visitor, a spirit one. I suggested she call Caroline."*

Now, Dimitris was really paying attention.

*"Do you know if she ever did?"*

Cora smiled softly to herself.

*"Oh, she did; I called the number and gave her the phone. She didn't have a lot of choice."*

*"So, what did she say?"*

Cora laughed and shook her head.

*"I've no idea. I left her to speak in private. I figured she would be more forthcoming if I was not eavesdropping. But she felt, and looked decidedly better, when she finished the call and returned my phone. I figured you could find out soon enough from her or your wife. They know her much better than I do."*

After dropping off Cora, Dimitris made a quick call to Angela, telling her he would be home in about 5 minutes. Then he pulled over and retrieved his mini recorder from his tunic pocket, rewound the tape, and set it to stand by. Aware that Angela would be watching for him, he switched the device to record and returned it to his pocket just moments before he turned into the apartment block. Angela met him on the front step.

"*Okay, darling, before we go in, I must warn you, you're in for a shock. Someone is here to meet you. Probably the last person you would expect.*"

Dimitris followed her into the apartment. He scanned the room. Everyone was standing. He recognized all but two of them and focused on them. Both were elderly, probably around 75 years or older. One had a goatee type beard and was well dressed; the other was clean shaven and looked oddly familiar.

Angela started with the well-dressed man.

"*Dimitris, this is Leander Kosta, an old acquaintance of mine. He knew your father during the war and has some interesting facts for you. You can thank your mother for tracking him down. Both Leander and your mother worked for the resistance, unbeknown to your father.*"

Leander stretched out his hand, and Dimitris took it. Then he turned to the other man, who seemed vaguely familiar. He studied him hard, and then suddenly he stepped back.

"*No! It can't be.*"

Caroline now stood up and spoke.

"*Earlier, Dimitris, you asked me if your father's spirt had contacted me. Well, I tried, but failed, and then I guessed the reason. To channel through me, you have to be dead. I suspected some time ago that Andreas was still very much alive, but kept that fact to myself until Christa told me he had made contact a few years ago. He had assumed a new identity and for a good reason. Only now am I beginning to realize the enormity of what has happened.*"

Dimitris sat down, a little shocked. Angela quickly handed him a glass.

"*Glenfiddich and Ginger on the rocks.*"

"*England's finest, according to Geoffrey. I was saving it for a special occasion, and this appears to be it.*"

Dimitris took the glass and uncharacteristically downed it in one gulp before replying to his wife.

*"Okay! I have plenty of questions. Whew! I'm not sure where to begin. Well, first off, I accept that this is my father, and will likely need the special talents of you, Caroline, to explain how and why he returned from the dead. But why is this the most pressing problem at the moment?"*

Christa answered for him.

*"It was absolutely necessary for everyone involved to believe he died during the war to protect him from a vengeful populace, but mainly to satisfy the Germans, especially the SS unit from the plant. They had orders to kill all witnesses. Andreas was top of the list."*

Now Andreas chipped in.

*"I knew my days were numbered after the explosion at the plant, and the fact that all other witnesses called to a fake meeting there quickly met with grisly ends. I don't know what they had planned to do with me, but whatever it was; it all went wrong when a group of communist partisans attacked the plant. I had just left the meeting there and heard a burst of gunfire coming from the checkpoint. I pulled over and abandoned the car. I took cover as a truck filled with partisans came into sight. They parked about 100 meters from the plant entrance and moved on foot to the plant. They were led by a young girl, I would guess, in her late teens. She approached the gate sentry with her hand up and called to him in German, asking for help. The guard levelled his machine pistol at her and told her to stop and put her hands on her head. She complied, and again said she needed help. He approached her and asked where she had come from and who was with her. To me, it seemed as if the young guard saw no danger from this pretty young damsel in distress.*

*It was his mistake. As he lowered his gun and seemed more interested in her body, without warning, she spun around and thrust a commando dagger into his throat. She clamped her hand over his mouth and pulled his head back, twisting the dagger as he fell back, dropping the gun. Cold-blooded and expertly done. Other partisans joined her and they ran into the plant. For a couple of minutes, there was silence, then a series of pistol shots. I saw three partisans run out of a small concrete building. It looked like a reinforced bunker of some sort. In seconds, the building exploded, and the three were caught in the blast. Only the girl appeared to survive and she was in a bad way. She staggered past the gate and onto the track. Then a lot of shooting broke out. It appeared as if the remaining partisans were engaging the SS men in a very one sided fight.*

*I took the opportunity to head back to the car. After a few moments, I came across the wounded girl. She seemed groggy and disorientated and was foaming from her mouth. I dragged her into the car, but she was in a bad way. She was retching and convulsing. I stopped the car about 50 yards from the gate. I could see the barrier was down and the two guards' bodies were concealed from the road, having been stacked behind the sentry box. I dragged the girl from the car and tried to sit her up. She made an attempt to reach for her dagger, but was unable to draw it. She rolled over coughing, and a small camera fell from her coat pocket. As I picked it up, there was a heavy and sustained burst of MP 40 fire from the plant. I was still close enough to hear screams, some of them female.*

*The firing stopped after about two minutes. I got into the car and drove back to Heraklion, and told Christa I had to leave and didn't know if I'd ever get back. I knew they would be looking for me and would come to the house, so I left. I drove out of town. To be frank, I was unsure of what I was going to do.*

*Then I saw the commandeered truck with the German deserters. I was still in my uniform and had my official car. So I pulled them over, I approached them, and when I got close enough, I shot all 3 in quick succession. One of them was approximately my size and build. I swapped clothes with him. Then I shot him again in the face, which destroyed much of the facial features. Not a pretty story I know, but the truth."*

The room remained hushed for a minute.

It was Leander, who then spoke.

*"We all had to make difficult choices, my friend. We may not like it or agree with it. But for those of us that lived through those times, survival was the prime motivator in our lives."*

He turned to Dimitris, and the stunned Angela.

*"Christa and I lived in that world, we fought in it, and some of us died in it, and not only in the physical sense. I'm sure that this makes little sense to you now. How could it. We live in the 21$^{st}$ century, the much vaulted Space Age. The war is something most of us know only through Hollywood films. But for Andreas, myself, and Angela, it was anything but a movie."*

Christa then spoke up in a voice and manner that neither Dimitris nor Angela had heard before.

*"For you, Leander, it was hardest of all. The rest of us knew how much you loved Sally, how much you blamed yourself for her death and could not understand what the point of it was".*

Angela was both confused and upset and she showed it in an angry outburst.

*"This should have remained buried in the past. What good is dragging it up now going to achieve?"*

Christa supplied the answer.

*"It would have, but for the camera."*

Angela countered.

*"Camera? What Camera?"*

It was Andreas who supplied the answer.

*"The one I took from Sally's body. Normally I would have handed it in, but by then I suspected I needed to steer well clear of the Police or Germans. The way I saw it, this young girl and her friends had given their lives in a seemingly pointless raid on a heavily defended German position. I needed to know what was so important. All these years I kept it. The war ended and slowly the world moved on. Then I met Carlos. This week, he told me that the Germans were involved in some top secret work here, on some kind of superweapon. Wunderwaffe, he called it."*

I gave him the camera, it has not been opened.

*"And I kept it locked in a cash box on my boat."*

All eyes then turned to Carlos, who had sat quietly during the meeting and had said nothing. Now he spoke up.

*"Christa gave me the name of a friend of hers, a retired photographer who ran a business here in Heraklion, before selling out 5 years ago. Yesterday we went over to see him and he opened the camera and developed the film and made some prints. There were 7 pictures on the film."*

He stood up and opened his briefcase, producing a buff coloured file and placed the photos on the coffee table. The others gathered around and examined them.

*"These pictures were, I believe, taken inside the plant on the day of the raid, most likely by Sally or one of her companions. They show several civilians wearing white overalls and who appear to have raised hands. Most likely, they were being held at gunpoint. But what interested me most is the large bell shaped cylinder, or tank, clearly shown in the last 2 pictures. I think these photos show a weapon called Der Glocke. I have emailed the pictures to our photojournalist department, who have the capability of enhancing and bringing out details. I hope to have a result soon.*

*Now, from what Andreas has told me and shared with you here today, I believe that something went wrong at the site immediately after these pictures we taken and before the explosion. The official explanation was that it was a massive radiation leak that killed all those present, and Sally shortly afterwards, which is why the plant has been sealed off since the war. Neat theory, but I, for one, don't buy it. And neither, I suspect, does Dimitris."*

Dimitris nodded.

*"So! What's your theory, Carlos?"*

*"A Massive burst of a mercury-based element called, Xerum. This was the compound that powered Der Glocke and was so volatile it killed many*

*of the scientists working on it. If my theory is correct, there are many agencies today that have a vested interest in ensuring it remains secret."*

# Chapter 22

### Reinforcements

Caroline was still unsure of what the future held. However, for now, her personal life took precedent. She knew that Geoffrey, a patient man, was also shrewd and long suffering, but the last two days would have tried the patience of a saint. She got back from her meeting around 7, which was what her husband had calculated. She fixed them both a drink and, for the next hour, accurately related the facts and purpose of the meeting. Geoffrey listened quietly and without too much interruption, occasionally sipping his scotch. As he listened, much of what was occurring now made sense. He was also too good of a police officer not to see the underlying dangers that this investigation could pose. Finally, he spoke up.

*"So, where do we go from here? It seems that Dimitris has discovered the truth about his father, which may at least ease his mind. Andreas and Christa are reunited, though somewhat belatedly. There's no contamination at the site, so Hanna can get clearance for her clients to build the holiday complex, and we can shake hands with everyone and get back to enjoying the honeymoon. If the dangers from this device are as serious as Carlos claims, then there are authorities that can handle it."*

Caroline smiled softly. That's when her husband sensed there was a 'but' coming. He sighed.

*"Okay Honey, let's hear it. And don't try flashing those 'come to bed' eyes at me, it won't work."*

Caroline knew this, but tried anyway, and was met with a serious stare.

*"Okay, it's Hanna. She's not here as a lawyer, she's searching for her grandmother. Unfortunately, she found her."*

*"Why is that so unfortunate?"*

*"Because her grandmother was one of the top scientists killed at the plant. Her spirit made contact and has really put the wind up with her.*

*I fear she has opened a can of worms, in this case, evil worms that could destroy her. She reached out to me for help. I just can't ignore her. I'm not even sure I should try.*

*I told you once that this gift is sometimes more of a curse. Some psychics exploit it or use it to make money, which is why there are so many sceptics in your world. In Hanna's case, it is not just making contact with her grandmother's spirit, it's the horrifying truth about who she was. I think I can help her with that."*

............................

In the Knightsbridge police CID office, the phone rang 3 times before being answered by a female voice.

*"CID, DS Turner."*

*"Hello, can I speak to DS Watson please?"*

*"Sorry, Ma'am, DS Watson is on vacation at the moment, can I help?"*

Caroline cursed under her breath before replying.

*"No thank you, it's not important."* before hanging up.

After a few moments, she switched on her cell phone and scanned through her contacts. She pressed a button.

.........

Geoffrey awoke and glanced around before spotting Caroline already up and loosely dressed out on the veranda in her silk Japanese Kimono. He sat up shaking the cobwebs from his head, a movement that was noticed by Caroline, who turned and smiled. Geoffrey heard her say;

*"Okay, Thanks Phil."*

Before shutting the phone off and stepping back inside. By now, Geoffrey was alert enough to sense something was afoot, to use an archaic British expression.

Caroline went straight into the kitchen.

*"I've just made the coffee. Do you fancy a cup?"*

Her husband mumbled, thanks, before getting off the bed. His wife turned to face him, the movement loosening the sash on her robe.

Caroline noticed he was no longer looking at her face. She smiled and untied the sash.

*"Not bad for a 40-year-old body, sweetheart, wouldn't you agree?"*

He smiled and approached her, slipping his arms around her waist and kissing her lightly on the neck.

*"You look like a Greek goddess, Caroline. So how is our friend, DS Watson?*

Caroline considered acting ignorant, but thought better of it. Instead replied;

*"Okay, so you overheard, no big deal. I was going to tell you, anyway."*

Geoffrey smiled and shook his head somewhat dismissively.

*"You can tell me now. All I overheard was the name Phil, and since we're in Crete and have not met any Philip's, to my knowledge, you must have been speaking to someone you know well, and if you are planning what I think you are, he would be an obvious candidate."*

Caroline sighed and sat down on the bed.

*"Quite frankly, honey, I don't see any way out of it. If I don't help Hanna, then she may finally go over the edge and commit suicide. Or try something even more stupid, such as try to sabotage the plant or attack the police there. None of which would be much help to us in returning to a peaceful honeymoon."*

Geoffrey could see the truth in her words and replied.

*"So, what did Phil suggest?"*

*"Well, he'll be here tomorrow afternoon. And I feel bad about that, believe me."*

Geoffrey looked surprised.

*"He's flying here from England just because you asked him?"*

Caroline shook her head.

*"No, from Athens; he's on vacation with his girlfriend and I don't suppose she's too pleased."*

Geoffrey tried unsuccessfully to hide a smirk.

*"Well, at least they're not on their honeymoon."*

As she turned away, Caroline countered quietly.

*"No, and this little episode may ensure they never will be."*

......................

Geoffrey and Carlos watched as Caroline drove out of the parking lot on the way to the airport. The veteran newsman sensed the unease in her husband as he accepted a glass of scotch and ginger with 3 floating ice cubes.

*"So, who exactly is this detective that has broken his vacation to fly to her side? An old flame?"*

Geoffrey shook his head.

*"Not exactly, he's a fellow psychic who has worked with her on several cases, including one that almost killed my daughter in law after 911 (Queen Ann's Curse). Although I know he is perhaps the only person who can protect her against what's coming, I'm beginning to wish we had chosen another honeymoon destination."*

Carlos studied his drink for a moment before replying.

*"Yes, I can see you would. Okay, so what's the plan?"*

*"Well, if my hunch is right, she is going to try to make contact with the spirit that's spooked Hanna, in what the layman calls a seance. That may put her in great danger. It's useless to try to talk her out of it, so I have to hope that Phil can protect her. That is, assuming that Hanna is agreeable to her trying. The last time it happened, the spirit was considerably older and more malevolent, 800 years older to be precise. This one, well, we know nothing about her, but she is Hanna's grandmother, and as an ancestor, one would think she would be unlikely to cause her harm."*

Carlos nodded, more in understanding than agreement.

*"So, is it possible for a spirit to actually harm a human being? Sorry, but I always thought that only held true for Dracula's movies and such. I must confess I know little about the real thing. In fact, I'm not really convinced it exists."*

Geoffrey nodded, totally understanding the quandary Carlos found himself in.

*"To be honest, I was in the same position; in fact, I'm still halfway there. Some things simply cannot be slotted neatly in the realms of what we call common sense. I am a Christian, and as such, believe in god and the resurrection unto eternal life, as is quoted at most funerals. But even the church cannot explain what awaits us in the afterlife. It is simply a matter of faith. Not just with Christians, but all faiths who profess to the afterlife as a real tangible fact. Caroline says it is not a paradise, Valhalla, or heaven as we describe it, but another plain of existence. Our bodies decay and disintegrate, but only because they are worn out. The spirit or soul, if you like, departs and finds a new host. Moreover, Caroline is not ever going to need to prove it. Her philosophy has always been that you can accept it or not. It makes no difference to her."*

........................

While Carlos and Geoffrey discussed the coming event, the subject of their concern was trying to wrestle with what Caroline had said to her during a 20 minute phone call last evening. She had asked to bring a colleague of hers who was also a psychic to help. Hanna had agreed, but was now having second thoughts.

She had spent a fairly quiet night with vivid dreams, but not particularly disturbing ones, mainly about home and her parents. In the dream they were kind and supportive, but with the cold light of dawn came realization. Her parents would never be supportive. They refused to ever mention Hanna's grandparents and told her on many occasions never to mention them again. Research had been difficult in Germany; the history of Nazi Germany was suppressed and not taught to any degree in the school system. The Nazi insignia and mementoes were banned and the advertising or sale of them brought stiff legal penalties. Hanna was only too aware of this, so had refrained from doing any searches or anything that may have compromised her university course for her law degree.

Over here, she felt like she had one friend that she could trust and had told her she would really like to know who her grandparents were.

That person was a police crime scene investigator who, though not a police officer, was working with the local police on the case involving the plant.

Hanna had been up for over an hour and had finished breakfast when the phone rang. She had been expecting Caroline, but was surprised to hear Cora Kronos from the other end of the line. They had not spoken since her hangover, and she wondered why now? A brief thought that maybe psychic forces may be at work was quickly dismissed.

"*Hello Hanna, it's Cora. I have been doing some digging on your grandparents and have dug up a lot of information on them. It's all unofficial, so I need to meet up somewhere and discuss it. When would suit you?*"

Hanna laughed.

"*Cora, I must ask you, do you believe in this psychic stuff, because I was at the point of calling you. I have a meeting with Caroline in around an hour; she is coming with another Psychic who is helping her. Frankly, I feel a bit outnumbered. I was at the point of calling the whole thing off until your call. I suppose there's no chance of you being able to attend?*"

Cora hesitated for a moment before replying.

"*Well, I'm not actually on duty yet, but I am on call. The autopsy reports are in and Dimitris is at a meeting with Deputy Director Adamos. So, I'll come, but may need to leave promptly, if that's okay?*"

# Chapter 23

### Hanna Comes Clean

*"Okay! So what are we facing here, some malevolent Nazi megalomaniac who wants to restart the war?"*

Philips' question was meant to be lighthearted, but Caroline was not smiling.

*"Don't think so. This entity is more a pissed off woman looking to complete a project that should never have been devised. The subject we must channel her through is her granddaughter, a product of the 70s women's lib movement and currently a high-flying attorney who is quite out of her depth."*

As they drove out into the Heraklion suburbs from the Airport, Caroline filled in the details. Philip listened attentively. His concentration was broken when Caroline's cell phone rang. She glanced down and saw Cora's name on the screen.

*"Yes, Cora. Can't talk right now. I'm on my way to see Hanna. Can I call you back?"*

Phillip could not clearly hear the reply, but gathered from Caroline's reaction that a snag had occurred. After listening for about a minute, she replied.

*"Alright, Cora. We'll be there in about 15 minutes."*

Then closed the phone and turned to Phillip as he spoke.

*"What's up? Hanna, get cold feet?"*

*"No! But there is a complication. That was Cora Kronos. She's a crime scene investigator working with the local police. She's kind of taken Hanna under her wing. Hanna wants her to sit in on the seance, for moral support I think. I don't like it, but I probably have no choice. I get the impression that if I refuse, Hanna will cancel the seance."*

Phillip delayed replying before giving his opinion, seemingly deep in thought.

*"Well, it might be to our advantage. The entity will be aware of her presence, and that may restrain her if she's planning some mischief."*

Caroline nodded.

*"Possibly, but there's something else. Cora has dug up some info on her grandparents. She has it with her, but has not shown it to Hanna yet. Apparently, she wants us to look at it first. Of course, that may just be a ploy to ensure I will allow her to stay. However..."*

Phil finished the sentence for her.

*"However, it may be that there is something in there that we really need to know before releasing this entity."*

Caroline smiled.

*"You always could read my mind, Phil."*

...........................

Caroline and Philip pulled up outside Hanna's hotel room. Cora saw them and called down for them to come up. Hanna had gone to some lengths to clean up, both the room and herself, and it showed. After the introductions, Caroline began to outline the proposed event.

*"Alright Hanna, first, I can assure you that you are personally in no danger. Before we begin, can you tell us anything you can remember or may have found out about your grandparents, anything, even a rumour or gossip?"*

Cora produced a file from her briefcase and handed it to Phillip, who opened it and scanned through the contents. Cora noticed this, but regardless, answered the question.

*"Well, not very much. My parents told me they died during the war and they did not know how. I did press them about it, but they simply said it would do no good opening old wounds. I think they were working with the German Government on something secret, or at least confidential. I'm not really sure they even knew what branch."*

Caroline spoke in a softer tone.

*"Do you recall anything said about them?"*

Hanna looked up with a flash of anger in her eyes.

*"Oh yes, when I was at collage. Some bitch started bugging me. She said I was a closet Nazi and my folks worked for Hitler. It started a fight, and we were both suspended for a week."*

Phillip cut in.

*"So, did you win the fight?"*

Hanna replied smugly.

*"Knocked the bitches' front teeth out. We didn't speak after that."*

Hanna may not have realized it, but what had just occurred was far from a random conversation. Phillip Watson was not just a paranormal investigator - that was his part time occupation. His primary job was as a Detective Sergeant in the Hampshire Police photographic dept. And as a police officer, he was trained to put witnesses at ease. Cora, of course, realized this and played along.

*"Well, you should never underestimate a pretty girl who knows how to swing a left hook, or so my boyfriend tells me."*

The comment brought smiles and light laughter all round, as Phillip quietly passed the file to Caroline. She looked through it with apparent casualty, but in reality with a growing dread. She noticed Hanna was getting a little nervous.

*"So! What's in the file, Caroline?"*

Caroline handed the file back to Phillip.

*"Oh, nothing of importance, just stuff Cora found on line. It does give your grandparents' names, though, Heidi and Gunther Vassal. Would that be right?"*

Hanna nodded.

*"Yes, but I couldn't find out anything else."*

Cora added.

*"Well, it appears they did work for the German Government. The research division of the ground forces armaments office, to be precise. That department was involved in mostly classified projects deemed vital to the war effort."*

The news seemed to satisfy Hanna. It was a true synopsis, but the parts missing were not included. There was a good reason for that.

..........................

# Chapter 24

### Violent Spirit

While Hanna, Caroline, and Philip were conducting their seance across town, Deputy Director Adamos and Dimitris were seated around a conference table at police headquarters listening to the senior pathologist from the medical centre, Professor Salvatore Romano. Behind him on a large screen was an image of one of the bodies from the plant. Other persons seated in the room included various military and police officers plus several officers from the Forensic Science Dept. The door was closed, and an officer was stationed outside.

Following his introduction and welcoming words, their host began the main *narrative*.

*"I think it is accurate to say that these autopsies have raised many more questions than any answers we had hoped to find. Firstly, all the subjects died in a split second, an instant in time. From the expressions on their faces, I would estimate death occurred in approximately one third of a second or less."*

The statement brought an audible gasp from the audience. Unphased, the speaker continued.

*"That is as fast as the victims that were uncovered perished in the pyroclastic flows that engulfed Herculaneum in 79 AD, from the Mt Vesuvius eruption. The official cause of death was myocardial infarction. In laymen's terms, a heart attack. The heart stopped because of a blood clot in the heart, a very unusual blood clot in that it was solidified. We have been unable to determine how that could happen. The brain was also abnormal, in that tissue samples show widespread burning to the nerve endings. We have been unable to find the cause, and frankly, the phenomenon is unknown in medical science. But it is almost certain that these conditions occurred simultaneously and at the same velocity. Additionally, they conducted tests on the bodies for toxins and radiation.*

*Apart from some traces of alcohol and nicotine, they were uncontaminated."*

The Professor paused to allow the information to sink in. Deputy Director Adamos then raised his hand.

*"Professor Romano, can you tell us what sort of weapon or condition could have caused this?"*

Romano smiled briefly before replying.

*"One of my junior colleagues did mention a Hans Solo Blaster, whatever that is."*

He paused to allow the joke to sink in before continuing.

*"And quite seriously, it's as good a theory as any we have at the moment. In other words, we have no idea. That will be your department, I think, Deputy Director."*


.........................

Leander was getting old; he had been troubled by the recent revelations from the newly resurrected Andreas, and this, in turn, had brought memories of the war years. Back then, he was a cold, efficient resistance leader, young and fearless. Now the years had taken their toll. Moving around was more difficult. Arthritis had taken a toll on his mobility and he kept a walking cane in the house, knowing that it was just a matter of time before he would have to use it in public. His Doctor had recommended a knee replacement, but Leander was stubborn. He knew that this would mean care and convalescence for several weeks, and since the death of his wife 3 years ago he lived alone, but he still maintained a good rapport with his friends. They met up for drinks in the local bar several times a week. Today, however, he had gotten up a little too early, and by lunchtime he was feeling the effects. He was watching a program on local politics when tiredness finally overcame him. He closed his eyes and pressed the TV off button.

A few minutes later, he awoke, strangely feeling cold. He shuddered and looked around for a blanket or sweater, but then, as his facilities returned, he saw the sun streaming through the closed curtains. A quick glance at his watch showed he had been asleep for less than 15 minutes. The outside temperature was 85 degrees, but in his apartment, it seemed at least 40 degrees lower.

At first he hadn't noticed her - until she spoke, a dimly lit figure in the armchair.

*"Hello, Leo, how's life with you?"*

Slowly, the figure came into focus. He recognized her immediately, but at the same instance knew she could not be here. Sally had been dead for over 60 years, but looked little different from the time he last saw her.

*"Sally, I don't understand, is this a dream, or are you a ghost?"*

*"Actually, neither, as Caroline would no doubt tell you, I'm an entity. What you may call a spirit. We inhabit the same world as the living, but on a different plain, mostly unseen, unless we want to be."*

Leander said nothing, but stared at her. He was aware that sometimes people dreaming are totally unaware they are dreaming until they awaken. They accept the most ridicules situations without question. So he wasn't dreaming. He spoke, choosing his words carefully.

*"So, you are saying you need me to see you. Supposing I accept that, I have to ask why."*

...............

*"If am able to make contact, I will have no control over my own speech. In fact, I will not be able to speak at all. A spirit will often use my vocal cords to express their thoughts."*

Caroline's words were measured and clear as Phillip prepared the equipment for the seance.

*"Now, to make this work, I need to clear my mind. Phillip will record the session."*

Hanna interrupted

*"But I had a conversation with my grandmother just like she was in the room. I was awake and knew what was happening. I was well aware of what she was saying. It was spooky, but I was not in any trance. I knew what I was thinking and expressed myself."*

Caroline nodded.

*"Yes, that is true. I said spirits prefer to use a psychic to channel their voice, but sometimes they choose direct contact. Not sure exactly why, but I believe in those cases, the need for communication is strong, such as to deliver a warning or to offer comfort to those grieving. Unless this is done during a seance, such channelling is not possible. Today I will attempt to call it out. Summon it, if you will. I expect resistance, but she will be compelled to reply."*

Cora switched her cell phone to silent, after telling the others that if she got a call, she would have to leave immediately without a comment of apologies.

Caroline sat back in the chair, eyes closed, and then she spoke firmly and directly.

*"Professor Heidi Vassal. I am Caroline De Winter, and I call on you to answer me."*

There was no response, so Caroline repeated the summons. This time, the room darkened and became cold. Caroline threw her head back and let out an audible gasp, and then Phillip pressed the record button. A deep, heavily accented female German voice emanated from her lips.

*"So, you desire to question me. Me, about the theory of quantum physics electromagnetic layered induction systems. Me, the greatest German scientific mind of the 20<sup>th</sup> century. You, whose education level barely exceeded grade school, dare to challenge me. This will, as you say, be most amusing."*

Hanna was suddenly fired up and, ignoring Caroline's warning, interrupted.

"*Greatest scientific mind, that's a sick joke. You worked for the Nazi regime, the architects of the largest mass genocide of the last century. Much worse, you did so willingly and freely.*"

Caroline turned towards her, but it was Heidi's voice that she heard.

"*So, my little granddaughter has also been brainwashed by the rewriting of history. Ignorant of the truth you refuse to accept that what you have been told is a fabrication. The Americans, the British, and even the Greeks have been lying to you, even today. Members of my team now continue our work in Russia and America. Had we prevailed, we would not have permitted this.*"

Hanna's eyes flared.

"*But you didn't prevail; you died alone with your precious Fuhrer and his entire evil regime. May they and you rot in hell.*"

All eyes were now on Hanna, but in reality, she was just getting started. Her voice now became softer and more sarcastic.

"*So, what was it like Professor, the day you died in the plant surrounded by your SS Thugs? Did you scream, beg for mercy, or whimper like the broken apology for a woman you had become?*"

There was silence; Peter was unable to suppress a smile, as was Cora, while they waited for a response. They did not have to wait long.

"*I am immune from your rantings, Jew lover. Soon you will realize that you have made a serious miscalculation. By then, of course, it will not matter. The Fuhrer's genius will be revealed and order will be restored across the globe. A Fourth Reich will rise from the ashes of its predecessor. And this time it can never be stopped.*"

Hanna started to speak, but stopped. The room was becoming lighter and warmer. Caroline stirred and opened her eyes. Even to Hanna, it was obvious the entity had gone. Peter stopped the recording and went to Caroline as she opened her eyes and took his hand.

*"Not the friendliest bitch, was she?"*

He quipped, bringing a weak smile to her lips.

Hanna, still in shock, stood up.

*"I'm sorry Caroline, I messed up, and you told me not to interrupt."*

Caroline shook her head.

*"Actually, I'm glad you did. While you were chewing her out, I got to see deeper into her psyche, revealing things she wouldn't reveal openly. For instance, that the dangers posed by the device called Die Glocke did not end with the plant's destruction. In fact, I'm now sure the completed device was not at the plant. What were there were essential components. Probably parts of the propulsion system. However, that is not what concerns me at the moment."*

Cora could sense that there was something else that was troubling Caroline. She realized it when she heard Heidi's words. Now she was sure.

*"Something doesn't fit, does it?"*

Caroline turned to face her.

*"No, Cora, it doesn't."*

Hanna was now totally confused. Cora gave voice to the thoughts.

*"The translation, and warning from the plant, they don't match. It was a different entity, wasn't it?"*

Caroline nodded and gave a shallow smile.

*"Your good girl, I'll say that for you, and right too. Heidi had no interest in warning us. She only cares about the fulfilment of the Hitler dream. This entity was at the plant with Heidi and died there, but appears to have realized the horrific consequences of what they did."*

........................

Leander was calmer now. He did not understand why Sally had come back from the afterlife, but despite the impossibility of the situation, he had to believe his own eyes. He had often thought of her over the years, but he still had questions.

"*Like all of us, I suppose we want to believe there is an existence after death, but you died so long ago. You haven't aged. Is there no aging process there?*"

Sally smiled before replying.

"*You that are alive always ask that. But why would we age? We have no bodies to wear out. I liked being 18, so I'm 18. Also, we like those that knew us in life to be able to recognize us. Mostly, we are content to watch those left behind to age gracefully until their time comes. When it does, we try to be there to help them across. Sometimes, though, we have to make contact.*"

"*Why are you here, Sally? Is it to see me safely across?*"

Sally laughed and threw her head back, dispelling any doubts as to her identity; he had seen her do this many times before.

"*No way, you old warhorse. You are nowhere near your time. I am here to help save a lot of lives, if I can, and to give you some information that has been worrying you since that day at the Plant. I cannot help physically, obviously, because I'm not, well, physically here; if you get my meaning.*"

Now it was Leander's turn to smile.

"*Still as crazy as ever, I see. But seriously, I do follow what you're saying. At least I think so. This Nazi device, Die Glocke, as you call it, still has the ability to endanger the world today. And this time, it's not the Germans that pose the threat. Is there anything we can do?*"

Sally shook her head.

"*Truly, Leo, I don't know. This is way beyond my comprehension. Hanna's grandparents were the science boffins.*"

"*Okay, but if they are also dead, can you not ask them?*"

Sally shook her head.

"*That would probably seem logical to the living, but it just doesn't work that way. It's difficult to explain, but in the spirit world, there is no rapport between the spirits unless they are related, families, and so on. I can make myself visible if I choose and ensure that only the person I want to contact is able to see me. But that's it. Oh, granted, some people are more psychically aware than others and sometimes see fleeting spirits or shapes. But in reality, the only person that could theoretically contact them would be Hanna. I know Caroline is trying to help. She is a practical link between our two worlds, but even that has its limits."*

Leander stared at the floor for a moment. To have Sally here was stirring old memories, a bit like getting a phone call from someone you used to know, but had lost contact with many years ago. He knew he could not touch or embrace her, but she did possess some answers that he needed to know. He finally looked up.

*"What happened to you, kitten? I mean, at the plant when you..."*

*"When I died?"*

*"Yes! Do you remember?"*

Sally looked out beyond him, as if staring into space and whispered;

*"Yes! I remember. We reached the plant without being challenged and I approached the gate where there was a single sentry. I played the helpless, lost girl, and when he got close enough, I eliminated him. We reached the main bunkers without being seen. Through the window, I could see several people inside. Some of them were wearing white, light fitting coats, about 6 in all, both men and women. There were also 3 soldiers, including an officer. They were SS, I could tell by the uniforms and the red swastika armband the officer had on his black tunic. We assumed the ones in white were Nazi scientists working for the Nazis. The officer was talking to a female scientist in her early 40s, I would guess. It seemed to be an intense discussion. Our mission, if you recall, was to get evidence of what was going on in the plant and kill as many of the occupants as possible. Ares knocked loudly on the door and it was opened by a guard who was brought face to face with Ares's MP 40. We entered the room and ordered all the occupants to put their hands up. They did, and while the others covered them, I started taking pictures. There were some bits of equipment in the back. I think it was some sort of tank components, like a small fuel or water tank.*

*They had pipes and valve fittings on them. I took some pictures. Then we took our backpacks off and spaced them out. On my signal, we broke the pencil fuses and pushed them into the explosive compound. We knew the fused would run for four minutes. We were intending to stay for just over 3, before leaving and dispatching the Germans as we left. We knew the gunfire would attract the garrison and hoped we could get clear. The rest of my team was ready near the gate. I really thought we had a chance. Then one of the SS men suddenly drew his pistol and aimed it at Ares. I shot him in the face with my luger, and then all hell broke loose. Ares opened fire and sprayed the group. I saw 2 of 3 fall. Then the woman, who was bleeding, grabbed a glass bottle containing a red liquid and threw it at me. I tried to deflect it off, but it hit my gun and broke. The red contents splashed over me, it was viscous, like molasses. I shot the bitch twice, and we ran out of the building. I wasn't hit, but was suddenly feeling very sick and dizzy. The others with me including Ares, turned to give me covering fire, but then the explosive packs detonated and they were caught in the blast. I managed to get clear and out of the gate. I was very ill. I think the red stuff that sprayed over me was some sort of toxic acid. I vaguely remember being pulled into a car. A man in a police uniform, I think. Then he dragged me back out of the car. I passed out and then nothing. A bright light that was intense and blinding. Then I knew. I had passed over. My grandfather was there, smiling. It was so, so beautiful."*

Leander smiled and looked at her, tears in his eyes.

"*Rest in peace, kitten,*" he said, stretching his hand out as Sally's image faded.

# Chapter 25

### Dimitris Reaches Out

*"So! Who is trying to warn us, and why?"*

Cora's question was on everyone's mind, but it was she who gave voice to it. Both she and Phillip looked at Caroline, hoping for an answer. She slowly shook her head.

*"Frankly, I don't know. The entity was making itself known only to a selected few. That, in itself, may provide a clue. If they should choose to channel me, then I can ask them. But I would need a name to summon them."*

Phillip then cut in.

*"I think Caroline's point is valid. Spirits generally have a reason to make contact. So, we start with those who got the warning. So, since I wasn't here then, it's up to you guys."*

Caroline nodded.

*"The first direct warning came from the injured guard who delivered it in German. A language he cannot speak. But before that, this young girl, Sally Knight, who I think she may be the catalyst here. It was she who made first contact with me at the bistro where we met Dimitris and Angela. Initially, I had assumed she was another tourist. That was until I realized I was the only one who could see her. She was, however, not trying to warn me direct, I feel she was actually there to connect me with those in the spirit world who need to give the living world a warning, and for that they need a medium."*

Cora had been following the discussion and chipped in.

*"You mean, Sally, was sent to find a suitable key to unlock a channel, and she chose you, Caroline?"*

*"I believe so, but she must have had a reason. On reflection, the conversation I had with her at the Bistro was the key. I inadvertently told her I was with my husband, who was a retired police officer. At the time, I didn't realize I was speaking to a spirit. To be honest, I was on my*

*honeymoon and had dropped my guard. But Sally, logically, would see me as an asset."*

Cora grinned.

*"I guess you could say you passed the interview and got the job."*

Caroline shrugged

*"I'm beginning to think you're right. Damn! If I can't get this sorted out quickly, this marriage may not survive the honeymoon."*

...............

Carlos had opened the PDF sent to him from his magazine's photographic dept. It contained 30 enhanced images and notes on each one. He studied them closely, and the more he did so, the more he was convinced this was not the mysterious Bell. In fact, it was a collection of parts with one picture showing clearly some heavy duty wiring. Whatever this was, it was designed to use very high voltage. One close up showed a partial data plate with a company name and some numbers. A note from one of the staff who had done some research had identified the company as an electronics company that supplied parts and equipment to the Luftwaffe during the war. Unfortunately, this just deepened the mystery. Whatever this device was, the SS had gone to great lengths to conceal it. Almost certainly, this included murdering all the staff working on it.

Then his cell phone rang. Carlos glanced at the screen and was confused, decided to answer.

*"Good morning, Captain, how can I be of service?"*

Dimitris came straight to the point.

*"I know you've been working on a story about Ronin Point and what went on there in 1944. I've just come from a meeting at the city mortuary; the bodies we recovered there appeared to have been killed in an instant, literally a split second. By some sort of high energy blast that left no residue. During your research, did you uncover details of any weapon or device capable of causing such injuries? This is quite off the record and I*

*am still hoping to come up with some rational explanation that satisfies the Deputy Director and brigadier."*

Carlos took a moment before replying. Trying to evaluate how much information to share and what would be the consequences if he did.

*"Well, Captain, it's a fascinating question. I know the Germans were involved in developing some kind of high energy weapon. It is possible that if they perfected it, then it could result in the injuries you describe. However, if they had, then they would have used it on the allies as they closed in on Berlin or earlier at the battle of the bulge. So, I think it would be very unlikely they possessed one. Of modern weapons, the Americans are testing some sort of laser beam that can shoot down aircraft. Apart from that, no, I have not come across any weapon that can do that."*

Carlos hung up and returned to the conversation.

*"Okay, the police are naturally focused on the present. As for us, I think we need to find out who the second entity is. Any ideas, Caroline?"*

For a moment she didn't answer, lost in thought, and then looked up.

*"My intuition tells me it's likely Gunther, Hanna's grandfather."*

Phillip nodded in agreement, Caroline continued.

*"Cora's research contains some clues to that."*

Phillip picked up the file and read from it.

*"According to information in the file, this part from the SS staff dossier, Heidi and Gunther, were brilliant physicists, but political opposites. While both were fully paid up party members, Gunther rarely attended meetings, other than when attending formal dinners with the SS Elite. Of course, employment with the SS required membership of the Nazi party. Gunther's lack of enthusiasm was noted in the file, but without recommendations. My guess is that the work was too important to risk upsetting the team. As Caroline has stated, the problem is, unless he wants to communicate with us, then contact with him would be difficult. I think Caroline has risked enough for one day and I'm sure Geoffrey would not*

*be happy if she attempted another seance. Since we both work together and understand the idiosyncrasies, I propose that I contact him with Caroline monitoring the session."*

.................

Geoffrey was relieved when he got the call from his wife saying she was on her way home. Now, hopefully, he would get to know what was going on. As her car pulled into the parking area, he poured a class of Baileys for her, as she had requested. She smiled and kissed him lightly on the cheek before accepting the glass.

*"Sweetheart, you've been very patient with me and I know you wish things hadn't got so fouled up. So, let me fill you in on what's been happening."*

Over the next hour, Caroline outlined the events of that day and stopping whenever her husband had a question. She finished with a bit of a bombshell.

*"Well, I feel we're now close to getting on top of this. Phillip has decided to do one more seance, this time with him in the hot seat. To be honest, I agreed because I feel guilty about being preoccupied with this and neglecting you. So this part is tricky for me. I really need your support. If Phillip goes ahead with this, he will face some danger. I could lessen that danger if I can assist him in backup and monitoring, to record and to an extent - control what is happening. It has to be done by an experienced psychic and I am the only one available. But I need my own back up; I need my uncompromising chief inspector of police to keep me together."*

Geoffrey was very familiar with Caroline's well used flirtations and those come along eye flutters when she wanted something. But this time, he saw no trace of this. Caroline was scared, even though she was trying to hide it. He stood up and walked over to her. Caroline rose to meet him. He gently lifted her head and kissed her, then carefully wiped a tear from her eye.

*"When do we start, my little ghostbuster?"*

He said with a slightly smug grin.

......................

Deputy Director Adamos stood to attention as the Brigadier read through the interim report that he had submitted the previous day. Finally, he put the file back on his desk.

*"Frankly, Deputy Director, I don't like it. Oh, the report is fine, but we both know there are still questions. I don't like this involvement of the De winter woman. What can you tell me about her?"*

*"Well sir, she's a fairly well known psychic who has published many books on the paranormal. She is in Crete on her honeymoon. Her husband is a retired senior police officer from England, former Detective Chief Inspector Geoffrey Spencer from the Hampshire police. I've met her and get the impression she's not too happy with being involved. Captain Dimitris and his wife have become friends with them, and he is giving me updates on what they are up to. For the moment I'm leaving them alone, I am confident that if they discover something important, I will find out, either from the good captain or his staff. If you wish, I could bring them in for questioning?"*

The Brigadier shook his head.

*"No, I think you are right. No need to rock the boat. I have one concern, though. The American FBI has put in a request that one of their agents be allowed to carry out discreet enquiries here on Crete. They say they are investigating a report of wanted Nazi war criminals living here under assumed names. We want to be cooperative and all that, so Athens has agreed to allow one of their agents to carry out discreet enquiries here on Crete, as long as we are informed of any arrests needed. In which case, we will assist and hold them ending extradition. I suggest you send a car to meet his agent and take her to Dimitri's station. Let him deal with it, but keep an eye open. The Americans may play it straight, but the Israelites have a history of ignoring international law and grabbing suspects off the streets, like they did with Eichmann in the 70s."*

Adamos saluted and replied

*"Right sir, I'll keep you informed. Do you have this agent's name?"*

The Brigadier glanced at his notepad before replying.

"*Paula Turner. She's from their Washington Office posing as a tour guide for Thompsons.*"

# Chapter 26

### Sally Has Gone

It was around 7 pm when Caroline answered the doorbell and invited Dimitris and Angela in. It was Dimitris who had requested the meeting and also asked if it could be held at their place. If he and Angela had shown up at the police station, Deputy Director Adamos would likely have been notified. Once seated, he got straight to the point.

*"I think things are getting a little out of hand. Today I was informed that the FBI is sending an agent to sniff around. Officially, she is hunting Nazi war criminals that may be living here under new identities, but I have my suspicions. It's a good story and even plausible under the circumstances, but something isn't right. These investigations are usually generated by the Simon Wiesenthal Centre and evidence passed on to the CIA or FBI. Sometimes even to Mossad. In this case, it's just a lone investigator."*

Geoffrey nodded.

*"That's true. But even Mossad have lost interest. The Nazis brought back for trial are being released with charges dropped because of their age. Understandable really; dragging elderly infirmed men and women in their 80s into court and asking juries to sentence them to death never seemed to be justified. We have moved on. So what's your theory, Dimitris?"*

*"Carlos mentioned that some of these rocket engineers had gone on to work for NASA and the Soviets. He has been sending emails to his office and we have all been using the internet to search for information on this Bell and the technology behind it. I called Carlos this morning, and he told me something that I was unaware of. The US has a clandestine intelligence department known as the National Security Agency. They were formed in 1952 and most of their work is classified as is their modus operandi. But they do monitor all internet traffic and cell phone chatter worldwide. Now, I may be verging on the paranoid here, but they would*

*be most likely aware of our little investigation here. And if so, it would make sense to check us out."*

Caroline was listening carefully, but sensed that this revelation was not the only reason for Dimitri's concern. She was correct in that analysis.as he continued

*"I feel that there may be some extra heat on me in the coming months. Now it seems to me that we are both working different leads, we are working toward the same end, but coming from two different directions. You are from the paranormal side, me and the Deputy Director from the traditional law enforcement direction. Although there is scepticism on both sides, I think we need to compare notes. Also, my father told me that he knows the Deputy Director. He was on his staff as a junior corporal in the 40s and was under some suspicion of cooperating with the partisans at the time of the Ronin Point episode. Of course, they have not met since the war, so they may not recognize each other."*

Caroline had been quiet up to this point, unsure of what to say. Obviously, she realized Dimitris did not know she had met Adamos at his request. Sharing the information would violate the code of confidentiality that was important to her credibility. However, this was no ordinary matter; if she kept quiet, someone may suffer or die. In England, she felt she could trust the police on such matters, here different rules applied. Both Dimitris and Adamos seemed straight up police officers, what Americans called straight shooters. She knew what she believed was the right course of action, but needed to speak to someone first, the only person that she could fully trust.

Having put her thoughts aside, Caroline then spoke up.

*"Right, I agree with what you say. So can I suggest a written narrative of what we know so far? For the moment, just the facts, regardless of the source, and let's start with the events in 1944."*

For the next hour, Caroline compiled a comprehensive set of details in chronological order. She included the information from Carlos and Cora, and from the seance Philip had conducted. Finally, she put the notepad down. The report, of course, did not contain evidence from Leander and his encounter with Sally, as Leander had not yet informed her of the incident. In fact, he had remained oddly silent in the past 24 hours, unbeknown to the group.

That would soon change.

Finally, Caroline was satisfied. She had added information to the file that he felt he could share. She, in turn, filled in the gaps that told a stark narrative of the events of 1944.

As Dimitris and Angela left, Caroline poured Geoffrey another drink. He took it cautiously, noting for the first time a worried look in Caroline's eyes.

*"Okay, so now we're alone again - what's spooking you?"*

Her eyes flashed annoyance at him over the top of her glass. He smiled briefly before quickly replying.

*"Sorry, terrible choice of words, but there is something on your mind."*

*"Yes, there is something I should have told you earlier. At the time, it did not seem too important, but now it's put me in a quandary. When you were a detective, you sometimes interviewed witnesses to get information from a suspect, and used that information to test a suspect's alibi, Right?"*

*"Yes, it often throws them off guard when they realize the police officer knows more than there're letting on. So what are you saying?"*

*"Well, I have a similar problem now. A couple of days back, I got a call from Deputy Director Adamos. Straight out of the blue, he asked for a totally off-the-record interview. Swearing if I reported it, he would deny it ever happened. I agreed, mainly out of curiosity. I expected some sort of warning to back off, in the event I was wrong. He wanted to update me on the events in 1944 when Sally was killed and afterwards, up to the time Andreas disappeared. Now, what he told me does fit in with what we already know. Had this been anyone else, I would have accepted it without reservations."*

Geoffrey cut in

"*But Adamos isn't any other person. He's the senior investigator of the Ronin Point incident. Yes, I can see your dilemma. Obviously, it's your decision; I know how highly you place on confidentiality. Is there any way you can check on the information without alerting him?*"

Caroline nodded.

"*I think so. He described an incident when a member of the resistance held him at gunpoint, but Sally Knight intervened and spared him. It was a case of two men falling for the same girl.*"

Geoffrey nodded understandingly.

"*But I still don't follow, or maybe I do, this resistance fighter, Leander?*

Caroline smiled faintly.

"*Yes! Exactly. He could confirm Adamos's story. If so, it could be done without Him knowing. In turn, it would give more credence to his story.*"

........................

Angela was still getting used to suddenly having a grandfather living with them, or at least in her life. Dimitris had rented a room in a small hostel run by the AHEPA, a military veterans' association who had agreed, after he assured them he had checked Kris's background and discovered he had served as a police officer in the Athens region in 1952 to1954. It was risky, but he suspected that the association would not check the story, especially as it came from the divisional chief of police, and he informed them he would only be staying a short while.

Even so, Christa stated she intended to visit him almost daily. However, before this arrangement was put in play, Christa got a call from Leander. That changed everything.

...............................

Leander's demeanour had changed. There was a look of sorrow and resignation on his face as Caroline opened the door to greet him.

She was, at first, unsure why he had asked for the meeting, but welcomed it as a chance to check Adamos's story. However, by now she suspected the reason for his visit. There was no opening questions,

Caroline had decided to give him the floor, while she and Geoffrey sat back, as Leander started to speak.

*"Thank you for seeing me, Mrs. Spencer."*

Caroline shook her head, with just the hint of a smile.

*"Caroline, please, Leo; Mrs. Spencer makes me sound like a frumpy married woman."*

Geoffrey shook his head, but wisely kept quiet.

Leander Continued.

*"Caroline, it's just that I had a visit, if that's the right phrase, from Sally. At first I thought I was dreaming, but I wasn't in bed. She appeared in the front room. I think I had dozed off, but something woke me."*

Caroline said softly.

*"The temperature, the room had gone cold, right?"*

Leander looked surprised, but just nodded before continuing.

*"Sally had come to tell me her death was not my fault. She described to me what happened that night - filled in the gaps, so to speak. I was going to tell Crista, so that you could use the information, but there was something else, something in her tone. It was as if she was saying goodbye."*

Caroline lowered her head and replied softly,

*"She was, Leo. I felt it before you got here. I'm so very sorry. Sally has passed on."*

Leo didn't understand, and said so.

*"Passed on? But how could she? She's already dead."*

Caroline looked up, Geoffrey noticed both Leo and his wife now had tears in their eyes. It was Caroline who spoke.

*"I mean, her spirit has passed on to a new host, a new body if you will. Somewhere on earth a new life has begun with an old eternal spirit. The new baby will, of course, develop a new spirit of their own. Sally Knight's memories will fade, but not disappear altogether, acting as a foundation if you will, for the new life."*

"You are saying that Sally was reincarnated. I have never really believed in that stuff. Then again, I never believed in ghosts until Sally came back."

Geoffrey could see that Caroline was emotionally drained and spoke up.

"Leo, I am glad you called today. You have had an interesting life and you deserved answers. However, we had intended to contact you anyway, because frankly, we need your help. It is regarding the War and an incident you were involved in shortly before Sally's death."

Leander looked up, a little surprised before saying;

"Go on"

"I understand there was a Christmas party, and that Sally had befriended one of Andreas's young officers. If so, can you recall his name?"

Leander thought for a moment, and he finally said;

"Oh yes, you're right, though I don't know how you could have known that. His name was Adamos, a good looking young lad who had taken a shine to Sally. That would have been reason enough for me to shoot him, but Sally had persuaded me to hold off until I heard what he had to say. She said he was anti German and was upset with Nomikos's cooperation with the Germans. In the end, we held him prisoner for 24 hrs. We would likely have shot him had the mission failed, but in any event, it didn't. The plant was destroyed, and the Germans left. With Sally gone, I didn't really have a reason to shoot the son of a bitch. So we let him go."

Caroline shot a glance at Geoffrey, who nodded, but said nothing. He didn't need to. Caroline had her answer.

"All things happen for a reason Leo, sometimes it's hard, if not impossible, to see the possible consequences of both our actions and inactions. The young police officer you encountered that night stayed in the force and survived the war. He is now a regional commander for the island with the rank of Deputy Director. He has been placed in charge of the investigation into the incidents at Ronin Point. That appears as pure coincidence, but I'm sure that the Brigadier who sent him has no idea of *his background with the case. He had come to see me privately and told me the same story as you have. And for a man in his position, that is a dangerous move that could have consequences for his career and continued employment with the Hellenic Police."*

# Chapter 27

### The Stunning Spy

Dimitris sat in the unmarked police car as he watched the Boeing 727 touch down at Heraklion airport. He glanced down at the faxed picture he had received from the FBI via Athens. The aircraft taxied clear of the runway as it approached the gate. The captain was not in his uniform by request, but wore a white open necked shirt and dark Ray Bann wraparound sunglasses. He wore a wide brimmed panama hat and blended in perfectly with the other tourists as he made his way to the arrivals lounge. He waited while leaning casually against a pillar as the arriving passengers left the customs bay and emerged out into the concourse.

Several were met by relatives of tour guide representatives, most in colourful uniforms. He spotted Paula Turner almost immediately, a blond woman in her late 20s also wearing Ray Ban glasses and a white wide brimmed sun hat. She was towing a luggage cart with a suitcase and a small attaché case strapped together.

Wow, he thought to himself, your picture does not do you justice. She was already attracting admiring glasses, and it seemed only a matter of time before some star struck man would approach and offer his assistance. Quickly, he moved to block her path.

*"Miss Turner, welcome to Crete."*

She stopped and studied him for a second, completing a top to bottom mental scan, before suddenly smiling and accepting the Captain's outstretched hand.

*"Dimitris Andreas, I presume. Thank you for meeting me."*

They spoke little as they walked to the waiting car. Dimitris guessed correctly that she did not want to be overheard. Once in the car and free of those constrictions she outlined her mission.

*"As you may know, this is a low key mission. As you may know, I have been assigned to follow up on some leads and determine if there is*

*anything to it. Personally, I do not believe Crete would be a safe place for a fleeing Nazi war criminal to feel safe to settle in. Following the war, the communists took over, and would have still if they had more support here had the Germans not agreed to stay on until elections. I believe your father was the commander here during those years of the war."*

If Dimitris was surprised, he showed no outwardly sign.

*"You've done your homework Paula, I'm impressed. And I agree with you. I doubt you will find Hitler or Gobble living here, maybe some German soldiers who stayed behind and married local girls, of which we have their addresses, but I suspect America has far more. All countries got scared of foreigners. Germany had internment camps that morphed into concentration camps. You also had internment camps for all Asian looking citizens. I think that is human nature, Paula."*

Paula was surprised at his candour and softened her tone with a barely concealed smile.

*"And what's your view on tracking down war criminals, Captain?"*

She said in a slightly seductive tone.

Dimitris looked at her briefly before replying. There was no doubt that she was stunningly attractive, and that was obviously a great attribute for a spy.

*"Do you really want to know Paula?"*

This time, the seductive look was unmistakable.

*"Yes, I really am interested."*

Dimitris stared straight ahead.

*"I think that it's a waste of time, yours, mine, and everyone else's. These former Nazis are in their late eighties and early nineties. Most are infirmed or in hospice care, some have been married for over 40 years with great grandchildren. Israel has no interest in prosecuting and executing such people now. And few courts will agree to accept the backlash that results. I'm surprised that the FBI doesn't have better things to do."*

To his surprise, Paula didn't snap back at him or try to defend the Agency. She sighed before saying;

*"Yes, me too, but orders are orders. I think I will go through the motions, enjoy the facilities your island offers, and have an unofficial vacation."*

...............................

*"So what's this FBI woman like?"*

Dimitris grinned before answering his wife.

*"You wouldn't be interested, Angela, trust me."*

*"No, seriously, I am curious."*

*"Okay, Paula Turner is an extremely attractive woman in her late 20s or early 30s, slim and very American. If you didn't know her occupation, you would take her for a Hollywood sex symbol. Most men would likely describe her as drop dead gorgeous."*

Now, instantly regretting asking, Angela responded.

*"I hate the bitch already."* before turning away.

*Fortunately, the phone rang, interrupting any further discussion. Angela answered it.*

*"Yes, he's here, Leo; just a minute."*

She handed the phone to her husband.

*"It's for you, Leander Kosta."*

Dimitris took the phone, and Angela moved discreetly away while Dimitris listened for a few seconds.

*"Yes, I do know her; she's here nosing around, but likely on a wild goose chase. She has no jurisdiction here and you don't have to speak to her unless you wish. I would be interested in what she has to say, though. Call it professional curiosity. Right, okay, let me know how it goes."*

He replaced the receiver and looked across at Angela.

*"Interesting. Paula has contacted Leo, asking if she could ask questions about the war. The question is, why?"*

...............................

Deputy Director Adamos was, of course, aware of the FBI agents' presence in Crete. He had been told by the Brigadier that Headquarters had decided it was better to let her poke around and leave, as opposed to putting up official barriers. Of course, the Deputy Director had agreed, but not for reasons the Brigadier was aware of. In fact, if this was more than just an enquiry about war crimes, then things could quickly develop out of hand. If the truth was known about what happened in the days following the plant sabotage, then the island would be swarming with not just the FBI, but Greek government officials and the world's press.

Adamos had not visited the plant for a couple of days and was now in his office reading the latest report from the ecological team. Twelve bodies had been recovered from the basement of the destroyed plant building. Four of them appeared to be German soldiers, part of the SS unit based there, and nine were civilians who were likely the science team working with them. One hundred twenty spent 9 mm casings, together with some live ordinance, 6 stick grenades, and 3 loaded MP 40 magazines. All were in pretty poor condition, consistent with being buried for 50 years. There was no radiation detected above the naturally occurring trace elements.

Adamos knew that this report would clear the site for any future development, which would, in itself, be the best outcome. Now perhaps he would be able to go back into retirement. He placed the report into a buff coloured folder. Finally, he took out his cell phone.

........................

While Adamos was digesting the environmental report, Caroline, Phillip, and Geoffrey had arrived at Hanna's hotel room. The equipment from the previous seance was already there and had remained locked in a bedroom closet for the previous 24 hrs. It took less than 5 minutes to set it up. It was now mid-morning and most of the hotel guests were out enjoying the hotel pool and city attractions. That meant that the adjoining rooms were unoccupied and that, in turn, lessened the chance of being overheard.

Caroline gave a final nod to Phillip, and he responded, Geoffrey and Hanna remained silent.

*"Gunther, Gunther Vassal. I am Phillip Watson. I summon you to answer."*

There was a pause, and then a sudden and brief female laugh. Philip persevered.

*"Gunther Vassal, I command you to answer."*

A heavily accented German voice now filled the room. To Caroline's astonishment and anger, the speaker was her husband, Geoffrey.

Silently she cursed herself for not realizing a male entity would most likely use a male conduit, but it was too late for regrets. She checked the recorder was still operating and continued listening.

*"I am, Gunther Vassal. Why do you summon me Peter Watson?"*

*"We in the living world are in danger from your Die Glocke device. We know it has the capability of causing great destruction. We need your guidance in preventing this. You can provide that guidance. The governments of countries that you termed the Allies in the war now seek to control its power. We must prevent this."*

Caroline looked across at her husband, he seemed inert and asleep, but his breathing was heavy.

Then Gunther spoke again.

*"It will be a dangerous journey for you and your companions. Die Glocke is not on Crete. It was moved to Gavdos by the SS in 1944. My wife and I supervised its relocation in 1944 and travelled there to assemble it. Our understanding was that it would be then transported from the Island to Argentina by U Boat, where there was already a thriving German community. We were then moved back to the plant on Crete to erase all traces of our work. Unfortunately, we did not anticipate that this erasure would include ourselves."*

Up till now, Hanna had remained quiet, but now she spoke.

*"I do not understand. My grandmother told us a young Greek partisan girl was responsible for your deaths, not the SS."*

*"I'm afraid Heidi could never see the big picture, my child. It is true that a small group of partisans did raid the plant led by a young girl. Heidi threw a flask of Serum 525 at her, which broke and caused her death. She shot Heidi and left with the others. We heard gunfire and knew the haversacks left behind likely contained explosives. We immediately ran to a back storeroom to take shelter, but the explosives detonated before we could close the door. Most of us perished in the blast. I was among those who didn't, but then the SS arrived and machine gunned all of us. Perhaps it was for the best. However, the danger is not passed. The U boat never arrived and Die Glocke remains on Gavdos. Now both the Soviets and the Americans have traced it here. Both countries have prototypes of the device, but need the modifications we incorporated in our example to make it work safely."*

Caroline now spoke up, trying to put aside her feelings that her husband was now being used by an entity; she asked the question that had so far remained elusive.

*"What can Die Glocke do exactly? What is its purpose?"*

All eyes were now on Geoffrey.

*"There is a fault with the drive unit. When powered up, it emits a deadly radiation type burst that will destroy life forms and tissue within 100 meters, accelerating to 200, then 300 and so on until shut down. When working correctly, it can fly over land in an area and destroy all life forms in that area, then move to another location and so on. There is no viable defence of the system. A simpler way of explaining it is to think of your automobile. You start it and the accelerator is pushed open and jams. The engine continues to race faster and faster until you switch it off. Now suppose the key welds itself to the ignition in the on position. Think on that and you can visualize the results."*

A look around the room revealed it had become all too clear, and furthermore, that they understood. Still concerned for Geoffrey, Caroline spoke up.

*"You say that the allies are aware of the bell's location and that they intend to retrieve it so they can utilize the technology. Can you tell us more?"*

*"I cannot see the future, which is yet to be. Like all entities, I'm aware of what is, what was, but not what is to come. As of now, the powers are unaware of the exact location of the device. I can tell you that if you can locate and destroy the device, then many souls trapped here will be able to pass on. I will break the connection now, as my host is becoming dangerously weak."*

As the room warmed, Caroline left the console and rushed to Geoffrey's side. His face was showing a grey pallor and his breathing was shallow. He looked up and smiled weakly at her before closing his eyes. Phillip was already on the phone to the emergency services. Hanna dug out a bottle of aspirin and poured a glass of water, which Caroline administered. Thankfully, she saw he had swallowed it before falling back into the chair.

# Chapter 28

### An SS Traitor or Hero?

Leander was intrigued when he saw Paula get out of her rental car and walk towards his door. Dimitris had not exaggerated; she was an extremely attractive woman. He had no doubt that some of his neighbours had noticed her and he would likely be quizzed by them at the bar later, but for now he was happy to prolong the intrigue.

*"Mr. Kosta, I appreciate you agreeing to meet me. I'm sure you had better things to do on such a fine day."*

She extended her hand and Leander shook it warmly.

*"I can think of nothing better at my time of life than spending some time with a beautiful woman. Please come in."*

After accepting a glass of white wine, Paula sat down and began.

*"Well, as I told you on the phone, my agency has asked me to follow-up reports of Nazi war criminals that may have settled here after the war. I understand that you were with the resistance during the war and, therefore, may know some things that may not be in the official record."*

Leander replied guardedly.

*"After the Germans withdrew, some stayed behind. They were younger ones who had formed attachments with some of our local girls. There was some resentment, of course, but we were thankful for the local gendarmerie for keeping order. Of course I can't be sure, but I don't think any were high profile Nazis. Most were in their late teens and of junior ranks."*

Paula nodded.

*"Yes, so I understand, but how about this person?"*

She passed over a FBI data card showing an old sepia print and the name Otto Kurtz. The picture depicted a man of about 25 in a German SS uniform. Leander studied the picture for a moment before replying.

*"He doesn't look familiar to me. When was the picture taken?"*

Paula took the picture back.

*"Probably at the end of the war, they didn't tell me. Well, it's likely unimportant, so tell me what was the situation like as the war ended between the local populace and the occupying troops?"*

..........................

Caroline had followed the ambulance to the hospital and had been sitting in the waiting room for almost 15 minutes before a nurse entered.

*"Mrs. Spencer, you can come in now. Your husband seems to have responded well. We are running an ECG on him, but all signs are good."*

Caroline followed the nurse into a side room. Her husband was sitting up, alert and looking annoyed. The ECG monitor had white pads with sensor wires connected to it, which dotted his exposed bare chest. His face brightened when he saw Caroline.

*"Well, look what the cat dragged in. I thought you had deserted me."*

Though said with a grin and obviously meant as a joke, Caroline was not laughing.

*"Don't joke about this, honey. Damn you, I thought I'd lost you. All because I forgot what was likely to happen. You should never have been there."*

She went to him and passionately kissed him full on the lips, her face now streaked with tears.

*"Hey, steady up there sweetie, you'll send my blood pressure through the roof and cause this machine to overload, setting off all sorts of alarms. They may ban you for life."*

He nodded at her as if to emphasize the threat. Finally, she smiled as she realized there appeared no danger. She paused as her cell phone buzzed; she glanced down briefly at the display before switching it off, muttering, you can wait Captain Almighty.

..........................

Deputy Director Adamos was on time for the meeting. He had chosen well, the small bar at the quayside was off the tourist routes, its only customers being elderly boatmen and a lobster fishermen. He had taken a bus to travel the 4 miles to Neoria Vechi, itself a well-known landmark, then walked the 500 meters down to the bar. Otto was already there. He looked every hour of his 82 years with well-trimmed white beard and moustache and his head covered by a white panama hat. He was reading a copy of the Patris Newspaper and put it down as Adamos sat beside him.

*"It's been a long time, Herr Meijer. Glad to see you are well."*

Otto nodded once before signalling the waitress and ordering another drink.

*"So, I'm curious to know what brings you to call me after so many years, my friend."*

Adamos took a sip of the beer before replying.

*"An American agent of the FBI is in Crete asking about you. Her story is that she is searching for war criminals, but I think that is just a cover. I think the real reason is that the Americans are interested in Die Glocke."*

*Otto did not respond immediately and took another swallow of beer.*

*"That is not altogether a surprise, Nico. I noticed a young couple that was taking pictures of the lighthouse yesterday, to anyone else they were just tourists, but they were speaking Russian to each other and then English to the locals. While at the bar I got a good look at the man's camera, it was a Canon EOS1D, an expensive piece of equipment in these days of cell phone cameras. Not the usual tool for holiday snaps. Of course, I may be reading more into this than it warrants. He could have been a reporter or travel magazine man."*

Adamos nodded slowly.

*"Yes, he could, but you have always been a shrewd judge of men. That is why the SS chose you. You may have aged over the years, but I would not bet against you. The local police suspect nothing, and I was called back into service just because I had some knowledge of the Rodin Point plant. So, I'm no more than an observer today. I must admit, though, I was, and to a degree, still am tempted to leave it to them. The chances are that Die Glocke will remain undiscovered and the Americans or Russians will*

*develop their own comparable weapon systems. However, there is another element I had not foreseen; Commander Nomikos's son has befriended an English couple here on their honeymoon. An interesting couple, he is a retired British police detective, and his wife a noted author and psychic in the paranormal field. I know that she and her husband are researching the SS Plant and have been assisting in excavations at the site. That could prove to be a problem."*

Otto smiled, as his mind went back to earlier years.

*"In my days, such annoyances were quickly snuffed out. Now life is more complicated."*

........................

Dimitris was in a bit of a dilemma. Leander had met with Paula Turner and had unexpectedly shown him a photograph. Although he said nothing to her, he had, in fact, called Dimitris to say he recognized the picture and the name. Otto Kurtz was indeed a former SS man and was living in Crete under an assumed name, but as far as he knew, he was not a wanted war criminal. He had asked Dimitris if he could check on that, a cursory check on google had not turned up any useful data, other than a load of namesakes and links to subscribe websites. That probably meant that he had a low profile in the SS. Even sites that covered Die Glocke conspiracy theories made no mention of him. So, the obvious question was what is the FBIs interest in him? Aware that calls from the station may be monitored, he then tried Caroline's number in the hope that she may have a contact for Carlos. But the call went unanswered. A second call to Geoffrey's phone was answered by an automatic message that the party was unavailable and to leave a contact number, all-in-all, frustrating to say the least. All Dimitris could ascertain was that Paula had a name of a former SS Officer living in Crete who was of interest to the FB1. Finally, he decided to confide in his father. He and Christa may know something. At all costs, he wanted to keep this development under wraps. Fortunately, he knew

Christa was visiting Andreas that evening, so he made a detour on his way home and headed for the Veterans hostel.

Both his parents seemed happy to see him, but he felt that this may change when they heard the reason for his visit. At least he could talk freely to them without wondering who may be eavesdropping. He came straight to the point.

*"Dad, I need to ask you something, it's very important. At the end of the war, did you ever come across a German SS Officer named Otto Kurtz?"*

Dimitris noticed that the question brought two very different reactions. His father shook his head, adding;

*"The SS were a fairly private bunch; they rarely left the plant, and never mixed with the Wehrmacht boys. Certainly, he may have been there. Who knows?"*

Christa's reaction was quite different. She appeared to be transfixed by something, staring straight ahead. Finally she said;

*"Where did you get that name from, Dimitris?"*

Dimitris was aware that both his parents were now looking at him. He considered making up a plausible story, but dismissed the idea. He had never lied to his parents, or for that matter, his wife, and he was defiantly not going to start now.

*"An American FBI agent is in Heraklion at present and looking for him. Officially, she is seeking war criminals, but I don't think this man is a war criminal."*

Christa sat back in her chair.

*"No, he isn't."* She whispered almost inaudibly.

# Chapter 29

### Geoffrey's In Hospital

*The meeting with Christa and his father had delayed Dimitris by almost an hour. He knew that he should have called Angela, but bearing in mind what he had just heard, it was the last thing on his mind. As he pulled up outside, he noticed she was at the door. She did not look angry or upset. If anything, she seemed concerned.*

"I'm sorry about..."

Angela impatiently cut him off.

*"Geoffrey's in hospital. Caroline is with him. Apparently, he collapsed during a seance."*

Now Dimitris realized why he had not been able to reach him and he felt pretty down.

*"Do you have any information on his condition or if he's still at the hospital?"*

Angela shook her head, trying to sound calm.

*"Not really. Hanna called me and said her grandfather had unexpectedly channelled him to pass messages to us. I read in Caroline's book that they sometimes do that if it's a male spirit and there are no males connected with the family there are present. Caroline is pretty upset and blames herself. For what it's worth, I think that is valid. She did tell me that he was pale and breathing shallow when the ambulance took him away. I was about to call the hospital as you pulled in."*

Dimitris replied;

*"I'll do that now. Hopefully I can get some information as the Captain of police. They may be reluctant to give a member of the public any information."*

Angela listened as Dimitris spoke to the doctor in charge, After a few minutes, he thanked him and hung up.

*"Okay, it seems things aren't too bad. His tests are all clear and they will be discharging him to Caroline's care in about an hour."*

"*Great news.*"

Angela remarked. Before adding;

"*Oh, Hanna also said she had information for you concerning the plant and how the occupants died. Under the circumstances, I think you should call her and leave Caroline and Geoffrey alone for a while. I think the matter is wrapping up anyway, isn't it? With the Deputy Director back at headquarters and the autopsy results in, maybe they can at last start to enjoy their honeymoon.*"

Dimitris smiled.

"*We need to try, certainly, but my parents have just dropped another bombshell on me. There is an SS man here on the island that holds the key to what went on just before the plant closed. The FBI is here looking for him, and most likely other agencies as well.*"

Now Angela was puzzled. She tried to digest what Dimitris had said before commenting.

"*So, what is the problem? This man must be 90 years old. Most of his henchmen will be dead or the same age. There is no Third Reich anymore. What can he do? Threaten to run you over with his Zimmer frame?*"

Her husband tried, but failed, to suppress a laugh, as the mental picture of what Angela had described flashed across his mind.

"*Frankly, I could probably deal with that, but this man is not what he appears. The Nazis and the Communists were hunting him for years after the war ended. Both wanted him dead. But it turns out he may be the catalyst here. The reason Die Glocke wasn't found, I believe, is that it is no longer on the island. The most disturbing thing of all was that the FBI has this man's real name, but he's living under an assumed one here. Somehow I need to protect him from these outside agencies and do so without alerting them. I have an idea, but it's not something I can do alone. My mother has supplied a fact I was unaware of, Deputy Director Adamos had a private meeting with Caroline at her request. As you know, the Deputy Director has been retired for a few years and has only returned because of his knowledge of Ronin Point. He is on the case as official*" *advisor and reports directly to the Brigadier. I would like to have consulted Caroline about this first, but under the circumstances, I think it's worth speaking to him directly."*

Angela shook her head.

*"That's too risky, honey. If he reports you to the Brigadier, then you risk everything. You need to find some other way. Look, Geoffrey's on the mend now and a quick call to Caroline wouldn't hurt, just to ask her advice over the phone. We're not asking her to do anything."*

Without waiting for a response she took out her cell phone and dialled the number.

*"Hi, Caroline, I need your advice on a question, but first - how is your old man doing?"*

Dimitris listened as Angela outlined the dilemma Dimitris faced. He could not hear Caroline's replies, but became concerned when he heard Angela say;

*"I really didn't want to involve you any more. You've done enough."*

Angela hung up and walked back to Dimitris, looking a mite upset.

*"Geoffrey's fine. She said it's a good idea to speak to Adamos, but wants to be there when you do. I told her not to get any more involved, but you know Caroline."* she said, throwing her hands in the air in a display of frustration.

*"There's no reasoning with her."*

......................

The Brigadier stood up to greet Adamos and shake his hand.

*"Nico, come in and take a seat. I have submitted your report to Athens, and they have agreed that we can wrap this paltry affair up. The bodies will be interred in a separate plot at the city cemetery. The environmental team has also submitted their findings and declared the site safe. So, our German lawyer can tell her clients they can submit a planning application. To be honest, I'm glad to be shot of this. Too many memories of the Nazis and the possibility that they may still be around is bad for tourism. So, me and the Department are grateful for your assistance, and*

*release you from active duty. I'm sure you're anxious to return to a quieter life."*

Adamos accepted the handshake, adding;

*"Actually, sir, it's been quite refreshing to get back to the job, but I think that at my age, a week is long enough. Thank you for the opportunity to oil up the old grey matter and make sure it still works."*

Otto Kurtz was driving slowly; the road was uneven and well fitted the description of the proverbial road less travelled. In fact, there were few buildings here and certainly no tourists. It was about 6 miles along the coast road when the small two-story cabin came into view. A wide gravelled area led around the building and to a 26 foot fishing boat on a launching trailer. An elderly man and a middle-aged woman were working on the boat's rudder assembly. They both looked up as the car approached.

The Woman greeted Otto as he pulled up close to the boat and got out.

*"Otto, what brings you out here on a weekday, a few fresh Amberjack for your freezer?*

*"Always welcome, Gaia, but I wanted a word with Paris, if he has a moment."*

Her smile faded slightly, and she nodded.

*"He's trying to free a busted bolt at the moment"*

The Elderly man stopped working and turned toward them.

*"I'll get the fish."* Gaia said hurriedly and moved off towards the house.

Paris approached and stopped in front of Otto. He said nothing; Otto's face gave him all the information he needed.

*"The Day we hoped would never come is here, my friend. I think we will have need of your boat."*

........................

# Chapter 30

### An Unexpected Visitor

Deputy Director Adamos was a little surprised to receive a phone call from Caroline. Knowing her husband had suffered a recent health scare, he had assumed she would have stood back from the investigation, but clearly he didn't know her. Caroline was not very forthcoming. She just came right out and asked him if he was still officially in charge of the Ronin point investigation. When he told her that he had submitted his report and therefore was again officially retired, she seemed pleased.

*"Well, in that case, I wonder if I can pick your brains? I have something that has come up involving the Ronin Point matter that I know is not in your report. Quite frankly, I could do with input from a Greek detective. For obvious reasons, I don't want to bother Geoffrey with this. In fact, he's unaware that I'm calling you. I would hope to keep it that way."*

Adamos was a little intrigued. He had come to respect Caroline's unusual abilities, but was wary of rocking the boat as far as the Department was concerned.

*"Of course, I have no problem with casual off-the-cuff opinions, but I no longer have any input on the departments' day to day operations. Can you give me an idea of what the problem is?"*

Caroline replied with two words.

*"Otto Kurtz"*

Adamos said nothing, but his mind was racing. A name he had not heard for many years and had all but forgotten; a name that very few knew, especially not the Hellenic Police Dept. And a name that stirred a lot of memories best forgotten. Finally, he responded.

*"The library is too public; can I suggest a more private location?"*

Caroline was hoping that Otto's name would trigger interest and was prepared.

*"Hanna Vettel's hotel room. And before you ask, she is not here representing her firm or anyone else. In fact, they think she's on vacation. The reason that she's here is her grandparents were chief scientists at Ronin Point. So she's looking for answers too. To date, I fear she has discovered more than she bargained for. But that's always a risk."*

It was a risky manoeuvre, but Adamos could see no negative comeback on him. He was no longer representing anyone but himself.

"Yes, alright; set up the meeting."

........................

Hanna was somewhat relieved when Caroline called her, as she had begun to feel a little alone. Her mind was still reeling from what her grandfather had revealed during the seance. And she was considering packing her stuff and returning to Germany while she still had her sanity. Moreover, Caroline had said this was not going to be another seance. Rather, a discussion on what had been discovered. Not only in the realm of the Paranormal, but in the living world, the known and recently discovered history of what went on as the war ended. She, Carlos, Santos, and Christa would be joined by two elderly members of the resistance, as well as a former SS man from the plant. The most surprising guest was retired Deputy Director Nicholas Adamos, and another man long since dead whose identity was being withheld; 7 in all. Notably missing were Dimitris and Geoffrey, the latter being understandable. To say Hanna was intrigued would be an understatement. The meeting had been set for the following morning.

Caroline had been determined to keep it from Geoffrey, but knew that not telling him would hardly help mend things between them. She did, however, believe that the meeting may well lie to rest on any loose ends. This was surely a problem the locals here could deal with without further psychic input. Both she and Philip could resume their holidays. It sounded great, at least in theory. The trouble with theories was they had a habit of going off script, as both Caroline and Philip were about to find out.

As the evening wound down, Caroline and Geoffrey had settled down for a rare, quiet evening. Angela had leant them a CD on Crete history, it did not mention the plant or the Bell, and Geoffrey was at least grateful for that. Philip was out on the veranda of his apartment, taking in the view and enjoying a beer. His thoughts were, however, far away with the girl he left behind a couple of days ago in Athens, 200 miles north across the Mediterranean. He really should have invited her along, but knew she was lukewarm about the whole paranormal thing. His thoughts were interrupted by a light tap on the door. He glanced at his watch, it was almost 8pm.

He crossed to the door and opened it. A young, attractive brunette woman stood in front of him. His surprise was total as he stared at her.

*"Well Phil, aren't you going to invite me in, or am I interrupting something?"*

She tried to look over his shoulder, but with little success.

*"Pam, how did you get here?"*

The girl replied;

*"Well, actually, there's a invention called an airplane that can fly very fast. I got on it and wham, here I am, it's called progress."*

"Smart Alec"

He quipped as he stepped aside and ushered her in. Pamela scanned the room, noticing the double bed and went over to it, sat on the side and bounced on it.

*"Cozy, isn't it?"*

She said with a grin. Phillip laughed.

*"Yes, very cozy. And before you get any ideas, Caroline booked it and said it was the only one left, due to a cancellation. I was going to check out tomorrow and fly back to you; the job here is complete, so you had a wasted trip."*

Pamela rolled onto the bed and struck an unmistakable provocative pose.

*"So we have at least one night in this magic island. Come here and tell me more about this psychic woman who has the power to drag you away at a moment's notice?"*

Phillip knew he had little choice, and was already working out in his head how he could extend their holiday for a few days. They had already done the Acropolis and most of the 'must see' sights. He sat down beside her.

*"Well, it's late now, but I'll set up a visit for us in the morning. You can put your mind at rest and judge for yourself. Is that satisfactory WPC Meredith?"*

Pamela smiled.

*"It'll do for now, but it's been a long flight and I'm sweaty in this heat. Can I use the shower?"*

Phillip snapped out of his thoughts.

*"Of course, take your time."*

Pamela got up from the bed and walked towards the bathroom, then turned and looked back over her shoulder as she unbuttoned her blouse.

*"Care to join me, lover boy?"*

Phillip smiled.

*"It's tempting, but."*

Pamela shook her head as she removed her blouse.

*"Chicken"*

She said as she closed the door. Phillip sat down on the bed, and then realized that he was not too fresh-smelling himself. He quickly undressed and stepped into the bathroom. The shower masked the noise he made and the steam all but hid him. He opened the shower door surprising her.

*"No one calls me chicken."* he said, as he put his arms around her neck, and pulled her close. She looked up at him, sliding her arms around his waist, pulling him close. Her hands moved to the front of his waist and down toward his groin.

*"Well, it seems as if you are pleased to see me after all, Detective Sergeant."*

An hour later, Caroline's phone rang. She glanced at the phone, then at Geoffrey.

*"A bit late for room service."* He remarked.

*Caroline picked up the phone and listened before speaking.*

*"That's Okay Phil, what's up. Yes, I see, well of course we would. Say about 11 am. No, I have a meeting first thing; it will take about an hour, no more. Okay, see you then."*

She put the phone down and looked up at Geoffrey with an impish grin.

*"Well, that's a surprise. Pamela has flown in from Athens. I think she was a bit lonely and suspicious of what was going on. Smart girl."*

Geoffrey laughed and said;

*"I'm pretty sure you would have done the same if you thought I had skived off for a dirty weekend. Anyway, I gather from the call that they're both coming over at 11 tomorrow, so you can judge for yourself."*

Caroline walked over and planted a kiss firmly on Geoffrey's forehead.

*"Yep, that's the plan; maybe there'll be wedding bells in the future."*

Geoffrey sat back on the couch and took another shot of whisky and said quietly;

*"So, tell me about this meeting tomorrow that you simply have to attend."*

# Chapter 31

## Loose Ends

Caroline had made a point of arriving early for the meeting to ensure that Hanna was on board with everything. As the guests arrived, she introduced them and Hanna provided morning coffee for those that requested it. The meeting began with a solemn warning that no one at the meeting was acting in any way as an official or law enforcement officer. After this, Caroline asked Carlos to outline the details known about the history of the SS Plant and its suspected purpose. He finished the synopsis by announcing that there are steps that need to be taken immediately in order to ensure the weapon known as Die Glocke is never made operational.

"I'd like to ask former SS Meijer Otto Kurtz, who worked on the project and was largely responsible for ensuring it was never used by the Nazis. In Fact, they put a price on his head, charging him with treason. Thankfully, with the aid of the resistance, some of whom are here today, Otto survived. His continued survival is largely dependent on us, Herr Meijer."

Otto got shakily to his feet and thanked the members for attending.

"The weapon that we developed was highly technically advanced; it was produced by the finest physicists of the German nation. Many people have suggested it was just a myth of some sort of devastating nuclear weapon. Neither is correct. The Bell was small, around 13 feet high and was powered by a propulsion unit comprising two counter rotating cylinders filled with a newly developed Mercury based solution produced by ultra-high speed rotation. The device required very high voltage to operate, and this was a handicap to its deployment. Initial testing was carried out in lower Silesia on the Czech border at a plant we called 'The Giant'. The purpose was to develop a machine using vortex compression, to induce an anti-gravity effect. This was actually achieved, but the intense *radiation given off was lethal, out to extreme ranges. At The Giant, we could control it by switching it on and off. But what was needed was an independent power supply, a nuclear powered generator that could achieve the voltage necessary. That is what we were tasked with designing and building at Ronin Point. A disassembled prototype of the device was shipped to the plant, ready for testing once we had perfected the power cell required. The unexpected advance of the allied forces made it crucial that we completed the weapon and were ready to deploy it. By then, I had realized that Die Glocke would never be completed in time and would most likely fall into allied hands. In any case, the weapon was indiscriminate. The weapon killed all life forms in the area and anyone could transport it to any location. Such a weapon could indeed have changed the course of the war. But by then, I had seen the growing horrors that were being committed in the name of the German people. I knew then I had to act and was able to contact the resistance and ask for their assistance. I knew that a young Gendarmerie cadet in the Heraklion police department was under suspicion for contacting a young girl who, in turn, was suspected of being a partisan. It was through this initial contact that I met Leander. I did not think he believed me and I half expected he would shoot me on sight."*

Leander nodded and smiled before adding.

*"It was most tempting, Otto. I'll not deny it."*

Otto continued.

*"Well, I gave him the location of the prototype and suggested he move it off Crete as soon as he could. I also provided him with the security details at the site. I had hoped that in doing so I would be proving my integrity. The device was snatched in a raid a couple of days later. I did not know anything else or even where it had been taken."*

Otto sat down. By now the meeting was alive with speculation as Christa now spoke.

*"For me, this has been a hard journey. Few other than my lifelong friend knew how hard, and even he didn't know the full story. Like many*

*occupied countries, Greece was a conquered land full of resentment. My husband, as most of you know, was commander of the Gendarmerie here when the city was a mere shadow of what it has become today. Most of you, including my son Dimitris and his wife, knew that my husband Andreas was killed in the war and I was left to raise my son alone. That is not entirely accurate. The Germans were sympathetic to me and often brought extra food and treats to Dimitris. They, of course, believed that my husband had been a collaborator and therefore they owed me something. In fact, there was an explosion at the plant and much speculation as to the cause. Andreas was summoned by the German commander, Colonel Steinberg, who asked him and several other city officials, including the mayor, to visit the plant and be briefed on what went on. What they didn't know was that immediately before his death, he came to me. He was agitated and told me that there were moves being made to clear out the personnel at the Plant and that he would have to lie low for a while. I did not complain, neither did the resistance, it provided perfect cover for me. Following Andreas death, I became aware of activities at the site involving the removal of something the Resistance had obtained that was highly secretive. This acquisition was made possible with the help of a member of the SS. As you now know, Leander and I were involved in arranging for the transportation of this device from a secure house to a sheltered cove where it was loaded onto a fishing boat operated then by my good friend Paris."*

She nodded at one of the elderly men, who returned the nod and half raised his hand in acknowledgment.

*"The device was taken to Gavdos, where it remains to this day. Well, as you know, the war ended and slowly things got back to normal. Of course, there were questions and rumours about what was being done at the plant. But all personnel, including the ones who had attended the meeting were dead, the latter ones in shall we say, odd circumstances; car accident, drowning, even an apparent suicide. In the early 60s, I met Carlos, he was an ambitious journalist and was looking for a scoop on*

*the Nazi secret weapons program they called the, Wunderwaffen. Dimitris was away in England getting a university education and Carlos and I became close. Okay, more than close, we became lovers. But his big scoop never happened. Okay, he was good in bed, but I never really trusted him enough to reveal what I knew about the device."*

She paused as Carlos became visibly uncomfortable and gave a half-hearted and mildly sheepish grin.

*"All this I had put firmly behind me until I got the biggest shock of my life about 6 months ago. I discovered that my husband had actually faked his death and was living under an assumed identity. If that was not a big enough problem, Caroline and Geoffrey suddenly arrive here on their honeymoon and disturb the sleeping spirits. No offence, Caroline."*

Caroline smiled and replied.

*"Blunt, but accurate."*

Hanna, who had remained quiet until now, cut in.

*"So, where is your husband now? Shouldn't he be here?"*

Andreas raised his hand.

*"Yes, he should, and in fact, he is."*

There was a shocked silence in the room as all eyes turned to the mystery man, who, until now, had not been identified. Only Caroline seemed unphased. Though, of course, Carlos was also expecting the revelation.

Andreas now had the attention of the meeting.

*"I find myself in a position that I had never hoped to be in. In 1944, I became suspicious when I was invited to a meeting at the SS Plant. The Germans put on an elaborate show and even had a fake Swedish professor explain to us the how the ground was highly contaminated with radiation and would remain so for years. However, they were unaware that I had been present at the time of the partisan attack on the plant and knew they were lying. I witnessed the raid and was the last person to see young Sally Knight alive. In fact, she died in my arms. Had she been highly radioactive, I would have also picked up a high amount. I*

*didn't. Whatever killed her, it was not radiation. We, of course, have had the assistance from what is known as the Paranormal, from spirits who have passed on. While some of us will understandably be highly sceptical, the information we got from them corroborates exactly what we already had gleaned from the facts. The Germans were no fools. They realized the account of me and the witnesses would not stand close scrutiny. So they had to be eliminated, not immediately, but after they had the time to relay the radiation leak theory among the populous here. Even so, they needed a scapegoat. Someone already suspected of collaboration with the Germans and would take the blame. The plan was to send me to meet an alleged informant who had information on a terrorist cell. I was to drive to the meeting place where the SS would be waiting. There I was to be taken prisoner and my car loaded with a large quantity of gold bullion and bank shares. After killing me, my body was to have been found in the car after trying to run a German road block. The matter would then be handed over to the Gendarmerie for investigation. The German authorities would be extremely cooperative in ensuring their story got out."*

Hanna was still reeling from this avalanche of information, but now she spoke up.

*"That seems pretty well thought out, so what went wrong?"*

Andreas turned to look at Otto.

*"Well, I was tipped off by a much unexpected source."*

Otto smiled.

*"Well, it seemed that I was in deep enough shit anyway, so I suggested he drop off the radar for a while, and being dead is pretty good cover.*

*I hadn't intended to kill anyone, but the deserters offered me a way out. I knew I had to get away. I had intended to leave Crete, but following the war, most of Europe was in turmoil. I grew a beard and paid for a trip to Athens and became a fisherman. As the years went by, I bought my own boat and returned to Crete, primarily to be close to Christa."*

*"So what happens now, do we all go home and forget everything?"*

Hanna's question was likely also on the minds of others, but she saw their expressions and knew there was something else. It was Leander who burst her bubble.

*"I wish we could. We all do, but now there is one more task the resistance must take on. Our last mission, if you will. The Americans and Russians are apparently aware of the bells existence and are already here making enquiries. We must destroy the Bell and the operating data from the plant before they discover it. But I feel we are past our prime for accomplishing it, but somehow it has to be done."*

# Chapter 32

## Destiny Angel

Paris Dukas had spread the chart out on the table in front of him and he had taken on the responsibility of planning the upcoming phase of the operation. His wife, Gaia, stood behind him. The small cottage was remote enough to ensure they would not be disturbed. Carlos and Leander were also present.

*"To be honest, the timing could not be worse. Last month, the multiple arrests on Gavdos of the November 17 terrorist group have put the Island under extra scrutiny. Initially, I thought we could just lay charges and blow the thing to bits, blaming the blast on an old Nazi arms dump that became unstable. With enough TNT, there would be nothing left. However, any explosion big or otherwise, will bring the Army and Hellenic Police down on us in swarms. So I suggest a change of plan, more risky, but just as effective. Approximately 150 miles North West of the island is the Calypso Trench that's over 16,000 feet deep and in a marine conservation area. Very few visitors are allowed. The only exceptions are, by special permission, only scientific teams. That would be an ideal disposal spot, but it would need good navigation and probably a better boat than mine. Any suggestions?"*

Carlos studied the map.

*"Well, we would need a team on Gavdos to locate and move the bell to your boat and then proceed on course for about three hours to a point off Kissamos. A fishing boat will not attract any attention with a night sea rendezvous about here to transfer the bell."*

He showed a spot on the map north of Crete. Paris nodded in agreement.

*"Okay, so where do we get a suitable boat to complete the trip?"*

Carlos smiled and replied.

*"Leave that to me, I know someone who would jump at the chance."*

.....................

190

Nico sat back in his chair facing Carlos, who had just finished outlining the initial proposal for the disposal of the bell prototype. It was only one part of the operation, but a vital one. If the bell was destroyed, then nothing else would matter.

Adamos listened and then gave a cautious reply.

*"I understand your request, Carlos. Destiny Angel would easily be able to make the trip, but there is a snag. Although I own her, my son and his wife operate her. I'm not sure if I want to involve them. I would need a convincing cover story, because if I replace them, I will need a reason."*

*"Well, that's a matter for you to determine, but there may not be much time. I think Geoffrey and Dimitris are working on a plan to derail the Russians and the Americans. The problem is we do not know how much they know."*

Nico looked up in surprise.

*"How did Geoffrey get involved? The man just had a bad heart scare? And knowing Caroline, I'm amazed she is letting him get involved in the first place.*

*"Truthfully, I don't think she had much choice. Dimitris cannot be seen to conspire in this escapade, which may end up costing him his job. Geoffrey is a retired detective from the British Police force, from a department called the CID, or Criminal Investigation Department. Of course, you need to appreciate that the British police force is not a branch of the Military, nor is it a federal or political entity. They do not carry firearms as a general rule, but of course, there are armed police units available. Despite this, the detection rate is pretty good. To do that, they are highly trained and good at what they do. I think his expertise would be useful. I feel sure that between them they will come up with a scheme that gets the right result, but I personally don't want to know."*

Andreas Nodded understandingly.

*"What you don't know, you cannot testify about."*

..........................

While Carlos and Adamos were discussing the core parts of their plan, Caroline and Geoffrey were meeting up with Phillip and Pamela. Caroline was delighted to hear that Philip had made arrangements for them to spend the remainder of their holiday in Crete. Both were, of course, aware that the Partisans group were planning a covert operation to remove and destroy the bell. They saw no reason to share that information. In fact, it seemed that everything would be over within 24 hours or so.

Pamela took an immediate shine to Caroline, and knowing that she was a celebrity in her field, had been looking forward to meeting her. Phillip had bought her a copy of Caroline's book, 'The Soul Never Dies' by way of explanation. Although Phillip was sure she had ignored it, in fact, Pamela had read it within hours of receiving it; primarily due to Phillip's cooperation with her, not only on the book, but during actual seances. Whilst in bed the previous night, she had asked him how the seance had gone, but received a less than informative reply, that 'nothing out of the ordinary had occurred and we gained some useful data. After meeting Caroline and finding her quite the opposite of what she had expected, she asked her the same question.

*Caroline shot a quick glance at Phillip, who shook his head slowly.*

*"I'm sure Phillip told you, but there were some hiccups that were unforeseen, but we got there and I am grateful he was able to assist. I'm not sure I could have done it without him. And I do apologize again for interrupting your holiday. Believe me, with a son and daughter in law in the force, not to mention an ex police husband, I do know how valuable police leave is."*

*If the answer was intended to reassure Pamela, it had the opposite effect. The words 'a few hiccups' caught her attention. She thanked Caroline and crossed over to Phillip, smiling like a panther sizing up its prey. She moved close enough to plant a kiss on his cheek and also to whisper.*

"We need to talk later, lover." Before turning with a beaming smile toward Geoffrey.

"Well, Chief Inspector, it's a pleasure to meet you at last. Your name is famous, almost a legend in Petersfield CID."

Geoffrey took her offered hand.

"I suspect infamous would be more accurate, Miss Meredith, but it is a pleasure to meet you too, and may I also add my apologies to those of my wife for interrupting your holiday."

Pamela glanced across at Caroline before replying.

"Oh, not at all. I think things are only going to get better from now on."

........................

Georgios Adamos recognized his father's name on his I Phone screen and pressed the answer button.

"Evening dad, what's up?"

"Can you get the Angel fuelled up for a long trip this weekend, and if possible, can you part crew her with me?"

Georgios replied.

"That will be awkward, Dad. We have a client booked for a corporate party, an evening cruise Saturday night. He's paying pretty well. What's the story?"

"It's a special operation, a favour if you like, for a group of wartime friends. Most are around my age, but only two will be making the actual trip. I'm afraid you will have to put off the client, tell him there's a problem with the boat or paperwork. But on no account mention this trip to anyone, not even your wife. It's vital that we keep it under the tightest wraps."

Georgios was more than a little perplexed,

"What are you up to dad, a bit of smuggling on the side?"

It was, of course, meant to be a joke, but it was obvious that his father was not joking.

*"Actually, the opposite, shall we say, disposal of something that should not have been created. Make sure we have full tanks of fuel, enough for a 500 mile round trip, and provisions for 4. I will not say any more over the phone, but I'll brief you on board."*

He hung up, leaving his son intrigued.

Just over 5,000 miles west, an operator at NSA, Maryland, had intercepted the cell phone call and made a recording. She passed it over to another operator at a desk marked FBI with an accompanying text, reading, 'Debbie, pass this one to the FBI. They are looking for info on Crete at the moment.'

# Chapter 33

## *Gavdos Island*

Paula looked up from the table at the roadside café as a well-dressed man in his late 20s approached. He studied her for a moment before speaking.

*"Miss Turner?"*

Paula nodded without looking directly at him. With a somewhat relieved look he sat down.

*"Mark Webster, US Consulate, Athens. Pleased to meet you. I have been directed to offer you any assistance I can in your enquiry. But initial enquiries have not been encouraging, I'm afraid."*

Paula looked up without any welcoming smile.

*"Sorry, Mr Webster, do you not carry ID in Athens?"*

Webster was taken aback and sheepishly took out his identity shield and handed it over.

*"Sorry, Miss Turner, stupid Error."*

Paula scanned the Card and shield before returning it, this time with the hint of a smile.

*"Indeed, the sort that could get you, shall we say, slightly dead?"*

Webster returned the ID to his inside pocket.

*"So, you were saying?"*

*"Well, the cell phone is registered to a Nicholas Adamos. He is a retired police Deputy Director here, not much else known. It was him and his son, Georgios, who was the callers' recipient. As to the message content, the boat they referred to is a 40 ft. former oceanographic survey vessel now operated by them as a charter hire base for celebrities and well-heeled elite, named Destiny Angel.*

*She is berthed at Heraklion marina and has been used on several occasions this year.*

*There is nothing known about the Bell device. Adamos was here during the war, attached to the local station Gendarmerie as a cadet. Of course, we know there was a facility run by the SS here in the early 40s working on clandestine rocket propellant, but the plant and its personnel were all killed in a mystery explosion about the time the Germans were withdrawing. CIA records show it was likely to have been caused by the SS as they withdrew, again, nothing to indicate the Bell or anything similar. All such research was being carried out in Poland and the Urals area. A facility here would, frankly, make no sense."*

Paula did not make any notes; instead the entire conversation was being recorded on a small Sony cassette recorder. She nevertheless was following the conversation carefully.

*"Well, that seems very logical, but I think some more digging is warranted. This German living on the island, there is little known about him, other than he worked at the plant and remained here afterwards. Ex SS men are never welcome in newly liberated areas. They know this and would never surrender to a partisan army who would most likely have strung them up from the nearest tree. So the question is, why is our, Otto Kurtz still alive?"*

Webster shrugged his shoulders.

*"Maybe he had something too valuable to be lost, something that would be well worth letting him off the hook in exchange for a new identity."*

*"Yes, that was what I was thinking."*

Paula replied.

..........................

Caroline and Geoffrey were just about to leave when they saw Pamela and Phillip approaching the hotel block. Hand in hand, they looked blissfully happy.

*"So, what are you two planning today?"*

Geoffrey's question was directed at both Pamela and Phillip. It wasn't said with any sort of suspicion, but merely because he was well aware that today was going to be a very busy one and knowledge of the couple's whereabouts would be useful. At first, Pamela's reply really alarmed him, but he slowly realized that it may be the break they really needed.

*"Well, we've been looking at the map and Phil found a gem of a resort. If you know your history, it appears that the famed Island of Calypso is close by. Legend has it that Odysseys was held captive there. At first, I couldn't find it on the map, but then one of the staff here told me that the island's real name is Gavdos. It's a two hour ferry trip from Crete. So, we were going to try it. Phil seems very keen on it."*

Caroline smiled.

*"Well, enjoy yourselves, we are going shopping for Greeks nick knacks that will no doubt cost a bomb, but provide special memories for us from our Honeymoon."* As if we were ever likely to forget, she thought to herself.

Once out of earshot, Caroline said quietly.

*"Is that going to cause a problem?"*

Geoffrey shook his head.

*"Maybe not. On the contrary, it may be the break we need. We'll be going to Gavdos with Paris in his boat; if we were to offer to take them as a gesture, it would give us a great cover story. Of course, we would not be able to bring them back, but we could make an offer to supply them with overnight camping gear and pick them up tomorrow. What do you think?"*

Caroline shook her head and laughed.

*"Geoff, you should have been a Hollywood screen writer, not a flatfoot."*

(UK slang name for English Bobbies)

Geoffrey grinned.

*"No director would accept this script, it's beyond credibility."*

*"Which means we have a shot."*

Caroline quipped.

*"I'll call Nico."*

Andros was with both Paris and Leander when he got Caroline's call; he listened carefully as she outlined the proposal. Finally, he replied that he would put the plan to the others before hanging up.

*"It seems we may have extra passengers on the trip to Gavdos, two more British police officers here on vacation, one male, and one female. Both are known to Geoffrey and Caroline, and were planning on going to the island on a sightseeing trip. They have no knowledge of what we are going to be doing there and are not really involved in the investigation. Although the male, is a Psychic like Caroline and has been assisting her here. It would be a risk to give them a ride, but probably less than allowing them to travel by ferry. No doubt, our FBI woman is receiving data and phone intercepts from the island. That is why I have rented these two cells from the town tourist centre, just in case they already have my number dialled into the system. So, what are your thoughts? We have to leave by 10 tomorrow to have time to locate the package and load it safely aboard."*

Paris spoke first.

*"I don't like it, if this psychic cop friend of Caroline suspects what's up, he may just walk away, or even call the police. That could blow the entire project open and likely hand the weapon to the FBI, or even Russia."*

Adamos had his reply ready, expecting some opposition.

*"Well, both he and Caroline have worked closely together for the past few years. I think as he was present during the last séance, he will, by now, realize what is at risk. In fact, I'm sure Caroline would have already recruited him, had it not been for his girlfriend. She is the unknown factor here. Either way, we have to decide now; we are quite frankly out of time."*

# Chapter 34

## Stopping the Russians

Igor Popov and Rena Orlov were operational agents of the SVR, but this was the first operation outside Russian Territory, Ukraine was their first operation, assigned to infiltrate the political campaign of Viktor Yushchenko, who was a potential rival to President Kuchma. Later, acting under orders, Igor had been part of the cell that kidnapped and beheaded troublesome journalist, Georgiy Gongadze.

The operation in Crete had been fairly recently put together. Of course, the couple had no information on where it had come from, only that they were to investigate, and if possible, locate a prototype of a German super bomb of aircraft hidden on the island. So far, the results had been mixed. That morning, a coded message had been received that the FBI were also looking for this weapon and had dispatched resources to Crete also. This information was the nearest they could get to conformation that this device really existed. Now they had their first lead. A local man had suggested they talk to an elderly Greek named Leander Kosta, who had been on Crete during the war and allegedly worked for the communist resistance. Sensing a possible kindred sympathizer, the couple had tracked him to a Greek bar in the old part of the city, but so far had missed him. Today they felt might be different as they prepared to leave their apartment. Outside, a marked police unit moved into position, at first they did not notice it. But Rena heard the car door slam, causing her to look up. She saw two uniformed officers approaching the ground floor apartment. She turned to Igor.

*"Police"*

She said rather nervously. Igor was not fazed. He moved to the rear of the apartment and without approaching the window, observed three more figures dressed in tactical gear marked with EKAM patches moving towards the rear patio doors.

He motioned Rena to sit down on the couch.

Dimitris approached the front door and knocked loudly. After a few moments, Igor opened it, feigning surprise.

"Mr Igor Popov" He said politely.

Igor replied equally politely.

*"Yes Officer, I am he. What can I do for you?"*

Dimitris took his cap off.

*"Perhaps we can speak inside, in case you have over inquisitive neighbours."*

Igor nodded and warily said;

*"Yes, of course. I hope it won't take too long. We were **about to** go out to the beach, for the morning."*

Once inside, Dimitris became more formal.

*"We have had information that you may be in possession of some stolen items that disappeared recently from the City Museum. It may be that you obtained these innocently, but with your permission, we would like to search these premises, unless you can produce them for us and save a lot of hassle."*

Igor looked at him and then at Rena, who looked bewildered. Then he spoke up.

*"Look, Captain, I don't want to sound uncooperative, but we have no idea what you are talking about. Now, I understand without my permission you will need a search warrant signed by a local judge or military commander."*

Dimitris nodded and pulled a folded document out of his inside pocket.

*"You mean like this one, Igor."*

He replied with a hint of menace before handing over the document. Igor scanned it with a growing sense of concern. This was obviously a pre-planned incident. But he decided to play along.

*"Very well captain, but I assure you, there is nothing here that should not be."*

Igor stood aside and motioned the two officers to move ahead. Dimitris crossed the apartment to the back entrance and admitted the three tactical offices waiting outside and then motioned Rena to sit on the couch while he watched the officers all but ransack the room. Dimitris himself, mostly, supervised and directed the officers to replace the mattresses and cushion covers they disturbed, assisting them at times. After 10 minutes there seem to be nothing of interest, then Dimitris remembered the couch. He asked Rena to stand up while he turned it over and ran his hands through the gaps between the cushions. With the upright couch shielding his lower body from the couple, he slipped his hand into a front pants pocket and removed a small black velvet bag that he deftly pushed down between the cushions. He continued the search for another minute, then pulled out the bag.

*"Well, well, what could this be?"*

..................

While the search was going on, Phillip had returned to see Caroline and Geoffrey.

He was not happy. The ferries for the next week appeared to be fully booked. Pamela was also not happy, because she had set her mind on the trip. But that was not all. It appeared that she was also suspicious that something was going on, that she had been shut out of.

*"Pam is no fool; she noticed a discrepancy between my account and yours of the seance. Of course, she does not know what's going on and, frankly, neither do I. But I know you Caroline; we don't have many secrets from each other. You and Geoff are planning something likely connected with the old SS plant. But if I were a betting man, I'd say you feel the need to put this case to bed for eternity. How am I doing?"*

Caroline gave a smile of, almost resignation.

*"Your right, of course Phil, I'm not good at keeping secrets, but your psychic abilities are as good as mine. I assure you that this little jaunt is no more than what you suggest, a tidying up of loose ends. We need no input*

*from the paranormal for this one. So, enjoy each other. I may even be able to arrange for you to get to Gavdos; we have made some pretty influential friends here. I should know later today."*

...............

Meanwhile, back at the Russians apartment, Dimitris had retrieved the object from the couch. He placed it on the coffee table and carefully opened it. Inside was a small egg-shaped ornament about the size of a large hen's egg. It was green overall, what appeared to be Onex or a similar stone. The egg was laced with gold straps and what appeared to be diamonds. He picked it up and examined it before turning to Rena.

*"Is this yours, Miss Orlov?"* He asked.

On realizing that the captain knew Rena's name, Igor's suspicion that this was no ordinary raid was now confirmed.

Rena was defiant.

*"No, it's not mine. Some dumb tourist is missing her cheap souvenir from the market."*

She snapped.

Dimitris was unphased.

*"Well, that may be, and I am no jewellery expert, just an ordinary unappreciated police captain, but we have a report of a valuable Fabergé egg matching this description missing from the city museum, believed stolen yesterday. If so, this 'cheap trinket' would pay my salary for the next 10 years. Until then, I am arresting you both on suspicion of theft. Come with us, please."*

Once the two were safely in the back seat of the car, Dimitris went to dismiss the tactical team. As they turned to go, he took out his cell phone and dialled a number. About a quarter of a mile away, Geoffrey's phone rang. He picked it up and a voice he instantly recognized said just six words, 'Number one target is on ice', before it cut off. He nodded to Caroline, who returned the nod. Phil was curious, but said nothing. It was Geoffrey who offered the explanation.

"*There's a space for you aboard the Fishing vessel, Aphrodite. Be at the ferry port at 7 tonight. We cannot pick you up until the following day. So you will need to get somewhere to stay. If that's not possible, the boat owner has offered two backpacks with camping gear. Pretty basic, 1970s stuff, I'm afraid, comprising a military pup tent, two army sleeping bags and two inflatable beds, plus a couple of torches with new batteries. Not exactly 5 star, but the weather forecast is good.*"

Phillip looked visibly relieved.

"*We won't mind roughing it for one night if needed. I'm grateful though. You see, this was going to be a life-changing trip for me. It was all going wrong until Pam turned up and got fired up about Gavdos. Now, well, it may just fall into place.*"

Caroline smiled and lightly embraced him before whispering;

"*Hope you have the ring.*"

# Chapter 35

## Barbarossa's Cauldron

The sun was lower in the sky and the harsh summer heat was at last abating. Aphrodite's old diesel engine was pushing the boat to close on 20 knots and carving a prominent wake as it left the ferry port. Unseen at the dockside, Paula Turner watched the departure; she had assumed that Caroline and her friends would be aboard the ferry. Her ticket had been pre booked from the FBI on line. Now she knew that she may be too late. The ferry didn't leave for another 30 minutes and it travelled at a more sedate 15 knots. All she could do was hope the Fishing boat was still there when she arrived.

Aboard the Aphrodite, a blissfully happy Philip and Pamela were standing in the bow, looking forward. Phillip stepped from behind her and slid his arms around her waist. She turned sideways, smiling, then suddenly stretched out her arms.

*"Look Jack I'm flying."* She grinned.

*Phillip chuckled. "You're crazy Pam, but I do love you."*

He bent forward recreating the famous movie scene exactly.

In the wheelhouse, Paris and Adamos also laughed while Caroline commented.

*"Do you think we should warn them to look out for icebergs?"*

As the ferry port slowly fell behind them, Caroline noticed the dark cloud on the horizon ahead had now become darker and more solid.

Ahead and below them, Pamela dropped her arms.

*"Gavdos, I can see it Phil, there, right ahead."*

At least for the moment, happy that Phillip and Pamela were distracted, Caroline and Carlos left the wheelhouse and retired to the main cabin where Leander had placed 3 faded sepia photographs over a chart of Gavdos Island.

"*This is our landfall point. The locals call it Barbarossa's Cauldron. It's a cave that opens up into a large lava cave that has killed more than one over inquisitive tourist. The cave entrance is submerged for most of the tidal cycle, but is above water around 45 minutes each day. We secreted the bell inside covered in an oilskin hatch cover. These pictures show the cave at low tide and as you can see, there is not much clearance.*

"*The plan is to enter the cave as it becomes exposed and roll the bell components onto a deflated Zodiac dingy and then inflate it. As the water reaches it, we drag it down and out of the cave and then fully inflate the zodiac. As the tide rises, Paris will bring Aphrodite inshore and recover the bell by crane then we leave for the Rendezvous with Destiny Angel. It's pretty obvious that we are no longer in the peak of condition. So we have assigned Carlos, Hanna, and Caroline to the cave, and me and the Deputy Director will wait at the entrance to assist with loading the cargo on board. Hanna is an experienced scuba diver and will lead the team. No dissent, please. Hanna may not be well known to us, but trust me, she has a very powerful reason to be on this mission. It will not be easy, especially as we will be doing this in the dark. The cave team will have waterproof LED headlamps, but you cannot turn them on until you are underwater. We have a waxing moon tonight, so that should help.*"

He folded up the map and stowed it away. Then they all adjourned to the deck as Aphrodite reduced speed and approached the harbour wall. Paris threw a line to a ferry crewman and asked him to secure it with a half hitch, adding they weren't stopping, just dropping off. Phillip and Pamela wasted no time in scrambling ashore. Paris threw them the two backpacks and wished them good luck. Adding;

"*We should be back around 6 on Friday. Have fun.*"

The couple picked up their bags and walked up the stone path that lined the harbour wall. Paris signalled the ferryman, who released the rope and touched his cap as Paris backed away.

He glanced up and saw the telltale wisp of smoke from the ferry as it appeared on the horizon.

Paula Turner was annoyed; the Consulate in Athens had identified at least three people on vacation in Crete that seemed to have a connection with the events in 1944. They had sent her images of 3 of them; one was a British police officer, Phillip Dawson, who had been on vacation in Athens with a female believed to be a girlfriend. But Dawson had then suddenly flown to Crete to join Caroline De Winter, who was already a person of interest. But this wasn't the only anomaly; his girlfriend had not accompanied him. Paula decided to check on her, but discovered she had left suddenly. FBI searches had revealed a person matching her description had booked passage on a TAE commercial flight to Crete the following day. Paula studied the picture of Phillip Dawson and Pamela Meredith. Her enquiries at Heraklion had revealed that they had gone on a trip to Gavdos, but she now knew she had made a mistake. Of course, she reasoned, this may be a total wild goose chase with a logical explanation. These kids were on vacation and could have just had a tiff; Dawson could have gone to Crete to join his friend Caroline. There was nothing remotely linking them to the SS plant. As the ferry approached the dock, Paula was already looking for an out clause. That was until she got a text from the FBI. Two Russian agents were arrested by local police under suspicious circumstances. Watch your back 'Petrel'; the use of her code name made it official. The Russians were here and looking for something big. Likely the same thing she was.

................

The trip to the cave was uneventful. As planned, Paris stopped at around 200 yards from the shoreline. The sun was already setting. Hanna dropped anchor on cue. After a good scan of the cliff top above the cave with binoculars, the equipment was loaded into the zodiac and it was lowered over the side. Hanna, Carlos, and Caroline were now all wearing wetsuits and assisted Adamos and Leander aboard the slightly overloaded Zodiac. They set out for the shore using a small and silent electric 3 hp trolling motor. Paris watched from the wheelhouse as they reached the short pebble beach.

It had been almost 60 years since Leander had made this trip, but his eyes, though dimmer with age, were still sharp enough to locate the submerged cave.

Quickly they unloaded the equipment and deflated the boat to around 25% before it was carried the short distance to the cliff face. The water was clear enough to see the entrance, about a foot below the waterline. Hanna stood up, striking a surprisingly slim figure in the wet suit; she then donned a pair of swim goggles.

*"Right, this should be relatively easy, but some of these caves have nasty surprises. I will check it out and set up a couple of lights inside before returning. In 1944, the distance was around 4 meters until it opens out. It may have changed over the intervening years. If all is well, I will be back within 5 minutes. If I get through, you may be able to see the glow of the lights inside when I turn them on."*

She stepped forward and knelt down, took a deep breath, and pitched forward. The others watched as she reached the entrance, her blue wet suit standing out clearly as she slid inside, then she was gone. Minutes passed; suddenly an enormous lobster emerged from the cave and moved over the clear bottom, then disappeared into the gloom. The falling tide was now becoming more noticeable and the cave entrance was more sharply defined. And now, something else, there was a faint bluish glow. Seconds passed, the sun was now on the horizon and its light diminishing. A Sudden swirling eddy of water brought Hanna's head and wetsuit into view and a second later she broke surface and took a gulp of air.

*"So far, so good,"* she said between breaths. *"The entrance is around 4 meters. Mien Gott, it stinks in there."*

She shook her hair, displacing some of the water.

*"I found the oilskin. It is above the waterline and quite soiled. The Bell parts are still there, wrapped in three sections. I was just able to lift*

*one, so I'm guessing that all three weigh around 60 kilograms total. Okay,*
*Carlos and Caroline, check your headlamps and follow me. Time is not*
*our friend."*

With Hanna taking the lead and Caroline and Carlos following,
dragging the crumpled Zodiac behind them, they made the trip
without any real problems. But the trip took longer, because of the air
still in the boat, which forced Carlos to release more of it. They made it
though, breaking the surface inside the cave, which was more than big
enough to stand up in. Now they moved faster, positioning the Zodiac
in front of the Oilskin, lifting and depositing each section carefully
inside, then wait 5 minutes to pull the boat further down. Seconds
later, the waterline left the top of the cave. Carlos glanced at his watch:
15 minutes to low water. One last heave should have the cargo afloat.
Caroline waded into the water and moved toward the front in an
attempt to get more leverage. It was almost a fatal error. She stepped
on something that moved and 3 sharp spines went through her sandal
and into the sole of her foot. She screamed and fell backwards into
the water, grabbing her ankle. The screaming intensified as Carlos and
Hanna went to her aid. They dragged her clear of the water. Her face
was a mask of pain as she shook her head violently. Carlos steadied her
as Hanna checked her ankle and foot. The three spines were clearly seen
pinning the sandal to her foot. Blood was seeping from underneath.
Carlos now saw the wound and yelled.

*"Hanna, get her sandal l off."*

Hanna snapped back.

*"No, that may kill her. Weever fish - I should have warned you both."*
..............

Around 2 miles away, Pamela and Phillip had set up their tent.
In fact, they had found a bar that offered to give them a room for
the night earlier, but neither liked the young landlord, or the way he
leered at Pamela. However, they were able to hire two bicycles, not in
tiptop condition, but serviceable. Now they settled down and found

themselves alone. The sun had just set and Pamela settled back into his arms. This is the time Phil, he said to himself as he reached for the ring box. Then he gasped and stood up, dumping a shocked Pamela in the process. Angrily, she got to her feet, but stopped as she saw his face. She had never seen him like this before. His eyes were staring, staring straight out to sea.

*"Phil, what is it, what's wrong?"*

She shouted, grabbing his shoulders. At first he seemed unaware of her, and then slowly turned to face her.

*"It's Caroline. She's in dire trouble. I think she's dying."*

# Chapter 36

### Caroline's dying

Ten minutes had passed; Caroline had stopped screaming, but not through lack of pain, rather by sheer willpower. Her ankle and foot were now visibly swelled and her breathing noticeably laboured.

Hanna spoke to her in a concerned tone.

*"Caroline listen, I know it hurts like hell. The pain will pass, but you will need medical treatment. Fast. Do you understand? You have been stung by a Weever fish; they are the most deadly sea creature we have here. You have to keep as still as you can."*

Caroline looked up at her and gasped through clenched teeth, she was sweating profusely.

*"Listen, you have to continue. I'll survive. You can't miss the window. Get that bloody thing out of here."*

Alerted by splashing at the cave entrance, she saw Adamos and Leander struggling through the half exposed cave entrance. They had entered the cave at the first of Caroline's screams.

As they reached her, Caroline yelled again.

*"The Bell, get it out now, the tide's turning."*

She then threw her head back in a stifled scream.

Hanna now took control.

*"Leave Caroline, she'll be okay. all of you help Carlos get the bell and Zodiac out of here. You need to inflate it and get it aboard Aphrodite, NOW. I'll stay here and join you later. Caroline cannot be moved, not yet."*

Reluctantly, the crew complied. As the Zodiac entered the water the weight partially submerged it, but with coaxing they got it clear. Quickly, they began re-inflating it using a 12 volt pump that was agonizingly slow, but finally it was firm enough. As they launched it, Carlos flashed his red signal torch twice; he could see the dark silhouette of the fishing boat under the moonlight. He gave an audible sigh of relief when he saw the two answering flashes. He looked back toward the cliff, it was now in darkness, but he knew instinctively the cave entrance was now totally submerged. As if to add to their problems, two lights had now appeared on top of the cliff and some people were now descending the path toward them. Leander turned to Carlos.

*"You and Nico, get the boat moving, take it slow, and keep her on course. I'll stay here and deal with these tourists."*

As the boat moved out into the incoming tide, Leander turned back to face the two cyclists, moving excessively fast. He turned on his headlamp, bathing them both in LED light. He then switched it off after he recognized the leading cyclist who saw him clearly in the cycle lamp.

"Leander, what's happened to Caroline? No double talk. I know she's been hurt"

Both he and Pamela abandoned their cycles.

*"Yes, she has Philip, badly I'm afraid; Hanna's with her right now. I don't pretend to understand how you knew or what brought you here, but it's a pity you didn't get here 15 minutes earlier."*

Pamela now spoke up.

*"Look Leo, I don't even pretend to know what's going on, but it seems you need our help. Where is Caroline, and what can we do?"*

Leander turned towards the boat and flashed his torch 5 times. There was a pause, then the crackling sound of the CB radio broke the still night air.

*"Okay, no worries, it's Caroline's partner and his girlfriend. Stand by."*

*"Alright, Phillip, I'll bring you up to speed. You brought Pamela here, so we will have to include her. First off, Caroline is safe and she's here, but not on the beach. She stepped on a Weever fish and is in a pretty bad way. There is a cave in the cliff face over here that the locals know as Barbarossa's*

*Cauldron. The entrance is below sea level most of the time. It's where we hid the bell components in 1944."*

For the next 10 minutes, Leander filled in all the details of what was planned. Pamela listened attentively, but said little. As he concluded, Phillip looked even more worried.

*"I know about the weever fish. I read about them while I was planning our holiday. I warned Pamela about them. So, how long will it take for the cave entrance to be uncovered again?"*

Leander sighed.

*"That's the rub, 24 hours is sunset tomorrow and we can't wait that long. Aphrodite has to make a sea rendezvous this evening with another vessel who will take the cargo and dispose of it forever. Caroline was insistent that we complete the mission quickly before we were discovered."*

Pamela was not happy with the discussion, and she showed it.

*"Phil, we can't leave Caroline in there for 24 hours without treatment. She could die. You yourself told me that. Forget the super spy stuff. Are you prepared to tell Geoffrey we let her die because we were on a secret mission from WW2?"*

Leander spoke out, waving aside Phillips' attempt to reply.

*"Yes, Pamela, you're correct. We cannot do that. The situation has now changed and the plan must change with it. I'll call the authorities and get a professional paramedic team out here. I'll tell them that you, Pamela, and Caroline were exploring the area with Hanna. They went in the cave to explore and Caroline stepped on a weever. Hanna told you to summon help, and while she was treating Caroline, the tide rose and cut them off. You saw me down the beach and called for help. The Bell is already aboard and they can leave immediately. They should be well clear when the authorities get here. There may be questions, but it's the best chance we have. I'll make the call in a second."*

He took out the CB and signalled Aphrodite, then called them, keeping the message short.

*"Emergency services have been contacted and are attending. Depart immediately, and god speed."*

He switched the CB off and glanced up at the fishing vessel. Almost immediately, the group saw the 5 red flashes, then heard Aphrodite's diesel engine burst to life. Leander took out his cell phone and dialled 112. A sudden shout from the cliff area made them turn around; they saw Hanna standing above the cave entrance and they hurried to her.

Hanna saw Aphrodite's navigation lights turn on as she set course out to sea. She turned to Phillip.

*"What's happening? Where is Paris going?"*

Philip replied.

*"They have a rendezvous to make. How's Caroline?"*

Hanna sighed.

*"She's not good. The pain is subsiding, but she's very pale and may be close to slipping into a coma. I seriously doubt she will make it 24 hrs. We will have to call it in. No alternative."*

Pamela nodded.

*"They're on their way."*

# Chapter 37

### The FBI Close In

*"A life and death rescue operation is now underway here at Barbarossa's Cauldron to rescue a badly injured woman trapped in the underwater cave. Behind me, you can see members of the police emergency support unit together with military support teams. At this time, we are awaiting an update from a police spokesman, which we will bring to you shortly. In the meantime, I have with me, Leander Kosta, who first raised the alarm."*

The local reporter for Chania TVs update was being watched in Heraklion by both Dimitris and his wife. Dimitris was aware that Caroline and her team were on Gavdos, so were interested enough to tune in to the 11 pm broadcast. The volume was low to enable them to talk. Suddenly, Dimitris saw Leander's image on the screen. He immediately turned up the volume. The reporter continued.

*"Mr. Kosta, I understand you were the first person to raise the alarm. Can you tell me what happened?*

*"Well, I was down here on the beach with my dog; we often walk here until sunset. It's a peaceful view. I heard two young people shouting for help and, of course, responded. They told me a friend of theirs had been exploring the cave and had stepped on a Weever. She was in a bad way and the tide was rising. One of her friends who has diving experience remained with her, but is now also trapped. The Police are optimistic that the cave does not flood completely and the two women can be rescued."*

The reporter nodded and continued.

*"Do you have any other details of the two tourists who alerted you, or the identity of the injured woman? Is she local?*

*"I wouldn't know ma'am, I am just visiting here for a little while. A pleasure we older guys get when we retire"*

The reporter was about to follow up, when her cameraman indicated a police officer approaching. She turned and continued her broadcast.

*"Well, it appears we may have some update."*

She stood aside as the police sergeant reached the microphone; he was followed by two other people, one in civilian clothes and the other a Police Captain. The reporter spoke briefly, off the microphone to him before standing aside. The Captain came to the already set up microphone first.

*"Good evening, I am Captain Thanos Condos, Chania Division. At 10:26 this evening, we were alerted to an incident involving one or more persons trapped in an underwater cave. Units responded and a rescue operation is currently underway. I can tell you that at this stage, divers from our underwater recovery team have reached the trapped woman, and she is receiving treatment for a toxic Weever fish sting. She is conscious and in pain. The medical team is preparing to move her to the hospital as soon as practical. Of course, this is going to be a critical operation in view of the location of the patient."*

The reporter then spoke up.

*"Captain, do you know the identity of the injured woman?"*

Thanos replied.

*"Yes, but we are withholding that information until we have contacted her next of kin. I can tell you that she is a 40 year old tourist from England."*

The reporter pressed the point.

*"We have received information that this woman may be the celebrity author and psychic, Caroline De Winter, here on her honeymoon in Crete."*

The Captain moved closer to the microphone before replying.

*"As I said, no Comment."*

He stepped back as the civilian stepped forward to identify himself as a professor of geology.

Dimitris turned to Angela.

*"I better call Geoffrey."*

......................

Dimitris and Angela were not the only ones watching the broadcast. Paula Turner was also more than a little interested in the Broadcast. Although it gave few details, it was the first lead to Caroline and her team she had received since landing on Gavdos. She correctly surmised that the bell or its components were no longer on Gavdos. The Fishing boat she had followed was absent. Also, she had made enquiries at the ferry terminal and found an employee who knew the boat, and confirmed it had dropped off a young couple of backpackers the day before, whom he did not recognize. There were at least two other females aboard, plus several others who were in the wheelhouse. Again, he did not know them. She, of course, had relayed this to the Bureau, but as yet had not heard anything back. But they had secured a hire car for her on the Island. It was not exactly comfortable, but did give her a place to sleep for a few hours. She drove out of the port and into the open country beyond, choosing a high point that gave a commanding view out to sea. That would also make communications easier.

...............

Dimitris' phone call to Geoffrey was no surprise; he discovered one of his officers had just left after informing him. Having no luck calling her, he then tried Phillip.

*"Phil, I've just been told about Caroline. What can you tell me?"*

Phil's reply was guarded; he had not forgotten Dimitri's warning about NSA surveillance. *"She's okay. they got her out of the cave and are preparing her for medivac flight to Heraklion as soon as she's stable. Everyone's safe. Pam and I will be here for another day. The police have said they may have more questions for us later. We'll be back as soon as we can get a ferry ticket."*

With his mind on his wife, Geoffrey replied unthinkingly.

*"Don't worry about that. Paris can pick you up."*

Dimitris gave a quick cut throat sign, bringing Geoffrey back to his full senses. He hesitatingly continued.

*"Or at least I can ask him."*

Geoffrey hung up and looked pretty crestfallen. He turned to Dimitris.

*"Sorry, old chap, that was stupid on my part. Still, if they are monitoring, I doubt that will tell them much. It appears as though they dropped Pamela and Phil off, then left, presumably to retrieve the bell. There was no mention of the Aphrodite in the media, so we can assume they are on their way. So now it's just a case of staying ahead of the FBI. That is a real poser. Miss Turner is no amateur. She is likely to go to ground and follow up what leads she has and what the FBI can supply her with.*

.......................

The sound of a Westland scout medivac helicopter roused Paula from her sleep. The sun was rising, causing a fine mist of dew to appear over the grass, which quickly began to dissipate. She started the Fiat and turned on the heater. Then she saw a text message on her secure decryption window.

It read.

*'Petrel'*

Paula the read the following transcript and shook her head.

*'The following cell phone message was intercepted by NSA at 0210 hours from Geoffrey Spencer on Crete, and Philp Dawson, who is on Gavdos. The call appears to reference an accident on Gavdos to one Caroline Spencer, who also uses the name Caroline De Winter. We have put out an alert for a local fishing vessel, the Aphrodite, based in Crete. It appears that these persons are acquainted with each other.'*

*"A damn needle in a haystack."*

She muttered out loud.

Geoffrey and Angela arrived at the Hospital about an hour after Caroline had been admitted. She was still sleepy from the effects of the painkiller medication, and the swelling in her leg was still pretty pronounced. However, she had been asking for him, so the treating doctors felt a visit would calm her down. Angela was however, was asked to remain outside, knowing she was the wife of the local police chief. The Doctor did not want her to convey sensitive information to him before the ongoing enquiry was complete, or at least until she was well enough to be discharged.

Caroline smiled as Geoffrey entered.

*"I told you to watch your step, sweetheart. See what happens when you ignore my advice?"*

Painfully, she stretched her arms out as he came close.

*"Yep, I really put my foot in it this time, or maybe that should be on it."*

Geoffrey smiled as he kissed her lightly on the forehead.

*"Well, according to the Doctor, you're on the mend. So lie back and be pampered. Is there anything you need, grapes, a book or two, a friendly Spirt?"*

Caroline giggled. Then her face became more serious.

*"I'd like to see Hanna. I'm sure she saved my life."*

While Caroline was at the hospital with her husband, Phillip and Pamela had been released by the police and had returned to their campsite. Phillip had been informed that Caroline, who they identified only as the injured woman, had been rescued from the cave and was now in hospital receiving treatment. They had, of course, been mobbed by half a dozen reporters, which visibly upset Pamela. Phillip, who was by now sure that their relationship was beyond repair, had been uncharacteristically sharp with them. Telling them that they were glad their companion was recovering and they will not be making any further comment, as they were here on an expensive holiday and wanted to get back to it. They got on their bikes and peddled off. Wisely, the press did not attempt to follow.

Now they were at last alone, Phillip sat dejectedly on the ground beside the tent.

*"I am so sorry, Pam. This was never meant to turn into such a disaster. I had tried to plan everything so perfectly. It was to be a perfect vacation.*

*Then Caroline got in the way as she has a habit of doing. And poof, just like that, everything goes sour."*

Pamela sighed and sat down beside him.

*"Gone sour? Well, that's not exactly one of the words I would have chosen. Let's look at this logically. My slightly wacky boyfriend persuades me to come on holiday with him to Athens, I agree, and in 48 hours I'm whisked away to the magical island of Calypso. There, I meet a group of old men and World War Two veterans who are planning a secret mission and are being chased by the FBI, and who knows who all else. I've been involved in a dodgy cave rescue and now have been dumped back here without even a ride home."*

She paused for a bit, enjoying Phillip's obvious discomfort before continuing.

*"So, what do I think? I wouldn't have missed it for the world."*

She pulled him close and kissed him passionately on the lips. For a moment, Phillip was stunned, as she gently pulled away.

*"So, let's pack up and get these bikes back before we lose our deposit."*

Phillip smiled and said;

*"You're crazy, but I still love you. Hope you realize that."*

Quickly, they dismantled the tent and repacked the backpacks. Then, Phillip reached into his jacket pocket, it was empty. In a state of rising panic, he quickly searched the other pockets to no avail; Pamela watched him for a while, smiling gently.

*"What's up Sergeant, have you lost something?"*

Phillip nodded.

*"Yes, a small box. I had it when we camped here."*

Pamela produced the gold gift-wrapped box from her waist pack.

*"Oh, is this it? You dropped it when you went queer after you realized Caroline was in trouble."*

Phillip took the box and unwrapped it.

*"Damn! This was not exactly how I had planned this, but whatever."*

He opened the box and smiled as he dropped to one knee.

"*Constable Pamela Meredith, will you please marry me? I need someone to sort me out.*"

Pamela started to smile, but then checked herself.

"*You certainly do, darling. Of course I accept, especially if life with you is always going to be this exciting.*"

Phillip removed the ring and gently placed it on the third finger of her left hand. She held it up close, five emeralds set in platinum. A stunning design that Phillip knew only too well,

# Chapter 38

### Sea Chase

Aphrodite was now well out to sea. The weather was still very calm, and the little fishing boat was nearing the designated rendezvous area. The crew were experienced sailors, but Otto was not faring well. He came up to the wheelhouse and looked pale as he sat in one of the wheelhouse chairs. Leander had earlier tried to talk him out of making the trip, but Otto was firm.

*"Since the war, I have been haunted by this dreadful weapon. Now the Spectre has returned. It is my duty to witness its ultimate destruction."*

Adamos, of course, was aware that there was no guarantee the mission would succeed. Discovery and seizure by the Americans was far more likely.

Adamos scanned the Horizon for signs of his prized Destiny Angel. They had maintained radio silence on Adamos's request and knew that they were not the only vessel, by far, in this part of the Mediterranean. Once sighted, the transfer needed to be carried out swiftly, out of sight of other boats if possible. There were, of course, no guarantees. While Adamos scanned the horizon, Paris was studying the radar returns, which were short range and inefficient. At a time like this, he wished he had the far more sensitive and long range radar system of the Destiny Angel. Fifteen miles to the west, Adamos's son had no such limitations. His radar had locked onto the Aphrodite echo and he was steering toward her.

.................

Meanwhile, the FBI had not been idle. They had compiled data from surveillance satellites showing live traffic in the Mediterranean around Greece. One hundred and forty one vessels were currently at sea. Of those, sixty eight were commercial tankers; nine were naval vessels from Greece, Italy, and the United States. The remaining sixty four were unidentified, but seemed to be private or corporate vessels.

It was these that were now under serious investigation. Paula had asked for priority on this, as she was certain that one of them, at least, was going to meet up at sea with the Aphrodite.

The FBI trackers were the best in the world; soon they had cleared fifty one as being too large or originating from a port outside the Mediterranean Sea. Of the remaining thirteen, only three were considered to be close enough to Crete to be suspect. The coordinates were passed to the Joint US Air force base at Aviano in Italy, requesting photo reconnaissance on all three.

Meanwhile, Destiny Angel had reached the rendezvous position and was holding on station with its four bow and two stern thrusters. Paris turned the Aphrodite into wind and came alongside. The little vessel had every fender slung out to absorb the impact. Carlos now moved into action, throwing three coiled mooring ropes in quick succession to the waiting hands on the larger vessel. It took 5 minutes to lock the vessels together and swing the loading crane over Aphrodite's deck. The crane was lowered into the rear fish hold and fastened to a heavy cargo net that now contained the disassembled bell. Aboard Aphrodite, Paris, Carlos, and Otto watched nervously as the cargo was lifted from the fishing boat and deposited aboard Destiny Angel, coming to rest on its aft deck. The net was unhooked and the three mooring lines were released. The fishing boat drifted clear. Adamos waved to his son as Destiny Angel fired up and turned away. With the twin diesel engines now at full power, the cruiser planed away, leaving a large white wake. Paris accepted a high five from Carlos as the Aphrodite turned toward Crete, rapidly drawing away.

Then suddenly from nowhere, a shattering roar filed the air causing everyone on board to clamp their hands over their ears. The crew looked up as a low flying American marked F15 fighter roared overhead at no more than 200 feet before banking up and away climbing rapidly. Carlos commented.

*"That was fortunate; 10 minutes ago, he would have seen us with Destiny. Not that he would have noticed anything, anyway. But these top gun boys are a law unto themselves."*

Aboard Destiny Angel, Georgios was concerned. The Bell was still on the aft deck and the same F15 that had flown over Aphrodite had also passed directly over them. He cursed that the delays caused at Gavdos and the wider course the Aphrodite had been forced to follow meant the transfer that was scheduled to take place at night, was now taking place 2 hours after dawn. It may have been that the F15 had been sent to check them out. If so, they could not have missed the bell and net on the aft deck. The mission was now in serious jeopardy. But for now, he had to make the disposal point, and the Calypso deep was still over 90 miles away. That was over 3 and a half hours at maximum speed.

.................

Finally, Paula got some news that the fishing boat, Aphrodite, had been sighted off the coast of Crete and seemed to be on course to land there. The coastguard had made radio contact and ascertained they were returning from an unsuccessful night fishing trip and his passengers were not happy.

At least, she thought, we may get some answers now. The coastguard had confirmed the Aphrodite's destination was the port of Kissamos in the north of the island, to drop off some of his passengers before returning to Gavdos to collect some friends. Despite her worries about local hostility, Paula decided to risk returning to Crete to meet the Aphrodite and check out her passengers.

In the meantime, the FBI headquarters at Langley had received aerial photos from the flyovers' computer analysis that identified the ships.

The FBI was pretty efficient in making things happen. A small Robinson R22 helicopter had collected Paula and deposited her at Kissamos. Now she sat at a harbour side bar outside table, as the Aphrodite approached. Paula adjusted her sunglasses as Paris and

Carlos secured the boat to the jetty. She immediately recognized Adamos from the consulate photographs. Then her phone buzzed with another encrypted message from Langley and a photograph from the F15. The text read.

*'MV Destiny Angel registered in Heraklion Crete, owned by Nicholas Adamos and managed by his son Georgios. Not responding to radio messages. Item of interest on the rear deck seems to be metal component parts of some sort of engine or cylinder. Vessel location; 60 miles north of Crete, heading NE at 25 knots. Awaiting director's authority to intercept.'*

Paula was elated.

*"Got you,"* she said quietly. She glanced across at Adamos, as if for the first time he noticed her, he turned to Paris.

*"That girl at the bar seems out of place here. We're well of the tourist beat."*

Paris looked up.

*"I've seen her before at the ferry terminal in Crete. She seemed interested in Phil and Pam, certainly a very striking woman. Matches Dimitri's description of that FBI agent, I think I'll make a call."*

Meanwhile, Otto disembarked and sat on a capstan on the jetty, still looking shaky.

*"Okay, Herr Meijer, the hard part is over. Just breathe deeply and relax. I should stay away from old boats; especially ones driven by old salts like me.*

Otto looked up and smiled weakly.

*"Danke mein freund, I will take your advice."*

......................

Back at Heraklion, Caroline was still feeling sleepy, an effect mainly of the painkillers. Geoffrey, who had been constantly at the hospital, had gone home for a few hours' rest when Cora arrived with a welcome visitor. Hanna had taken the ferry back, having heard that her patient had been asking for her.

Caroline was visibly happy to see her and immediately thanked her for her actions in the cave. Hanna smiled and took her hand.

*"I'm relieved to see you on the mend. You know, at first I didn't pay you much attention. The paranormal is not my bag, and to be honest, you scared me a little. I have Cora to thank for changing that. She's a remarkable woman."*

Caroline smiled at Cora.

*"She certainly is that. So, how did you get Dimitris to let you off at such a busy time?*

*It was he who told me that you were asking for me. He's gone up north to meet a contact at Kissamos.*

# Chapter 39

### Where Is The Bell?

Almost two hours had passed with nothing from Langley regarding the Destiny Angel. It wasn't usual for the FBI director, Robert Mueller, to prioritize requests for a vessel to intercept on the high seas, especially from an agent working on little more than a theory. The request had been brought to his attention, and he pressed for further information before going on to other matters. Meanwhile, Paula had decided to return to her helicopter, which was still waiting outside the port. She greeted the pilot and climbed into the passenger seat.

"*Okay, Carter, let's go back to Heraklion. I think we are about to put a lid on this case.*"

The pilot looked up and shook his head.

"*Sorry, Paula, we're on hold. I'm waiting for the flight clearance. There seems to be a hitch.*"

For the first time, Paula became suspicious. That suspicion grew when she saw Captain Dimitris approaching them.

"*Well, well, if it isn't our sceptical Police Captain, why am I surprised?*"

Dimitris smiled and bowed his head before speaking.

*Well, well, if it isn't America's top Nazi hunter. I don't think you'll find any war criminals here, Miss Turner, nor do I believe you expect to. So, may I ask why you are here?*"

"*I told you, I decided to take an unscheduled vacation. Is that a crime, Captain?*"

Dimitris shook his head.

"*No, but I fail to see why the FBI should pay for it, because the Robinson is a private charter - the client, the FBI. I don't think you've been exactly honest with me, Paula. Your mission here has nothing to do with war criminals. The FBI has no interest in such matters. Strange, in the last 48 hours the Russians have also sent agents here. Are they hunting war criminals too? Let me give you my theory. There is a rumour that during*

*World War Two, the Germans developed a Wunderwaffen, a super device*
*well ahead of its time. It was captured by the allies, but was found to be*
*unstable. Realizing that the Germans had sent it here for modification,*
*America and Russia both desire to make the weapon available for their*
*respective militaries. So, they send agents here to search. How am I doing?"*

Paula looked at him with a defiant glower on her face.

*"Delightful story, Captain, but too imaginative. You've been watching*
*too many James bond movies. So if you're done, can you get air traffic to*
*clear my flight?"*

*Dimitris replied;*

*"Sorry, but you see, there is a problem. Sorry, but you see there is a*
*problem. We revoked your visa an hour ago when we discovered your true*
*mission here. That, in fact, you had made a false declaration on your visa*
*application, officially makes you persona non grata. We have informed*
*the American consulate in Athens, and in the interest of international*
*relations we have agreed not to detain you. I'm therefore under orders to*
*escort you to Heraklion airport where a seat has been reserved for you on*
*a flight to Athens, where I understand you will take a connecting flight to*
*Washington, DC. Your personal luggage and effects have been picked up*
*and will be waiting for you at the airport."*

...........

Aboard Destiny Angel, Georgios knew that time was likely
running out. As a former marine research vessel, the Angel had a useful
feature. That was the main reason Adamos had chosen her for the
mission. There was a centre diving pool with hydraulic doors that could
be opened under the keel, allowing diving teams to enter the ocean
from inside the vessel. The pool chamber was pressurized to create a
diving bell effect. As they approached the Calypso Deep area, Georgios
had decided it would be too dangerous to stop. He glanced at the
cabin's chronometer and the sonar returns, depth was still only 300
feet. Radar showed several vessels within 10 miles, but none were
changing course.

.....................

Back at Langley, the Director had been informed of the deportation of Paula and had also been examining the photo reconnaissance pictures. He also had a classified report of the weapon known as Die Glocke. After conferring with several military advisors, he gave the order to stop and search the vessel on suspicion of smuggling drugs. The encrypted message was then sent out to a US Naval destroyer, which changed course. Aboard Destiny Angel, Georgios saw the vessel change course and knew he was on borrowed time. He ordered the crew into action and immediately they unsealed the aft storage hold.

Meanwhile, Paula's phone buzzed. She glanced down at the message.

*'PETREL' 'Intercept underway.'*

Dimitris looked back at her.

*"Good news, Miss Turner?*

Paula smiled back at him.

*"Oh yes, Captain, the best."*

.....................

The Destroyer was now matching speed with the motor cruiser and flashing Morse code signals. Georgios slowed the engines as he read the signal.

*"This is the USS destroyer Bowie. Stop your engines and prepare to be boarded."*

Georgios pulled the throttles back and slowed to a dead stop. He spoke over the tannoy.

*"US Marines about to board us offer no resistance."*

A zodiac was launched from the Destroyer with 6 men aboard. Georgios instructed the crew to help them aboard. Moments later a US Navy Lieutenant entered the wheelhouse.

*"Sorry for the interruption, captain but I have orders to search this vessel. Can you tell me what cargo you are carrying and how many crew you have on board?"*

Georgios shrugged.

*"No problem, Lieutenant, I have 5 persons on board. We have no cargo except what you see on the aft deck. You are welcome to inspect that."*

The object on the rear hold cover was lashed down with a thick cargo net, making it difficult to discern. While the other marines went about searching the ship, Georgios led the officer to the load. He released one of the strops holding the net in place, revealing a collection of crushed aluminium sheets and very rusted metal framework. The Lieutenant was confused, and he pulled the netting further up. Finally, he spoke.

*"What is this?"*

*"Well it may not look like it now, but it is, in fact, the remains of a P51 Mustang fighter, shot down in 1945 and recovered by a local history group. Mr Adamos purchased it last month and we are taking it back to Crete for him. Personally, I think it's a hopeless project, but, well, he is my dad and it is his money."*

Within 15 minutes, the boarding party had returned, having searched the vessel and found nothing. The Lieutenant saluted and thanked Georgios for his cooperation. One of Georgios crew waved them off as they boarded the zodiac. He turned to him commenting.

*"Well, I certainly don't want to go through that again. Can we go home now?"*

Georgios nodded.

*"I think so Christos. Break out the beer."*

# EPILOGUE

The lights were burning brightly aboard the moored Destiny Angel with the boat quite crowded. It was a well-deserved celebration and Adamos was happy to play MC. Caroline, now released from the hospital, along with Geoffrey, were the principal guests. Not all of the guests were happy, however. The death of Otto Kurtz, from a stroke a few hours after landing, had affected both Leander and Paris. Leander was, however, comforted by his reassurance from Sally's manifestation to him that he had passed on to a different plain. Phillip and Pamela were present, at her insistence. And she was attracting a lot of attention with her ring. Caroline of course, recognized it and at an opportune moment took Phillip aside.

*"That's a stunning replica, Phil; she said softly, where did you find it?"*
He shook his head.

*"Queen Ann's ring was unique; there are no others, at least not until now. I commissioned it from a photo I took. They made a pretty good job, don't you think?"*
Caroline nodded.

*"Excellent. But why that ring? It had a dark a history, as you know."*
Phil raised his glass and said clearly.

*"It was a gift from a King to his Queen, so is this one."*
With that, he walked away. Caroline was in no position to argue.

Pamela was quick to join him as she steered him towards Georgios. Phillip introduced him, and ever the Gentleman he took her hand, and congratulated both of them. Pamela then spoke up.

*"There is one thing I'm curious about. If I understand this right, you were boarded after Paris, and the crew had transferred the bell. But it had been switched for that old plane wreck. How did you pull that off?"*
Georgios got up.

*"Follow me, I'll show you."*

Accompanied by her fiancée, Pamela followed him below deck. She was visibly awestruck when she saw the pressure pool and Georgios explained its function.

*"This is our most innovative feature. The bell parts were laid out on the keel doors, loosely. It was a tight timeline window. The Destroyer was already in sight, so I had to risk dropping the parts while still travelling at 25 knots. I knew we were likely under binocular observation. I operated the doors from the bridge. It takes 4 minutes to fully open them, and I didn't have that much time. I opened them enough to dump the Bell parts and closed them again; I did so as we made a tight turn. I estimate that the pieces will have been strewn out over a 4 mile area at a depth of just under 16,000 feet. They likely buried themselves in the silt. The plane wreckage was picked up last week, and we hadn't had the chance to land it yet. When the mission came up, well, we figured it might be useful as a decoy."*

Back in the briefing cabin, it was now transformed into a compact reception area Dimitris and Angela had joined Geoffrey and Caroline at the makeshift bar.

*A week ago you arrived here on your honeymoon; I knew nothing about you, other than Angela, telling me you spoke to dead people. But had you not arrived when you did, the world would now be far more dangerous than it is. Crete and its people are indebted to you both, even if they will never know what you did here. We here in Heraklion and the people on this vessel do know. We would like to make up for ruining your honeymoon."*

Geoffrey put up his hand.

*"There is no need for any apology. Honeymoons should be memorable, and I think you would agree that ours will be unforgettable."*

Dimitris chuckled, and Angela giggled briefly. However, Dimitris was not done.

*"Nevertheless, the fact is that we felt we owe you an extension.*

He handed him a folded piece of paper.

*"This is conformation of one week's extension of your hotel stay with all amenities included; plus a week's extension on your rental car."*

Geoffrey scanned through the document before handing it to Caroline. While reading it they failed to notice Cora and Hanna approaching, and they were not alone.

Geoffrey took Dimitris' hand.

*"Well, we're both very grateful, but I don't know if my daughter will be. She has been making plans for us to house decorate and such."*

He looked up as a familiar voice interrupted.

*"I think England can do without you for one more week, Dad."*

Debbie ran forward and threw her arms around his neck; David sheepishly came forward and shook his hand.

Geoffrey was naturally pleased to see them, but confused nevertheless.

Angela cleared things up.

*"I thought the least we could do was to invite your family to share in your party. So Dimitris and I paid for a plane ticket for them, with a little help.*

She shot a wry smile at Adamos, who smiled but said nothing.

Debbie then reassured Caroline.

*"Don't worry. It's only a weekend. They fly back Monday. Two's company, right?"*

........................

Phillip slipped his arm around Pamela's waist and guided her out onto the Angels deck with two glasses of Deutscher Sekt champagne, complete with cherries. He handed one to her. She looked up and smiled before looking out across the marina. Phil smiled at her again.

*"The island of dreams, darling, with maybe a dark past."*

He kissed her lightly.

*"The Dark Island, I'll drink to that."*

Pamela said, before tapping her glass against his. For a couple of minutes, they were silent, deep in thought. Then Pamela snapped back to reality.

*"So, where are you taking me for the Honeymoon?"*

Phillip turned away from the harbour scene before replying.

*"Well, there is this haunted Castle in Scotland Caroline mentioned, Appa..."*

He never finished the sentence. Pamela put her hand over his mouth and carefully poured her champagne over his head.

**~ *Finis* ~**

## About the Author

Steve Challis was born in 1948 in the United Kingdom. The son of a farmer, Steve, grew up in the rural Cotswolds where he learned to shoot and hunt on the farm where his father worked. Following 5 years of service in the military (Royal Air Force), Steve joined the Hampshire Constabulary in 1969 and served as an officer for 21 years. In 2006, Steve met his wife Eva via the internet, and then in 2007 they became engaged. The following year in November, Steve moved to the USA and he and Eva were married in Ketchikan, Alaska.

In 2009, the couple settled in Kentucky where they bought a farm, then in 2010 opened a firearms training school. Now a permanent US resident, Steve is the author of several books on gun rights and historical fiction. The Dark Island is the second in a series of paranormal thrillers.


Follow me on Facebook: Stephen C. Challis Author
Contact me at S.C.Challisauthor@gmail.com

# Don't miss out!

Visit the website below and you can sign up to receive emails whenever Stephen C. Challis publishes a new book. There's no charge and no obligation.

https://books2read.com/r/B-A-JCVCB-KACUC

**BOOKS 2 READ**

Connecting independent readers to independent writers.

# About the Author

Steve Challis was born in 1948 in the United Kingdom. Steve grew up in the rural Cotswold's where he learned shooting and hunting on the farm where his Father worked. Following 5 years of service in the military (RAF), Steve joined the Hampshire Constabulary in 1969 and served as an officer for 21 years. In 2006, Steve met his wife Eva via the internet, and then in 2007 they became engaged. The following year in November, Steve moved to the USA and he and Eva were married in Ketchikan, Alaska. In 2009, the couple settled in Kentucky where they bought a farm, then in 2010 opened a firearms training school. Now a permanent US resident, Steve is the author of several books on gun rights and historical fiction.